MAAT-
KA-
RE

MEMOIRS OF
A TIME TRAVELER

W. J. CHERF

Foxbat Publishing
ISBN: 978-0-9834814-6-1

Cover image: limestone raised relief of the Eighteenth Dynasty Pharaoh Hatshepsut as the goddess Hathor. The front and back cover's reversing clock image is adapted from the apple.com time machine logo.

ALSO BY W. J. CHERF

The Manuscripts of the Richards' Trust

Bow Tie
Recovery
Children of Ptah
Imhotep
Maat-ka-re. Memoirs of a Time Traveler
Iron from the Sky

The Adventures of J.J. Stone

The First Soul
The Lictor of Magic
I Am the Storm

Adventures in Paranormal Archaeology

The Magician's Tomb
Netherworld's Gate
Dhampirica
Hallowed Promises

DEDICATION

An author's first line of defense is made up by those brave souls, who are willing to place aside their sanity and common sense to plow through an early beta draft. They are a remarkably patient and hopeful lot and without them, frankly, any author would be at a total loss.

Consequently, it is with deep and heartfelt thanks that I mention Joni and Jim. Their honest assessments and observations were all invaluable.

To my good friend Kalin, I owe so very much, as once again his keen and sharp observations on Russian culture made this book far more accurate, authentic, and hence, believable.

Last, but hardly least, I must mention my ever-endearing wife Sue, whose presence and support had this book possible. In fact, the germ of its creation was her idea all along. What would I do without you? Bless you.

Author's Note

Memoirs are considered sacred to us Russians. And rightly so. After all, they were our only place of solitude during the Czarist and Soviet eras. Within its pages we absolutely knew that we were free to think what we wanted, and to express what we must. To read a Russian's memoirs was to open a portal into their very soul, for they contained disjointed thoughts, transient feelings, illogical emotion, and moments of extreme happiness, disappointment, and even horror. But if you think about it, that was what life truly is, a toss salad of ingredients that were put before you, not chosen, and hardly ever controlled. It just is.

So, here I write about what is most important to me, and also about matters that are considered to be extremely secret. Fortunately, I remember a remarkable amount, and in almost superhuman detail, even down to the specifics of a certain conversation, as my recall has been so enhanced.

These things I must share with you. Why? Because throughout my extraordinary existence, it has always been about the people, those who had so touched my life. They need to be remembered, hated, and even in some cases to be praised. So I write about that which is forbidden, sometimes based directly upon my own sure recollections. Sometimes based upon others whose hearts I trust and believe.

As for the "rules" on Russian names and their forms of address, kindly see, "A Note on Russian Names" at the back of this book.

CHAPTER I

My First Drop

My Cyrillic-English identification badge read:

VESNA BORISEVNA GREGORIEVA
TEMPORAL FIELD AGENT, NR. 3
RUSSIAN-AMERICAN ACADEMIES OF
SCIENCE

That I was the third temporal field agent pleased me, almost as much as I had succeeded my mentor Alexander Andreovich Piankoff.

I, with my American counterpart, was tasked with preserving our current reality. And to make a very long story short, I have been busy. My first incarnation was as Maatkare during several deployments to ancient Egypt. Next, I was sent as Lieutenant Valerie Gregg back to Princeton, New Jersey of all places. Finally, I journeyed back as Veer "the Bloody" in eighth century France. Like I said, I have been busy.

As anyone will tell you, they never forget their first unassisted ride on a bicycle, or for that matter, their first love. So it was for me, that first drop into the *somewhen* was quite memorable. After all, we, Joey Richards and I, were only sent to assassinate a minor pharaoh of the Eighteenth Dynasty. What possibly could go wrong?

*   *   *

"You know Vesna," I remembered hearing Doc Allen say so many times, "what you are about to undertake is something that few humans have. To date,

I count only two, who have risked their bodies within such an electro-magnetic field, and they were males, who over time developed a serious reaction to that temporal field. So that makes you special, very special indeed. We really don't know whether your body will react as theirs did, or entirely in some other way. So Vesna, do you really want to do this?"

As I have always considered myself special, I swallowed my fears and pushed on. *If my Sasha could do this, so could I! To hell with the potential risks involved.*

Then there was the minor task of the assassination of the young Pharaoh Ankhkheprure Smenkhkare. He was certifiably a very mad and psychopathic telepath, who was telekinetic spawn and successor of the alien Pharaoh Akhenaten. He and his hybrid genes had to be stopped and prevented from being passed on. Otherwise, humanity's future was destined to be divided between those who could, and those who could not, exercise telepathic and telekinetic abilities. Accomplish that, and then Joey and I would get to come home.

To prepare us for the aforementioned psychopathic Smenkhkare, Doc Allen played a considerable role. He implanted in both Joey and me deep psychic blocks that would protect and preserve us against the young pharaoh's genetically augmented mental powers. He also inserted mental images of our own choosing meant to confuse the errant teenager. Finally, and perhaps most importantly to our survival, the good Doctor then placed a trigger in us that would quickly raise our metabolisms and adrenaline levels. This would allow us, for a brief period, to go into a sort of physiological overdrive. This period of frenetic exertion had to be brief, otherwise, a terrific crash would level us. I was told that my Sasha and Joey had already used such a ploy, when they eliminated Smenkhkare's alien father, Akhenaten.

*   *   *

To be perfectly honest, I really didn't know what to expect the first time I deployed through the American's temporal field. Given all the technology and power required, I wondered if that transition from one time to the next would be painful. I worried whether I would remember all my hard earned landing lessons, which had been drilled into me during those two intensive weeks at the Fort Bragg parachute school. Would my muscle memory come through? Would I break or sprain something upon landing, just as my beloved Sasha had?

Yes, I freely admit, I was scared, but since I had come so far, I refused to wash myself out. So I swallowed my fear and pushed on.

That first drop was exhilarating! There I was, standing above the energized ring as the temporal field coalesced, the braids of my black wig flew in all directions because of the van der Graff effect, while my white, single-shouldered dress stuck to me like paint, because of all the electromagnetic static. With my bare feet and toes tingling as if I stood at the edge of a high cliff, I looked at the very center of the ring's field, took a small jump forward into the air. I locked my knees with a slight bend as I had been instructed at the jump school, and *dropped*.

The divine slipperiness of passing through the temporal field and its ion stream, into the *somewhen*, felt nearly orgasmic, and infinitely more pleasurable than a hot baby oil message after a long sweat session in the sauna.

*   *   *

The very next thing that I remembered was gracefully landing on the balls of my feet and performing a classic tuck and roll.

Oh, how I blessed my parachute instructor!

Then, quite suddenly, my senses rudely kicked in. I was assaulted by the smell of the intense incense, the light of gently fluttering shadows from oil lamp tapers, and the life-sized, seated golden presence of Amen Re in the near darkness. It was precisely then that I finally got it. I finally understood my Sasha's first love.

Then my teammate and Egyptologist Joey Richards landed in the sanctuary with a plop like a sack of potatoes, groggy, and incoherent. He and Doc Allen had warned me about his post-drop syndrome, a condition that affected his electrolytic balance. As I anxiously hovered over him in the near-darkness, his unconsciousness quickly passed, just as Doc Allen said it would. But Joey's his first words at coming to were confused.

"I am upside down," he quietly announced in the language of ancient Egyptian.

After another moment or two, blessedly, he blinked, smiled up at me, and came fully to his senses.

"I am in good health my sister. We must go. But first find our leather pouch. It's around here somewhere. It contains our expense money."

We left the intimately sublime beauty of the inner-most sanctuary of the Great God Amen Re by carefully squeezing ourselves between the massive cedar wood door leaves. My Sasha had somehow discovered that an alarm system was attached to the opening of the doors. But he found that if one gently opened them by only just so much, the old and overstretched ropes would not release the hammers of bronze alarm gongs.

So now beyond that towering portal, we were greeted by the near darkness of the main temple. I say near darkness due to the scattered oil lamps that passed for lighting. Encountering a black granite statue of the fierce lion-goddess Sekhmet, we passed behind it to a cleverly obscured side passage hidden in the statue's shadow. Once through the thick walls of the temple proper, Joey surprised me by saying, "Look up."

The star field I beheld was so overwhelming in its complexity and brightness that I staggered back unconsciously wishing to take it all in. In this ancient atmosphere, devoid of any pollution, the many flowing streams of Milky Way made themselves self-evident as breath-taking tendrils of light. The intense density of the stars assaulted my straining eyes to the point that I had to look away.

Joey whispered conspiratorially, "Is it any wonder that *Kemet* included such stars in their religion? Why they adorned the ceilings of their pyramids and tombs with them? But we must go now to my adopted father's house. Hopefully, it will still be vacant."

As we walked in the dark, mindful to be as silent, I found myself amidst a maze of low slab-sided mud brick structures that seemed to glow white in the moon and star light. After many twists and turns between them, we approached a modest solitary building with a portico of columns that marked its entrance.

Joey approached first to confirm whether its new tenant had yet moved in. Finding that he had not, we entered and made ourselves comfortable within its walls. I was led to a side room with two bed frames. All at once the excitement and tension of the drop bled off in a rush. Practically collapsing onto his bed, Joey let out a moan of nervous exhaustion and fell to sleep.

As for myself, I was still quite awake with the newness of everything. Besides, I had to answer a nagging personal question. So I quietly joined Joey on his bed frame, naked, wrapping myself around him in a most possessive way, and communicated my hunger. To my happy surprise, Joey indeed responded to my affections, took his good time about it, was attentive and gentle. As a result I enjoyed myself greatly, several times, and found myself crying tears of pure joy in his cradling arms. I had no idea how erotically sensitive a shaved head was. But Joey showed me. As we finished, both physically exhausted, slippery in each other's sweat, we fell asleep entwined. To me, in my mind, our team had been sanctified.

The next morning, I must admit, was a bit awkward for me, but Joey just smiled and said, "Time to get up and get moving. I'll check out the pantry to see if there is anything to eat."

We took care of our personal needs and Joey showed me where and what. He then announced that the house had indeed been cleaned up and stocked with beer and wine, but since it was not yet occupied, the household still lacked any fresh cheeses, dried fish, breads, or fruit. So, with Joey jiggling his leather pouch, we ventured out to visit the market place for breakfast, and thereafter, to arrange for our passage north to Akhetaten, and our target, the mad Pharaoh Smenkhkare.

On the way to the marketplace, I went over in my mind why I had initiated last evening's passion. I guess that I wanted to know, first hand, whether the American was a real man and not some robot. Well, now I knew. Besides, I shamelessly admitted to myself, I was more than just a little bit curious. I just hadn't expected Joey to so promptly return the favor, so well, and for so long.

As for the marketplace, I found it to be a riot of color and smells, many of which teased my stomach into voicing its need. Hearing this, Joey smiled and steered me over to a bread vendor.

"Venerable One," he said in a kindly manner to the elderly woman, "two of your most delicious sweet breads with honey. My sister's stomach must be silenced."

Smiling back, the vendor selected not two, but three of the sweets, and served them on a date palm leaf cleverly fashioned for the purpose.

"Why three sweets, Venerable One?" Joey asked.

"I heard your loud stomach as well, priest of the gods. Now eat, as my old ears can barely stand all the commotion from you two."

Turning to share his breads with me, Joey then plucked a tiny gold ring from the leather pouch around his neck. He reached across and placed the tiny treasure in her hand and closed her fingers around it. Surprised by the quickness of the act, the woman gasped at opening her hand and showed a look of wonderment in her eyes.

"Venerable One," Joey said, "you have just fed two hungry servants of the Great God of the White Wall.

Do you not think that He thanks you as well?"

As we turned and walked away toward the docks in search of a boat, I distinctly heard the woman loudly whisper to her nearby vendors.

"Look there, it is he, the kindly priest of the House of Horemheb. I remember him! I would recognize those brave scars anywhere. And just look what he gave me for just three sweet breads!"

While this was my very first interaction with the ancient Egyptians, it was memorable in many ways. The *sem*-priest of Ptah, Mayneken, my Joey, had just shown me a side of him that I would never have imagined. As I ate the delicious sweet pyramid laden with honey, I had a lot to learn about my temporal teammate in this most ancient land.

* * *

While there were several river craft available for our transit north to Akhetaten, the then royal capital of Egypt, I watched at how Joey negotiated with the boatmen, querying as to their provisions for the journey, their speed, and also rather bluntly whether their boats carried lice or fleas, much to their surprised and indignant protestations. What a practical education I was getting!

We left Thebes that morning on a swift river craft and a day and a half later arrived at the capital. I freely admit that I marveled throughout the river journey north at all the sights, sounds, and smells. Countless flocks of colorful birds clouded the sky, only to land and blanket the bank and its nearby waters. Basking crocodiles with their mouths opened wide allowed prancing birds to clean their teeth. Endless verdant fields of what Joey explained were wheat and barley crowded the river banks. Their ripe stalks bowed. Braying donkeys and splashing children playing in the reeds filled my ears. And the many cooking fires, frying onions and garlic and meats, made my stomach speak.

Upon reaching the busy docks of Akhetaten, by their attire, I could see that it was populated with a broad mix of cultures. Joey, ever attentive, kindly explained everything that I was witnessing.

"See that one over there with the beard. He's most likely from one of the cities along the Levantine coast. And that well-muscled one with the long, snake-like hair, he's definitely from Crete. As for that one, my guess, by the pottery that he is hawking, he's from mainland Greece, maybe even from the city of Mycenae."

Lost in the moment, I grabbed Joey's strong forearm like an excited child. Then, when he looked down at me, I blushed, and let go. I could not believe it, but I was beginning to trust that stubborn American. I felt at ease in his company, with his broad knowledge and experience, not to mention his presence, even his smell.

Now on the dock with our growling stomachs primed by the delicious smells of roasted something, I wanted to gorge myself, but Joey firmly made the point that we needed grooming first, and so he led the way. Little did I know that this would be my first challenge, not only to negotiate the service, but also to experience the touch of a total stranger washing and shaving my body! It took all the control that I could muster, but after a while, much as with a hair shampoo at my favorite salon, I began to settle down to the ritual. By the time I had been massaged with oil, I did feel and smell delicious. So I made a note to myself that such experiences can become extremely dangerous, if not habit forming.

Now for something to eat!

Joey, again showing the way, made some suggestions, even let me sample some of his favorites, and I then and there concluded that Americans do have the oddest of palettes when it comes to food. So while he indulged himself with a portion of roasted garlic hen, I became adventurous and meandered among of the many stands of freshly cooked foods, fruits, and many others unidentifiable, and decided to act upon sheer curiosity and impulse. To be honest, the assault on the senses was considerable. Roasted garlic, onions, breads of all sorts, meats, and fish, both cooked and dried. They all made up a kaleidoscope of possibilities. But through it all, and before I sampled anything, Joey found me, and again with that subtle American respect, no, it was deference, would politely ask the vendor.

"Which of these fine fish would you offer to your own sister?"

Or, "Of these fine sweet breads, which would you select for your own mother?"

These diplomatically pitched words from a priest truly impacted the commoners' ears as they spoke volumes, again. As with the old woman in Thebes that had sold us the sweet breads, this elderly one, nearly toothless, offered the American a ready smile of her gums as she passed over her offerings, in this particular case, a whole dried fish. But when Joey attempted to pay, his hand was gently brushed aside.

"Dear priest," he quietly said, "Pray for my *ka's*

survival, for I know you will. Your eyes are clear and guileless, unlike the others."

Thanking the man with a respectful nod, Joey performed his trick again as he took the his hand and simultaneously slipped a small gold ring unto one of his heavily callused fingers. Gasping in disbelief and wonder, he clutched the finger tightly with the other hand as if the finger had been injured.

Looking up, Joey only smiled. "Venerable Father, let it be known that He of the Great White Wall will care for you in the West, as you have cared for one of his lowly priests among the living."

With heartfelt tears streaming down his weathered visage, Joey turned to leave, and then I heard as he did so, yet another all too familiar gasp of recognition.

"By the Aten! It is he! He's the one that I saw entering our dear Queen's own household! Those magnificent scars only prove it!"

Twice now, Joey's approach with those of the marketplace told me of an inner strength and generosity of spirit that I had not before seen. It warmed my heart and made me smile. Such a simple thing.

Imagine, I thought, *a Christian abroad within a pre-Christian world. What a revolution that would make!*

But before we left the marketplace, Joey led me over to a public well, which he deemed very drinkable, if not delicious. And, once again, he was right. For I didn't realize just how thirsty I had become, especially after that dried and salted fish. While others waited their turn at the well, we drank until our bellies distended.

*　*　*

Knowing where the royal palace was did not present us a problem, for all knew where the edifice was located. Frankly, one could not miss it. The palace's sheer mass and its centralized location made it the natural nexus of the town. And it was located next to the truly massive Aten Temple, actually connected to it by a bridge across the main north-south thoroughfare of the city. But such centrality also meant getting past a veritable gauntlet of courtly bureaucrats, in order to attend the daily royal audience, where we hoped to find our target. Getting access, I could now see, would present us with a challenge.

However, as I had learned so well while at the Directorate, one's sense of presence and attitude can go quite far when confronted with such challenges. Besides, the *sem*-priest of the god Ptah, Mayneken, and I his lovely sister, Maatkare, possessed these qualities in abundance. Joey's ambassadorial ring from the royal household also provided its own unique privileges. But when the situation called for sheer, brazen moxie, that too has its place, and that was where I came in.

Joey, freshly groomed, bare-chested, and striding forth powerfully in his white linen kilt, surprised me as he walked proudly along through the crowded streets. It wasn't that he was acting like a strutting popinjay. It was just what they call in the military "command presence."

So, when he walked up to the two tall, blue-black Nubian Medjay guards at the palace's side entrance, I wasn't really all that shocked. That Joey's direct approach had been effective was clearly evidenced by the way the guards hands had unconsciously slipped to the pummels of their vicious-looking chariot scythes, their *khopeshu*, which hung heavily by leather straps from their magnificently muscled shoulders.

Stopping before them with a smile, Joey, quietly addressed them, all the while he focused upon the bigger of these formidable twins.

"Worthy guardians of the royal palace. I, Mayneken, *sem*-priest of the god Ptah and ambassador of Queen Nefertiti, and my sister, Maatkare, seek entrance to the royal palace."

Now standing to Joey's right, I noted with pleasure that the guards had acknowledged their granted "worthiness," as their backs fractionally straightened and chests swelled with pride. I could almost read their minds. "Finally, someone appreciates who we truly are." But then, in an instant, the taller of the two recovered, and asked.

"So what is your business, priest of Ptah and ambassador to the Queen?"

To my utter amazement, Joey continued to smile up at the towering man and quipped.

"That, my powerful friend, is the concern of the Great One within. May we now pass?"

Recognizing the gamesmanship of Joey's reply and no doubt taking into account this priest's impressive warrior physique as well, we were allowed to pass.

Once within the first shadows of the palace and out of earshot, Joey sighed heavily and said.

"That was close, now for the next barrier. For a moment there, I wasn't sure whether that brute was going to let us in."

I could only smile and said, "Not so, my dear

Mayneken. Both were entranced by my presence."

"Oh?"

"Yes, my dear *sem*-priest of the god Ptah and ambassador to the Queen, their kilts betrayed them."

* * *

The side entrance of the royal palace opened to a blessedly cool, long, and narrow passage, which emptied into a rectangular receiving chamber. Along the base of its two long walls were low masonry benches. Every square inch of them was occupied with seated petitioners.

I wondered what we would do next as we had stopped in the room's center. Joey pivoted around to slowly survey the scene. He later told me that what he saw were a good many petitioners from all of Egypt: traders, businessmen, and even some foreign merchants. But none held any significant domestic or foreign stature. This he surmised by the worn edges of their garments. Finally, Joey espied just who he was looking for, the peacock that guarded the doorway opposite.

Turning back to me, he rather wickedly smiled and said, "This beautifully colored water fowl is all yours my sister."

Smiling back with the most mischievous grin that I could muster, I said, "Watch me pluck him bare and then steal his eggs!"

Standing boldly in the center of the room as we were, our presence had been noticed, as the gentle purring of conversation had dwindled into silence. So had we recognized that this chamber was only the second vetting, the second barrier to overcome in order to gain access to the king's presence. With this fact firmly understood, I smoothly glided toward the peacock, much like a stalking cobra would a preoccupied, feeding rat.

As for the peacock in question, a palace bureaucrat officiously titled The Royal Fan Bearer, he was a soft middle aged male. His fingers held far too many rings. His fat layered neck was far too burdened with a heavy pectoral necklace of lapis lazuli, carnelian, faience, and gold. He even wore lotus hemp sandals decorated with gold leaf and a short white linen kilt that sported a leopard skin girdle. This last supported his extended, near pregnant stomach like a sling. This palace official, who flicked his ivory pummeled horsetail fly swatter this way and that, more out of officious emphasis than anything else, watched with considerable interest my sultry approach, as did the rest of the petitioners in the chamber. The anticipated confrontation all knew would be epic. You could have heard a pin drop.

As far as I was concerned, the fan bearer was toast. Here I was, finely formed, beautiful, and wrapped in a white, single-shouldered, and near diaphanous linen with my taut left breast fully exposed. In the coolness of the chamber, my hard nipple distended.

Perfect.

That was only the prelude. As I reached the proper distance of address for such an official, I stopped, bowed low toward the man's kilt, and noted with satisfaction his ever growing bulge.

Ah, I do indeed have his full attention.

Rising from my bow I stood erect and proudly before this disgusting worm of an official, my left nipple fully ripe.

"Most Noble One," I purred. "I am Maatkare, sister of Mayneken, *sem*-priest of the god Ptah and personal ambassador of Queen Nefertiti."

I paused for the information to sink in as his eyes were still locked on my perfect left breast.

"We wish audience, this very day, with the Great One, the very Son of the Aten," I breathed.

As calculated, and as I had practiced in the modern era, the heady mixture of perfume, visual stimuli, sheer lust, pheromones, and the words "*sem*-priest of the god Ptah and personal ambassador of Queen Nefertiti," this stimuli caused this insufferable and imperious slug of a man to stop his blatantly affected and incessant flicking. After a few seconds of stunned silence, while he continued to feast his eyes on me, he finally blurted out a bit too gruffly and loudly.

"So, where is this so-called personal ambassador to the exiled queen?" All in the chamber had heard his imperious and intemperate words.

It was then, almost theatrically, that Joey appeared behind my left shoulder. His upper body was hard, chiseled, and in full flex, which he could effortlessly maintain. This sudden vision of pure masculinity, which stood beyond my gracefully feminine shoulder, shocked the bureaucrat with widening eyes.

"Here Noble One," Joey smoothly answered. "I am Mayneken, *sem*-priest of the god of the Great White Wall, and here is my signet ring of ambassadorial authority."

As Joey slowly extended his powerfully sculpted arm forward, with a fist to better display the symbol of the Queen's granted authority, a low murmur broke out among the other petitioners, as they not only saw the muscular display, but also the ragged scarring across the whole of Joey's back.

"Such a priest!" one whispered.

"No, such a warrior priest," his neighbor pointedly corrected. "Cannot your eyes see those brave scars?"

Then Joey continued in a steady low voice and a slight sneer. "But regarding the current station of the 'true' Lady of the Two Lands, I seriously doubt that she considers herself in exile. In fact, such news would amuse her. Would you like me to share with her your ill-advised indiscretion?"

Panicked and in full spiritual retreat, the official stuttered out that was not ever his intention, that he was ignorant of the queen's true situation, and even more, that she had at her disposal such a personal ambassador-at-large. Amid many hidden snickers, the cowed Royal Fan Bearer allowed us to pass on.

As we made our way through the narrow passage, I breathed a sigh of relief. But with two barriers passed, now came the let down. The royal audience hall was actually a quite small, even intimate. The chamber was only about two-thirds the size of the previous one. Certainly not what one would consider pharaonic.

Rectangular, it was smoothly paved in limestone. Its high ceiling of cedar timbers was supported by six brightly painted papyrus-form stone columns. Only one piece of furniture adorned it. At its far end stood camp stool-like throne atop a low, three-stepped, stone platform.

A total of six Medjay guards stood within this confined space, framed within the columns. Sixteen important people of various nationalities and cultures filled out the audience. Some were engaged in hushed conversation. Others waited in stony silence. All, excepting the Medjay who kept watch on the gathering from either side, faced toward the raised throne in anticipation of the Great One's arrival. None noted our arrival. None except the Medjay.

We glanced at one another, smiled, and realized we were within striking distance. All the mat training, all the psychic implants from Doc Allen, were now about to be put to the test. Was I nervous? Yes. What fool would not be. But we were prepared in ways that no ancient, and most assuredly, no alien hybrid had ever seen.

So we casually looked around, took stock of our surroundings, and noted the armament of the Medjay. Each had a dagger scabbard, in addition to heavy and vicious chariot sickles slung over their massive shoulders. Next, we took in the others within the royal audience chamber. Were any of them a potential threat? The answer was clearly no, and so we split up, each to our own side of the chamber.

After waiting for some twenty minutes or so, the sounds of scraping sandal bottoms could be heard from a small doorway located to the left of the raised throne. Through it shuffled an ancient looking man, who I assumed had to be The Royal Herald. After a few moments, he reached the first step of the throne. There, he turned to us and barked out.

"Abase yourselves before the brilliant and magnificent presence of the Son of the Aten! King of Upper and Lower Egypt, the Master of Kush, the Master of Libya, and Master of all the Great Green."

As commanded, all of us, excepting the Medjay of course, fell to the floor face down, with the back of our necks ritualistically exposed in the classic pose of submission. As seen from the perspective of the throne, the floor of the royal audience chamber had been transformed into a sea of colors, textures, and human heads all directed forward.

Several minutes passed before we again heard the sounds of scraping sandal bottoms. But during that period, I inwardly chuckled at the audacious vanity of the herald's announcement.

'Master of all the Great Green!' Hardly did any pharaoh, much less this monster, command the entire Mediterranean!

This rebellious train of thought I stifled once the sound of a solitary pair of feet entered the chamber. They briefly stopped to survey us, the groveling multitude, and when apparently satisfied, only then did they crisply ascend the divine throne of Isis.

What we heard next was the voice of a bored young man, who dully stated with a tone of complete disinterest, "Arise. We wish to see your faces."

Upon pharaoh's command, we all did so, albeit some levered themselves up with considerable difficulty, others rose quickly, but Joey and I purposefully got to our feet slowly so as to remain partially hidden behind the others assembled. Separated as we were to the opposite sides of the audience chamber, we had done on purpose. We did not wish to catch the attention of this hideous psychopathic telepath, Smenkhkare. Oddly, his three royal names translated as "Living are the Forms of Re," "Vigorous is the Soul of Re," and "Holy of Forms." This monster did no justice to any of them.

As we had expected, the young king did indeed

perform a cursory scan of his gathered flock. In the process he managed to miss us, as we had blacked out our personality signatures. *Bless Doc Allen for that trick!* Where we stood, each of us was, practically speaking, an incorporeal entity. Our two physical forms were all that remained behind.

Within such a packed gathering, and since we both were partially if not wholly hidden by those who so dearly wished to be recognized and noticed, our initial concealment from the young pharaoh's sixth sense, his divine *sia*, had been total. Still and all, I had felt the heat of the pharaoh's less than gentle scan. It had caused goose pimples to rise on my forearms and neck.

Such an intrusive monster!

Seated on his throne, sitting stiffly erect with his hands pressed flat against the tops of his thighs, I noted that the pharaoh chose this day to wear the blue military crown, the *khepresh*. Not that he had ever seen a battlefield. Quite literally, at his feet and sitting cross-legged next to the first step, was the chief scribe, who purpose was to dutifully read the petitions and then record their judgment. He entered the chamber after the king, unnoticed. To his right stood proudly, and with appropriate gravitas, the aged royal herald. He now leaned heavily upon his stout wooden *w3s*-staff of authority.

Looking straight forward and fixing his eyes on a point above everyone's head, the king then intoned, "Read to Us the first petition."

So the royal audience began, with the chief scribe reading a legalistic statement from three foreign dignitaries from the Levantine area. At the start of the reading, they had stepped forward to be recognized and receive the king's judgment. Their plea involved a request for Egyptian troops and financial aid, as their cities were threatened by a military power, called the Mitanni. To this plea, the king listened, considered for a moment, and then sent the trio on their way with a talent of gold, but no troops.

"Read to Us the next petition."

This time four petitioners from the audience stepped forward as the scribe began to read. At issue were the boundaries of four administrative districts that required the king's wisdom as to how to resurvey lands altered by the recent Nile inundation. The lands in question were prime agricultural plots that had been lost by one district and now claimed by the other three. To this petition, the king again listened, dramatically thought for a moment, and then rather cleverly declared that what the river god Hapi had deemed worthy of moving, should remain in the hands of those so fortunate to receive them. Clearly, reasoned the pharaoh, the lands must have been mismanaged by their former owner.

"Read Us the next petition."

Two merchants stepped forward upon hearing their issue read aloud. At this point, Joey and I were, for the first time, out in the open and without cover. A shared glance signaled that the time had arrived. I, Maatkare, was the "designated batter" in this diabolical assassination plot. So after the two merchants had moved forward, I too moved forward five full steps to take their place, which placed me next to the nearest Medjay guard on the king's left. At this distance, less than twenty paces from the king, he was a dead man. But to the Nubian guard, I was not seen as a threat, but rather as a sweetly smelling morsel of ripe fruit ready for picking. In actual fact, the guard was so distracted by me that he was getting a bit flustered as well.

While the king had not seen me stepping forward, he nonetheless had felt its affect upon his nearby guard. Easily distracted from such boring proceedings and curious, he looked up in my direction, and flinched, as this was the first time that he had beheld me in all my loveliness.

I knew he was asking himself where I had come from. When he looked again, but this time with his *sia*, or telepathic sixth sense, he clearly flinched a second time as there was nothing there. Here I was, a beautiful woman standing before him. Yet, he could psychically read nothing but a black void – a living body without a *ka*!

While I distracted the king, Joey chose to move as well toward him. Taking some six paces, Joey stopped, and then turned his head as if he was either hard of hearing or particularly interested in the reading of the current petition's substance. While the nearest guard on the king's right duly noted Joey's movement, he ignored it, as he too had become totally captivated by my beautiful form.

Nonetheless, and despite his perception of a living void before him, Smenkhkare had indeed both seen and felt Mayneken's approach. I saw the moment Smenkhkare scanned Joey with his *sia*. I imagined his blood chilling again as this one too was a black void, a living body without a *ka*.

How can this be? The panicked young pharaoh's mind screamed.

As the first scribe finished his reading of the trade

dispute, the two petitioners moved forward so as to receive the king's judgment. After one heart beat, so did Joey and I, two full steps each. Now both of us were within sure kill range, for all six guards were behind us. Only two petitioners, a sitting scribe with his head down, and one very old royal herald, albeit with a heavy staff, were between us and our target.

I saw as Smenkhkare's sense of self-preservation took hold, as he realized that two *ka*-less ones now stood to his right and left. He quickly calculated that his escape routes were blocked. His two nearest guards, totally smitten by me, were out of position to act on his behalf.

It was at this truly delicious moment that I was near enough to literally smell the young pharaoh's fear. And in response…

WHO ARE YOU!

The young man pulsed out with a devastating mental power that even staggered Joey and me. Then, suddenly, he saw who we were, for in my mind stood my beloved Sasha, with his arms crossed across his chest, who glared back, daring any passage past him whatsoever. With clear shock on his face, he then quickly turned to Joey, and the mental image there was of me holding two golden royal cobras entwined on each arm. Out of my mouth a forked tongue extended, lasciviously licking, beckoning, in his direction. And with these distractions now planted, Joey snapped his fingers and triggered our primed and ready metabolisms into an adrenaline overdrive.

And we moved.

Instantly recognizing our first step as an encircling movement, a telepathic shriek of "NO!" boomed out from the teenage king. Seeing that his command had had absolutely no effect, the panicked pharaoh next pulsed out a generalized and devastating shotgun-like death wish that affected all those assembled in the chamber. We were only slowed by the authoritative command projected by the young man's highly developed *sia*. The death shriek, however, had rendered the rest of the chamber lobotomized cretins, as blood gushed freely out of their ears, noses, and mouths. Their collective eyes rolled back due to the overwhelming onslaught of the pharaoh's telekinetic power. Moments later, they dumbly dropped to the floor as lost cerebral function and gravity took its course.

Thudding to the ground right and left like so many sacks of potatoes, I, as rehearsed, reached Smenkhkare first. I delivered the telling death blow as I expertly rammed the palm of my left hand up into the king's delicate nose, sending splinters of bone and cartilage into his fore brain, in effect, physically lobotomizing him. How poetic.

I must admit that the act was immensely liberating, as I experienced a further surge of adrenaline when his head sharply snapped back at the impact. I, Vesna Borisevna Gregorieva, had successfully taken vengeance upon the Akhenaten's own spawn. And this, I knew, my dear Sasha would have truly appreciated.

Now stunned and with his eyes wide open, the king next saw the floor rush up to his face as Joey had swiftly decapitated him with one of his guard's chariot sickles.

Kicking his head over, he spoke directly into the king's face, Joey said, "Your seed is no more."

Then all sensation left the dying pharaoh as his

skull was crushed with the heavy back edge of the weapon. That act instantly evacuated the blood supply from the king's brain, which now formed a messy pool of splatter.

"Why did you do that?" I asked in sudden shock.

"Habit," Joey grimly replied. "Piankhotep did the same to his wretched father, Akhenaten."

Now all silent except for our heavy panting due to the exquisite effort, we staggered our way toward the exit of the audience chamber, which had already filled with the heavy aromas and foul smells of a battlefield. But before we could leave, we removed our soiled clothing and wiped off the bloody splatter from each other with a bit of handy cloth taken from among the fallen. While Joey stripped a fresh loin cloth off of one of the fallen guards, I was challenged to find an unsoiled garment. In the end I selected a beautiful multi-colored sash of a foreign ambassador to simply wrap around my waist.

While so doing, I whispered to Joey, "Noble Mayneken, you did well this day. Indeed our beloved Piankhotep would have been most proud of you."

Joey answered. "It is indeed best that we leave this place."

*　　*　　*

Our return to Thebes was blissfully uneventful as there was a strong and steady wind. Joey, in a moment of inventiveness, had talked our boatman into rigging an extra sail that greatly increased our progress. And, as at our arrival at Akhetaten, Joey insisted again on grooming before eating. *That man!* But to my great surprise, that rather gaudy multi-colored sash that I had been wearing, I managed to barter for my entire grooming and even a new dress! Apparently, the groomer had never before seen such finery. Joey had given me a tiny gold ring that I put it on my right hand, third finger, as I was now feeling marvelous and playful as well.

Thereafter, with our stomachs attended to, we wandered Thebes, hand in hand, he explaining, me listening. It was an extraordinary experience having an expert of two worlds as my very own tour guide. And truth be told, I think that he was learning as much as I was. After all, his first brush with Egyptology was from its ruins. He was seeing first hand those very same ruins, but now as entire structures, complete down to their inhabitants. In fact, I actually caught Joey marveling to himself about the details.

* * *

Under the rubric of "small towns are all eyes and ears," I must report that Prince Horemheb was informed of our presence from his chief houseman, Ramose, who chanced to see us in the marketplace. And while we were touring we managed to bump into the man, while he was out inspecting some public work projects, or so he said.

Allow me to say, here and now, that while Horemheb was quite a fine specimen by ancient Egyptian standards, he couldn't match that of Joey. Nonetheless, he was a kind, generous, and charming man, who invited us back to his household for a quite memorable dinner.

It was during that soirée that I learned firsthand many things, and in particular, about my Sasha's and

Joey's social station. While I knew that Joey acted as the assistant of late Piankhotep, my Sasha, and had succeeded him as a *sem*-priest of the god Ptah, he was considered a learned wizard of sorts. He was also the personal ambassador to Queen Neferiti, and knowing Joey, perhaps much more.

What I did not know was that Joey was also the adopted son of the late Meryptah, a High Priest of Amen Re no less, *and*, the adopted older brother of Prince Horemheb! Talk about connections!

These facts explained to me why Joey was so kind and almost deferential to the locals. He knew he had clout. They knew that he did as well, but he chose not to misuse it. And while I learned of these things, it was important for me to hear what the locals "felt" about this relationship between my Sasha and Joey, not to mention what those inherited titles implied. What I found was a deeply reverent respect for my Sasha, and an ever growing appreciation, and yes, even love, for Joey. And once again, I found myself thanking the gods for my good fortune.

*   *   *

After having enjoyed the Theban prince's hospitality, we took our leave, saying that prayers were owed to the Great God for our safe journey to and from that "other" city. Upon arriving at the temple compound, we reached the house of Joey's adopted father, which, to our surprise, was still unoccupied. We entered its cool spaces, its kitchen area, and there and then Joey broke open one of the many beer jars that had been stored there.

To this very day, I do not prefer beer, but that beer, that day, at that moment, tasted like the very nectar of the gods. Our bellies full of food and drink, and now even more beer, our eyelids began to droop. And then something unexpected, yet something so right, happened. Joey took me by the hand and led me to the guest room.

Never before in my life had I so enjoyed another. I would like to say that was was just the release of so much pent up stress and energy. But I knew better than that. I couldn't fool myself. So while our retrieval point was only a scant one hundred meters away, we had time to kill, and we did so celebrating our very survival, our clean escape from that "other" city, and each other.

While Joey will never admit it, we almost missed the hour of our retrieval! We had so exhausted each other that we almost overslept. Waking with a start, seeing that darkness had fallen, we dressed, removed as best we could all evidence of our passing, and left for the temple proper. To our best knowledge, none was the wiser, excepting of course, that one missing jar of beer.

*   *   *

When I emerged from the temporal field, while grasping tightly onto the retrieval rope, I was greeted by a great electric roar of cheering soldiers. As the wooden crane swung me high up to clear the ring, I was gently deposited before Colonel Charles "Tuna" Cartwright, who met me holding open a rather large military fatigue shirt. Seeing the surprised look on my face, he explained.

"Ms. Gregorieva. For the men. Please put his on, for them."

While doing so, I caught the Colonel carefully looking me over, up and down. I realized he was seeing the evidence of our encounter that was clearly displayed as mild abrasions on my neck and skin.

When Joey emerged from the temporal field, the soldiers' roar was repeated, along with a few congratulatory whistles and cheers that signaled good-natured male envy and appreciation.

* * *

That was my first deployment. While we had managed to escape the palace unnoticed, it was only during our trip back up river to Thebes that I had the time to truly put all the pieces together. My first naïve thought was that we had been incredibly lucky to have pulled off the assassination, and then even more so just to get out with our skins intact.

Upon further consideration, my second thought was that we weren't meant to survive at all. In no respect were the odds in our favor. Yes, the Americans had given us the tools to succeed, but when I had gotten back to Russia, it became obvious that my handlers had considered me expendable, and just as obviously wanted Joey dead as well – come what may and whatever impact that might have had on our current reality. It was one thing that the Americans had control of the temporal device. But for them to have their own seasoned temporal field agent was entirely another. The more I thought about it, the more that scenario made sense.

Chills ran up and down my spine as I considered all the cold and dark ramifications. At the same time, I found myself warming to the Americans, especially the likes of John Milson, Doc Allen, Peter Borov, and of course, Joey. *My, what a surprise he turned out to be, and in so many, many ways. So young, and yet, so very wise.*

That left my cool Russian colleagues on the outside, a group that had to be watched most carefully. What I could do about my situation remained murky, but I was determined to remain patient, and above all else, vigilant. My return to Moscow would be unexpected. Clearly, I was on borrowed time.

CHAPTER II

The Early Years

I was born in 1979 in the Yugoslav capital of Belgrade. That country, that city, at that time, with the heroic image of Tito everywhere, was not the best place to raise a highly impressionable young girl. Still and all, the Yugoslavian flavor of socialism remained a far cry from that practiced in Bulgaria, or for that matter elsewhere behind the Iron Curtain.

As time passed I became aware, for I never went hungry as did some of my schoolmates. My clothes were always clean and neat and were never second-hand. In fact, I never really wanted for anything. My father, Boris Alexandrevich, was Russian and a professor in applied engineering at the university. My mother, Ljubica, was a Yugoslav apparatchik within the state's security system. Both of my parents were members-in-good-standing within the Communist Party.

We three made up a loving family, but a family at times on display, especially for me. Excellent grades in my school subjects were expected, as nothing less was tolerated. For sport, a mix of dance, ballet, and gymnastics were my only options given my slight build. As with my academics, only my very best efforts were acknowledged. It was a pressure-cooker environment, where I learned early that with discipline, knowledge, focus, and a certain amount of deft ruthlessness, that virtually anything could be accomplished.

I was raised an atheist without any knowledge of the divine. The State and Party were both "mother" and "father." All in all, I felt loved, secure, and happy. In retrospect, I find this rather odd and hard to swallow. Nonetheless, that was my reality.

When I was barely twelve, this structured and relatively privileged environment abruptly came to an end, as the Soviet Union disintegrated into a quarrelsome patch-work quilt of nation-states. Our family had to move. I found myself in a strange city, located far to the north. It was only September, but already it was a biting, bitter, humid cold. Even though the newly renamed St. Petersburg was the western-most port city of Russia, being thin of build, my bare knees actually ached in that never-ending arctic wind that blew across the Baltic.

To my surprise, the administrators at my new school didn't know where to place me, so I endured four days of rigorous testing. When finished, I was so wrung out that I barely remembered how to write my own name.

I must have done well, as three days later, in our micro-sized flat, one among many within a huge concrete complex, we had an impromptu party. It wasn't much really, but at the time was grand. We shared one small chocolate sweet, a solitary candle, some fresh black bread and butter, fried onions, and three rather large and tasty sausages. Father was beaming as his little genius had scored so well in science and mathematics, while mother was near tears as I had aced the literature and history sections.

Because of my examinations, I was placed at an advanced level where only the very best, or select children of the former Communist Party's elite, attended. Then, the following week, we were moved out of our flat and into a five-room apartment that was within walking distance of my new school. Our new home was spacious in comparison to the previous postage stamp flat, was decorated with fine furniture, freshly painted walls, and even had a standing refrigerator! When I first opened it, I discovered that it had been filled to the brim with milk, juices, fresh meats, cheeses, and eggs. It even had a freezer where father could store his vodka!

When I had asked why all of this had come to pass, my father just said, "There's nothing that my little girl should want for."

*   *   *

It did not take long for me to realize that there was a distinct pecking order in my new school. The boys and girls of the politically well connected were treated with deference and were granted surprising latitude by the academic staff. I, on the other hand, was seen as an interesting intellectual prospect, but an outsider, an anomaly from a provincial state.

While I struggled through some of my subjects, I earned every mark that I made with my own effort and more than a few well-hidden tears. This was not the case for the "special children," who blissfully skipped from class to class seemingly without care. When I told my parents about the situation, my mother frowned while she brushed out my long hair, bit her lower lip, and shook her head in silent rage. But my father said something that to this day I'll never forget.

"Vesna my dear, do you remember when we fled from our beloved Belgrade? Do you remember all the changes, all the uncertainty? And yet, through hard work we have managed to adapt and succeed. Now consider this. How well prepared will these children be if such drastic change would be thrust upon them? Do you think for a minute that they will be able to compete with you on a level playing field?"

That simple statement sparked within me a warming sense of pride, a self confidence that I cherished. His softly spoken words, matched with the pure love that emanated from his robin's egg blue eyes, always touched my heart in a very special way.

*   *   *

In the gymnasium, personal performance was far easier to measure. Body types were matched and placed on athletic "tracks." In my case, I was initially placed during my first two years on the gymnastics team, where my dance and ballet background were seen as an advantage.

In my third year, I was transferred to the track and field curricula. I had grown too tall to be the prototypical, pixy-sized gymnast, which at that time had become so fashionable.

Damn you, Nadia Comaneci!

But as with so many things, the change was a good thing. Since my background in dance and ballet had blessed me with a limber and graceful form, I found that I was a natural on the track surface, which nicely matched my ever-lengthening stride so very well. With my long and silky hair trailing behind me, I imagined being the wind, sometimes a wild horse. I easily became lost in the moment. Running became a near obsession. It became a sanctuary where all my academic frustrations could be released, a place where my mind cleared. Track calmed me so that my academic marks improved, to the point that by the end of my fourth year, I placed second in my class.

*   *   *

The year was 1995, I was fifteen, and many worrisome political rumblings were breaking out within the young Russian Federation. The broadcasts were filled with daily clashes between the Chechen revolutionaries and the Russian Army. Accusations of atrocity were made by both sides. The times were grim and uncertain.

Thursday, January 12, I was told that I had been promoted two years ahead of my class. I was simply exploding with the news! As soon as I had arrived at our family's apartment, I set the table for dinner, and put on the stove mother's heavy soup pot. She had filled it with all of her magical ingredients.

By five-o'-clock, neither my father nor mother had arrived. Six-o-clock came and went and still no father and mother. The soup by this time was piping hot and ready to serve. The apartment smelled divine. I had even sliced up father's heavy black bread and put out the butter to soften.

Then a kindly woman from the Directorate arrived and gave me the news. No less than five terrorist bombs were detonated within the city limits of St. Petersburg during that evening's rush hour. All five targeted the main train stations, killing hundreds, and maiming even more. As for my parents, they were no more.

I, in a moment, had become orphaned by a shadowy, distant nationalist war. I had been orphaned by faceless agents, who had purposefully traveled to my city, far, far away from their homeland. The woman from the Directorate had said that the bombings were the acts of misguided nationalism and radical Islamic terrorism.

While I could intellectually comprehend all the "isms," I remained an emotionally crushed, angry, and dazed teenager. Again, my world had been turned upside down, but this time, I was on my own and without my parents' support and guidance.

After the Directorate's representative left that evening with a firm promise to return in the morning, I resolved not to fail. I would not turn my back on the many hopes and dreams of my parents. Above all, I would not let myself down. I remembered my mother's dictate: "Can't was killed in the Battle of Try." I remembered my father's blue eyes and loving words of encouragement in the face of adversity. So I sat down at the table alone for the first time, and with an empty stomach full of grief, I buttered my black bread with my own tears.

* * *

Much to my surprise, I learned that my parents had long prepared for such an eventuality. It was their way. The next morning the kind lady did indeed return with the news I was to pack all that was near and dear to me. I was being relocated by the Directorate, as their special charge, to live in Moscow. There, I was to begin my first year of tertiary education, or university, at Moscow State University, the very same prestigious Russian institution where my father had once gone to school.

* * *

Once again, as had happened to me so many times before, change had made all the difference. At last I found myself on a level playing field. It was exciting. It was intoxicating. It was hard. It was rewarding. I loved every bit of it. And yes, I purposely lost myself in it to forget.

At least twice a week, my mentor from the Directorate, Valentina Ivanova Piltova, and I would meet for lunch, which meant the faculty lounge, a very special privilege for a mere student to enter, but she had arranged it all. There, we would talk and she, unknown to me at the time, would assess my mental state. This striking, middle-aged, and crisply clothed woman provided me a marvelous model of what a truly professional woman looked like. But best of all, she was my sounding board. We would discuss how I was doing in my classes, my work load, sport – which was track, and even women's styles in dresses and how to properly use makeup. Valentina Ivanova, bless her, became a much-needed big sister.

After my first month at university, Valentina Ivanova arranged for faculty to join us at our table. Mathematicians, physicists, engineers, historians, linguists, chemists, archaeologists, biologists, it did not matter, as she seemed to have an endless supply of them. Each such luncheon would begin with her shyly introducing me to Academician So and So, and before long, I would be immersed in their pet research subject. Remarkably, all were interesting. None were boring, no matter how theoretical or obtuse the subject.

I will never forget it, but during my second year at university, during one of Valentina Ivanova's planned faculty get-togethers, I was introduced to a man named

Alexander Andreovich Piankoff. Unlike the other faculty that she had exposed me to, Piankoff worked for the same department that she did within the Russian Academy of Sciences, The Special Projects Directorate. Even to my then young eyes, Alexander Andreovich, dressed in a flatteringly tailored dark suit, possessed an erect posture that screamed military. And, of course, I was right. But it was his demeanor, his kind eyes, and his absolute passion for his subject that instantly captivated me – ancient Egypt. So much so that two hours later we were still talking.

Alexander Andreovich's story was fascinating. His grandfather was also named Alexandre, but spelled in the French style. This once famous and well-respected Egyptologist, among many other things, had published translations of all of the royal inscriptions found within Tutankhamen's tomb. As a boy, young Alexander Andreovich would eagerly await his grandfather's letters and lessons, posted from Paris, on translating hieroglyphic inscriptions.

So had begun Alexander Andreovich's interest in that most ancient culture, but the State had other plans for his future, and it was not Egyptology. Not to be denied, Alexander Andreovich continued his studies on the side to the point that he could sight-read Middle Egyptian quite well.

To my impressionable ears, this man's message was a different one from the other academicians, but one that was quite clear. Follow your heart, and do not be detoured from that which you are truly passionate about. Taken by his honesty, to my great surprise I opened up to him and cast to the wind my usual reserve. I found myself sharing with him my passions for mathematics and physics, my joy of running, and the important synergy in maintaining a strong body and a healthy mind. Perhaps I had said too much, but I had felt that a kinship had been discovered, a bonding had taken place during that luncheon.

*   *   *

At the beginning of my fifth and last year of university, which in the Russian educational system is considered the norm, I received an invitation from The Special Projects Directorate of the Russian Academy of Sciences. Not knowing what to make of the letter, I shared it with my friend Valentina Ivanova, who clapped her hands together and smiled so broadly that I thought her face would split!

"My Vesna! My beautiful and intelligent Vesna! The Directorate wishes to meet with you! We must have a party! We must celebrate!"

"Why?" I asked.

"Because to work for the Directorate is the opening of so many doors! So many possibilities! We must celebrate your good fortune."

With wide eyes I said, "How? Where?"

"Do not trouble yourself! I know just the place. They even keep their Vodka in the deep freeze!"

At this last, my face must have fallen as Valentina Ivanova's demeanor instantly changed.

"What's wrong Vesna? What's with the suddenly long face? Do you not want to celebrate?"

Recovering, I remember quite distinctly saying to her, "Yes, I do wish to celebrate. My father and mother would have heartily approved."

*　　*　　*

Years later I learned that the Directorate's interest in me was not by chance, but rather had been the result of a long process. In the final analysis their decision to pursue my candidacy was because of my parents, my exemplary academic achievements, my physical gifts, and a certain luncheon that had been in reality an intensive fitness review.

Upon entering the Directorate, I found to my surprise that my supervisor was none other than Colonel Alexander Andreovich Piankoff himself! When I entered his office for the first time, and once we were alone (but as I again realized later, you are never "truly alone" in the Directorate), he took both of my hands in his and warmly welcomed me to the future.

At the time, I thought how odd that statement was. Now in hindsight, I know the full truth of his well chosen words.

CHAPTER III
The Directorate

The purview of the Special Projects Directorate within the Russian Academy of Sciences is omnipresent. It was first established during the Cold War years, when security was everywhere and presumably spies as well. So it was decided early on that bright individuals in the sciences and social studies should be recruited, who would quietly "accompany" scholars to their many conferences. Such "watchers" might deliver lectures, publish papers, articles, and even write books in order to establish their academic *bona fides*.

Once the Iron Curtain had fallen, Russian scholars and scientists, hungry for contact with their foreign colleagues, remained a liability as post-Soviet Russia was ever paranoid that one of their own might leak something of vital national interest to the West. Now the "watchers" not only looked after their own, but also the foreign competition, who with the least bit of provocation tended to be egotistical magpies and gabby-Gus's. In short, they were absolute gold mines of potentially useful information.

I, with my background in the sciences and mathematics, was assigned to this academic security subgroup. It became plain to me that I was a natural at such covert observation. Valentina Ivanova's many get-togethers at the university faculty lounge had made me quite artful at formulating, and then fearlessly asking, that critical first probing question, which would trigger the typical western academic to reveal and discuss, *ad nauseum,* their most cherished research project.

What I was not prepared for, however, was the non-intellectual side of such an encounter. While blessed with natural beauty and a taut physique to match, I was not adept at western make-up, clothing, and the all-powerful use of perfume. Such tactics were all new to me, as were the strategies and tactics of sex. Not that I was a prude. It's just that the difference between one's personal love life and the needs of the Directorate took me some time to straighten out. All the "skills" nonetheless had to be mastered if I was to succeed, even if I never had to employ them. As Colonel Piankoff was so fond of saying, "A loaded gun is a direct threat. But a simple smile can make a willing friend." So I applied myself, since I wished to succeed for the sake of my parents' memory, and to please my mentor.

*   *   *

I can say with pride that I never had to use my body as I had been instructed. Instead, I used my mind, my wits, and yes, my devastating smile. The weak ones misread that smile, letting their ever-swelling groins led them into submission. The strong ones, however, saw me and my intellect for what they were, and out of such encounters, mutual transactions of substance occurred, and professional, and sometimes even personal bonds, were made.

Sadly, I have found that there are very few strong ones among the foreigners that I have met. The American John Milson, an extraordinary Egyptologist, was definitely one, as was the Russian engineering genius, physicist, and ex-patriot Peter Borov, the fatherly physician James H. Allen, and grudgingly, even Joseph Richards, another Egyptologist, but I am getting way ahead of myself. And when it comes to Joey Richards, well, that situation became quite complicated. Quite complicated indeed.

My training continued and eventually I developed my own style of dealing with the weak or strong, and in the process became an ever more competent "watcher." Along the way, I delivered the occasional paper, wrote an article in a well-placed journal, and became a regular attendee at the important international conventions and congresses devoted to physics and mathematics. With my second language being British English, my persona was crafted as that of a mid-range scholar. I learned to play that to the max, all the while shadowing one of our own on one occasion, or, noting something significant that a westerner said during a cocktail party.

I made myself appear as the ultimate librarian figure, wearing dark and heavy-framed, prescription-less eye glasses, my long dark hair worn up in a tight bun, subdued wool suits with knee length skirts, low heels, and tasteful silk blouses in muted shades, all finished with pearl earrings. Those last personal adornments I dearly loved as my Sasha, Colonel Piankoff, had given them to me. He had said that my chosen persona was far too severe to be approachable. Some ornament of feminine vanity was sorely needed to complete the ensemble, to complete the image that was Vesna Borisevna Gregorieva, of the Russian Academy of Sciences.

*   *   *

After a year of being a "watcher," several odd things transpired. First, I was summoned to Colonel Piankoff's office. Apparently, he had just gotten back from a rather important meeting in the United States with an organization called the Philology Annex. Curious about it, I went online and could not find anything definitive about it.

Then, in the course of an intense conversation, I was informed that I would be shifting to a new specialty for my "watcher" duties, ancient Egyptian philology and culture of all things. Also Colonel Piankoff wanted me to meet with an academician named Markova, who ran the Center for Egyptological Studies in Moscow. Henceforth, I was to drop the subjects of physics and mathematics, focus solely upon the international congresses pertaining to this new area, and "absorb like a sponge" as much as I could about this discipline's latest research.

I have to say that this entire development was a rather rude shock, because until that day, I had thought myself a pure scientist, and not a humanist. The difference between the two cannot be underestimated. In fact, the vast chasm between the two cannot be easily bridged as it requires a dramatic shift in one's outlook on the world at its most basic underpinnings. Put bluntly, in science, theory can be rigorously tested, confirmed, or rejected. But in the humanities, there exists an uncomfortable vagueness, an imprecision, and a complete lack of exactitude that humanists can tolerate with ease. I was not initially very keen on this reassignment.

Nevertheless, and to his everlasting credit, Colonel Piankoff saw the look on my face that betrayed my rather obvious distress at this shift in my assigned duties. The result was one of his classic and disarming smiles.

Then he said with a casual wave of his hand. "My dear Vesna Borisevna, consider this task that I have put before you as a supreme personal challenge, one that will tax your intellect. It will be an opportunity to shed logic and consistency upon a sometimes beautiful, but oftentimes disorganized subject. Frankly, I think that you, of all the "watchers," are the one most capable of adapting to and succeeding with this task. Why? Well, because you are someone that I know will not give up. You also have a proven track record of overcoming adversity, you're adaptable, and have a remarkable sense of purpose and pride in whatever you do. That, frankly, the others lack."

I was floored by my superior's frank and open assessment. I distinctly remember feeling privileged in some way, but mildly dizzy, sitting there in my chair, my head all abuzz with the possibilities.

"Colonel Piankoff," I asked, "When will I be introduced to this Academician Markova so that I may begin?"

Piankoff's reaction to my question was reflected in a sudden softening around his eyes that I had never seen before. It was as if a pent up pressure had suddenly been relieved.

When he spoke, his voice clearly cracked with emotion. "Vesna Borisevna, my grandfather Alexandre was an Egyptologist. He was a man who had greatly influenced me as a young man. I guarantee that if you put your heart and soul into this undertaking, you will not be disappointed. In fact, I think that you will rediscover yourself. Perhaps even find the real you. But beware that a deep dive into the humanities can do that to you.

"As for Academician Konstantina Iosifeva Markova, she is expecting you at two-o'clock today. You can get the logistical particulars from my secretary on your way out."

And then he paused for a moment.

"Academician Markova will be very suspicious of you, a scientist, as possessing any genuine wit of interest for her field. She will assume that you are an opinionated pragmatist who can explain all of mankind's most cherished mysteries in the cool language of mathematics or within the sterile confines of physics. That, Gregorieva, you must overcome. You must sell yourself to her, must convince her of your passionate interest in ancient Egypt. Fortunately, your innate sense of rigorous empiricism and skills in technology will be a great help given her current situation, which, as you will no doubt find out, is a formidable one.

"Good luck."

CHAPTER IV
Center for Egyptological Studies (CESRAS)

Academician Konstantia Iosifeva Markova saw herself as both the protective mother and prime force behind the Russian renaissance in Egyptology. She refused to allow the first efforts, scholarship, and acquisitions of Golenischchev, Lemm, Stuve, Piankoff and de Rachewitz to be lost to the voracious greed of the antiquities black market, or merely forgotten. A recent addition to the Russian Academy of Sciences, CESRAS was all that remained of a once promising legacy decimated by the Soviet winter. Founded in 1998, the first directive of the CESRAS and its sister institution, the Russian Institute of Egyptology in Cairo (REIC) was to catalogue the contents of the former Soviet Union's many museums and enter all of the information into a single database.

Political, cultural and agricultural relations between the former Soviet Union and Egypt had been strained for decades. Being a Russian in Egypt was much akin to the ugly American in Southwest Asia. This was the world that I was stepping into.

* * *

Moscow State University fronts Leninskije Gory and within its multi-towered, gray stone walls can be found the CESRAS office. Not surprisingly, I had never been in this part of the university before, but after some hunting around, I finally found its basement location.

To say that the journey was like finding a long lost ancient tomb would be an understatement, but upon entering its narrow entrance corridor, I felt strangely warm, at home, and not at all at odds as I had first feared. Perhaps it was the smell of the fresh coffee in the air, perhaps it was the posters depicting antiquities on the walls, or the immense cork board that was covered with several layers of pinned-up notices, with the oldest nearly buried and yellowing at their curling edges.

The next room, this one a square, was to the right and along its far wall was what I believed to be the department's reception desk. Behind it sat an older woman, sixtyish, dressed in an oversized woolen sweater, with a riot of dark and gray curly hair. She was furiously typing on her computer's keyboard, her fingers energetically striking the keys as if they were daggers. So I politely waited for a convenient break in her frenetic activity.

"May I help you?" She said as a curt, declarative than as a courtesy, without looking up from her screen.

Startled I said, "Why yes. I have an appointment with Academician Konstantina Iosifeva Markova at two. Would you be so kind and let her know that I'm here? I'm a bit early."

Now glancing at her wristwatch, the woman smirked, looked up revealing her deep brown eyes, and quipped, "Indeed you are. You must be Vesna Borisevna Gregorieva. I am Academician Konstantina Iosifeva Markova. Welcome to my kingdom."

What followed were several moments of stunned silence, while I attempted to find my tongue.

"Th-thank you." I eventually managed.

Now leaning back in her chair and crossing her arms across her chest, Markova slightly tilted her head and said, "So, how may I help you, Vesna Borisevna?"

Standing straight and tall I replied, "Actually, I was told that you were the one who was seeking assistance. I am a mathematician and physicist. I possess a ruthlessly logical mind, and, understand computer databases."

Now smiling a half-smile, Markova parried, "How refreshing. An honest answer."

Sigh.

"Excuse me Vesna Borisevna for my current attitude. It's not a reflection on you. It's just that I thoroughly despise academic bureaucracy, begging for research funding, and struggling with imbeciles who do not know the difference between a royal scarab and a cheap copy regurgitated by a goose."

For some reason I laughed, and as it turned out, that had made all the difference, as Markova rose and pulled over the room's only vacant chair.

"Sit." She commanded. "I like your laugh. It is refreshingly genuine."

"Why, thank you again, Academician Markova. I think that you will find me quite genuine, warts and all."

"So, Vesna Borisevna, again I ask. Why are you here?"

So I began, to bluntly and directly explain my situation, what I had been tasked with, what I wanted to know and why. It took some time as Markova had plenty of her own questions, and I, answered each and every one of them with no evasions. The whole experience was emotionally draining as I really wanted

Markova as my mentor, and, of course, I did not want to disappoint my Sasha. Finally, as all such interviews eventually run out of steam, it ended.

Markova, still with her arms crossed over her torso, stated with finality.

"So, I like your energy Vesna Borisevna. I like the way you logically presented your impressive academic credentials and somehow managed to remain humble about them. You know what you know, and, know what you want to know. That, I like as well. But as you probably have guessed from these surroundings, my funding budget is extremely tight. As for wages, I cannot promise much right now. My department is not a rich "scientific" or "strategic" one like those that you are probably used to dealing with. We are a very modest shop here, but you will learn from the basement up, that I can guarantee.

"When do you wish to begin working on the database?"

I began that very day as a green-as-grass data entry clerk. I entered catalogue numbers, matching them with an artifact's photo or drawing, typed in descriptions and a myriad of other arcane details. What aided me and insured my success was Markova's uncanny organization and ability to anticipate my novice's needs with lists of useful abbreviations, ancient sites, names, and a chronology of Egyptian civilization. In short, if her database was to be accurate, I had to be accurate as well. Then there were my seemingly endless questions about this and that, all of which were patiently and concisely answered.

Remarkably, Markova started me transcribing from a very old volume that dated to 1891. It was the

Golenishchev Inventory of the Egyptian collection at The Hermitage in St. Petersburg. That, she said, would be our base from which we would next add the collection at the Pushkin Museum in Moscow, and then the other minor collections scattered across the federal republic.

By the end of day three of this database immersion, Markova announced to the room in general and to me in particular.

"Vesna Borisevna! I will make a proper Egyptologist out of you yet! By the way, I have just received confirmation of your appointment as my assistant. No more black bread and butter for you. And no more of this 'Academician Markova' crap any more. I am Konstantina Iosifeva."

* * *

Konstantina Iosifeva's enthusiasm for her subject was absolutely infectious. After six hard months of data entry, I could recall by sight almost the entire Egyptian collection at The Hermitage and Pushkin Museums. As for the minor collections, I must admit that they remained a bit more blurry. With the Egyptian chronology indelibly etched into the convoluted folds of my brain, I could now effortlessly distinguish between periods of art, coffin and sarcophagi types, pottery, the many gods and goddess, not to mention a plethora of cultural items from the ancient Egyptians' life.

What was far more lasting were the occasional "field trips" that Konstantina Iosifeva and I would take to the Pushkin collection. Photographs and sketches cannot accurately depict scale and on more than one occasion, I was simply astonished. It was during one of those insightful expeditions that I murmured, a bit too loudly, how nice it would be to understand what that inscription actually said.

Konstantina Iosifeva, hearing me, said, "Take care Vesna Borisevna, for what you ask."

Later that week, an ancient Egyptian primer appeared on my desk. The attached note said: *Read, memorize, master. Then ask me your questions! – Konstantina Iosifeva.*

* * *

I received surprising news from Konstantina Iosifeva one morning. All smiles and eyes bright, she said, "Vesna Borisevna, I have some extraordinary news for you! I have just received approval from the Colonel Piankoff for you to spend some time at the University of St. Petersburg. Next month, you will begin an intensive program in ancient Egyptian. I expect you to finish it in twelve months time, as I will need you back here by then. I told you that I would make an Egyptologist out of you!"

* * *

The year of study in St. Petersburg was an exhilarating intellectual experience that I will never forget. I was lodged in a cozy and marvelously appointed flat that usually was reserved for visiting foreign scholars from the west. On top of that, I received a generous monthly stipend, much of which I managed to save. I truly wanted for nothing within this lap of academic luxury, and so, and at a tremendous rate, I immersed myself in Middle Kingdom Egyptian.

For some reason that I cannot adequately explain, I, an avowed empiricist, excelled to the point that I was working on average two to three chapters ahead of the class. I found myself absorbing at a terrific rate, quickly memorizing the bi- and triliteral signs, mastering the many determinatives, and making marked headway with verbal expressions. I pushed my instructor to the point that we met in his office for my philological questions, which had begun to disrupt the class. I suppose that my motivation was to please Konstantina Iosifeva. But, to be honest, I could not let my Sasha down either. I must admit, I wanted to understand his passionate interest in ancient Egypt, his cultural first love.

I found out later that the year in St. Petersburg was nothing more than the execution of a long range, pre-planned curriculum. The timing behind the implementation of that plan, however, occurred because the Directorate wanted me temporarily out of Moscow.

Why?

Because my dear Sasha was recuperating from a brutal mental injury, which had scrambled his mind, impaired his speech, and even upset his sense of balance. It was thought that if I had caught wind of his condition, that I would have become unstable. So, the Directorate in its infinite wisdom whisked me off to St. Petersburg, where I could immerse myself in the minute details of ancient Egyptian hieroglyphics, and in so doing, had insulated me from getting any whisper of the torments that my mentor was going through.

That was the plan, and, it had worked, but in a way that was unexpected. And they were absolutely correct. For if I had gotten any inkling of my Sasha's condition, than I would have lost it. First my parents, and now him? My evaluator Valentina Ivanova had been correct in gauging the fragility of my psyche. But when I did learn of his injuries and how he had come by them, I then and there silently vowed to wreak havoc and somehow collect a brutal revenge. The real question at the time had been, how? My second, just who did this to my Sasha?

CHAPTER V
Secrets

After the completion of my studies in St. Petersburg, I returned in triumph back in Moscow and my work with Konstantina Iosifeva. But I also was eager to visit the Directorate as well, so that I might surprise my Sasha, and tell him of my many successes with the Egyptian language.

When I called ahead to arrange for an appointment, his secretary at first nearly choked at my request, but after some cajoling, she finally found a fifteen minute slot the following late afternoon. Although I thought that the secretary's reaction was a bit odd, I passed over it, so happy I was to see my Sasha.

So that afternoon I made my way to the university and surprised Konstantina Iosifeva. To say that it was a warm welcome home would be an understatement! After a shriek of surprise, Konstantina Iosifeva hugged me, and then sat me down for a download. This, I gladly did, even offering to attempt a cold transliteration and translation. Instead, Konstantina Iosifeva just smiled, got up, and moved me over to the computer.

"Translations later Vesna Borisevna," she stated, "but right now I need your eyes on our database. It seems that several items of the 1891 Golenishchev Inventory are not currently in The Hermitage collection."

* * *

The following day, excited and full of anticipation, I arrived at the Directorate. As I waited in the small reception office with Colonel Piankoff's secretary, my appointment time came and went. Then, finally it seemed, the secretary's phone rang. Answering it, she listened, shook her salt and pepper head once, and said, "*Da*." Replacing the receiver, she looked up at me, smiled, and cocked her head toward his office's door.

I really did try not to jump up and run to it, but I probably had as I heard a quiet chuckle from behind my back. Rapping twice, I turned the door knob, and boldly entered.

In retrospect, my obvious excitement most likely was misread by the secretary, and hence her mirthless cackle, but what I saw froze me in my tracks. Sitting rather stiffly behind his desk, my Sasha, head shaved and with a high polish, took me in with vacant, yet strangely haunted eyes. Unsmiling, he gestured with his open hand to the lone chair.

"Sit Vesna Borisevna." He said with a crisp, military directness. "We have much to discuss."

I sat down rather awkwardly before the changed human being, who sat before me. One that was almost robot-like in his movements.

"I understand that you have completed your philological studies in St. Petersburg. Tell me about them," he simply stated.

So I began, haltingly at first, as I tried to read his eyes, the stiffness and twitching muscles of his jaw line, and his overall intensity. *What had happened to my Sasha?* I asked myself over and over in my head.

At my summation, Colonel Piankoff had merely grunted. Then, he picked up his phone, listened, and then ordered that his car be brought around. Rising from his chair, he announced.

"Vesna Borisevna, I have never seen the Pushkin Museum's Egyptian collection. Today, you will be my tour guide."

*   *   *

I had never ridden in a Zil before. It was big, black, with comfortable seats and a good heater. After about a five minute drive, we arrived at the Pushkin Museum, a magnificent white stoned Ionic-styled temple dedicated to the fine arts. Opened to the public in 1912, and still breath-taking from a distance, its need of restoration was now quite apparent. Stopping before its monumental entranceway, we got out, mounted the steps – no, we assaulted them, and entered the edifice unmolested, as the colonel had flashed his credentials before the face of the surprised attendant.

Now in the museum's main hall, Colonel Piankoff abruptly turned to me and said. "Now, you are the leader. You are in charge."

And lead I did, directly and unerringly to the Egyptian collection on the museum's first floor. Then I noticed a subtle change in my Sasha. As I prattled on about this *object d' art*, or that, Sasha's face began to ever so slightly soften. The fingers of his right hand began to lovingly touch this statue and trace the hieroglyphs of that monument's inscription. At this point, I stopped speaking and just watched the man as he seemed to be reacquainting himself with something lost, but newly found, and warmly familiar. His fingers stopped and seemed fixed, hovering over one of the lines of a hieroglyphic inscription, that prompted me to translate.

> The God's First Wife, Lady of the Two Lands, the most beautiful Nefertiti. May she live long, with health and prosperity. Forever.

"Yes." He said with a small smile. "She indeed was a beautiful woman. So strong. So alive. If she could overcome what I have experienced, then, so can this old soldier."

I must admit that at hearing these personal thoughts so expressed, I blushed with a mixture of self-consciousness and jealousy at not being that "beautiful woman."

Then his eyes filled and the tears began, slowly at first, then with greater force. Finally turning to me, my Sasha's eyes were back, alive and strong.

"Thank you, Vesna Borisevna. Your translation had a most poetic quality to it. It reminds me of another, a particular young lion, who can make your heart ache with such soothing words."

Allowing his hand to drop to his side, my Sasha then checked his wristwatch, and surprised me again.

"Vesna Borisevna, I find myself suddenly famished. Would you like to join me for an early dinner? I believe that we have much to discuss about your future."

*   *   *

I have always believed that in everyone's life there occurred a watershed moment that placed into focus one's life purpose, the identification of a particular passion or endeavor. That dinner with my Sasha was such for me, for it defined the course of the rest of my life.

"Vesna Borisevna," He began during the after dinner coffee. "I believe that you are now ready to discover your future. In order to do so, will require some explanation on my part, so kindly grant me your patience.

"The story began just prior to the Nazi siege of Stalingrad, today's St. Petersburg. A young man, only eighteen at the time, called Pyotr Valerievich Borov, had just received his doctorate in quantum mechanics and theoretical engineering. His thesis topic was as remarkable as his youth. His dissertation, rather brazenly, outlined the theoretical basis for time travel.

"Somehow, and I suspect that your mathematics and physics background provide you with many proofs against such a notion, his arguments were taken seriously. The Soviet government became very interested in what he had to say, and so funded a very obscure panel, called the Hourglass Seminar, to discover the actual feasibility of such a daring notion. As you might appreciate, the members of that seminar were the period's heavy-weights in physics and mathematics. You might even recognize some of their names: Alexandr Gregorievich Koslov, Nikolai Alexandrevich Fedorov, and Dmitry Nikolevich Giga."

"My God," I exclaimed, "I know of them! That's the Terrible Three!"

"The very same. In addition, the seminar's chair was a philosopher named Suvurov, Gregor Veniaminovich Suvurov, a pompous ass if there ever was one, but also a very dangerous one as he had the ear of Stalin himself, if I read the security files correctly. Finally, the seminar's membership was completed with an odd choice, but one that proved to be extremely seminal, a humanist, a Byzantine papyrologist by the name of Victor Petrovich Latysev. That alone, given your own background, should give you some idea of what the chemistry of this group must have been like: extreme empiricists and two humanists.

"Well, their first, and as it turned out, only tangible result was the creation of a set of rules for the practical use of time travel, which they boldly entitled, *Rukovodyashiy Ukaeaniya dlya Tymporalie Eksploratsiya*, or The Guidelines for Temporal Exploration. Abbreviated *RUTI* for short.

"The points enumerated within this rather remarkable set of rules included," as Colonel Piankoff gripped his right forefinger for emphasis, "first: that Time had to be considered as a single instance, and thus, an alterable dimension. In their minds, Time could not be immutable nor subject to multiple parallel iterations. Today this rather dogmatic position is not one shared by many theoretical physicists, mathematicians, and philosophers. Regardless, the seminar adopted this very conservative position. After all, their purpose was not to produce a theoretical exercise, but rather to provide guidelines for the practical use of a temporal device.

"Second," now grasping his fore and middle fingers, "paradoxes were to be avoided at all costs. In other words, any situation where two propositions are simultaneously true and false cannot be allowed to occur. The best example would be meeting yourself or your immediate ancestors in the past, but of equally importance is to do no harm. In other words, do not terminate yourself or your ancestors, and, do not injure indiscriminately or consciously instigate change.

"Third," now holding his first three fingers of his right hand, "any authorization to use the temporal device can only be made by the designated scientific representatives of at least two national entities. This rule, as you can easily imagine, was rather controversial, as the members of the seminar were all Soviet citizens. They clearly did not trust their own government. Why, you say? Because what was at stake was our present reality, something that even these avowed atheists did not wish to tamper with.

"Fourth," now holding his entire right hand, "to emphasize the sanctioned use of the temporal device, it was made abundantly clear that the device was not the property, nor would be placed under the control, of any national entity. Instead, it would be the property of at least two scientific academies. Fascinating, isn't it, Vesna Borisevna?

"Fifth," Colonel Piankoff now held up his right fist, "all temporal devices must be deployed with self-destruct protocols and provided with such devices to prevent their falling into the hands of unauthorized persons, organizations, or national entities.

"Sixth," now raising his left forefinger, "authorized temporal insertions are to be unobtrusive events designed to avoid any unintentional temporal alteration. Further, all authorized insertions must be judiciously planned in advance with their scientific or operational tasks designed to produce specific results. And for your information, the final calibration of the temporal device was the primary reason for the initial temporal insertions. More about that later.

"Seventh," now holding up his left fore and middle fingers, "it was judged that minor cultural impacts are inevitable. While major ones were to be avoided at all costs, since such an alteration may have an adverse temporal impact, much like ripples in a still pond. Such effects, it was judged, might produce changes to the future as the past 'propagates' into the present, the so-called 'butterfly effect' that you sometimes read about in the literature.

"Eighth," while grasping his first three fingers of his left hand, "all temporal field agents must seamlessly blend into the temporal horizon into which they are deployed. This implies that they must be provided with a full briefing on the period, wear appropriate clothing, speak the language of the period, and assume an unremarkable persona, all to lessen the potential temporal impact of their presence.

"Ninth," tightly holding all of his left fingers, "any act of procreation during a temporal insertion represents a major alteration to the temporal stream and so must be avoided at all costs. The introduction of a person, who should not exist, must not be allowed to occur.

"And, tenth and finally," he indicated with a left fist, "all objects and temporal field agents must return back to their own time, whether damaged, alive or dead. Furthermore, objects are not to be inserted or extracted from their rightful place in time."

Finally, coming to an end, my Russian mentor took a drink of his coffee and grimaced as it had gone cold.

Is he really serious about all of this? Time travel?

Smiling back at me across the restaurant table, my Sasha said, "I have seen that look from you before Vesna Borisevna. It usually shows up just before you bark out an objection. But, and here you must trust me, these rules I have memorized for a very good reason, as I am that first temporal field agent. It was I who gathered the much-needed chronological calibration data. It took me three trips back into the *somewhen* to accomplish my mission."

I put my hand to my mouth in astonishment. I remember consciously trying to stifle all sound, but I suspect that I had failed. Besides, the sheer size of my eyes must have betrayed me. But, finally, after a few moments, I asked rather disjointedly, "Why? How?"

"Those are excellent questions. As to 'why,' I suppose that my duties at the Directorate had become too boring. Besides, when the Americans came to us, seeking a 'volunteer', as they so cavalierly put it, I was the perfect candidate. I possessed the philological background and the military training. I, once bronzed by the sun, could pass as an ancient Egyptian.

"As to 'how,' well, that was up to the Americans themselves. You see, that eighteen-year-old PhD, Pyotr Valerievich Borov, the one who had argued for the practical application itself, had defected to the United States. Now that story is worthy of an epic narration all by itself, which would rival Homer's *Odyssey*.

"But to make a long story a very short one, he quite literally walked his way through the German lines outside of Stalingrad, through occupied Poland and Czechoslovakia, all the way to neutral Switzerland. Once there, and now with funds in his pocket, he grabbed a train south through Fascist Italy, took a boat to Sicily, and one more to British Malta. From there the Brits transported him to England, and from there to Philadelphia, and the house of an old family friend, the very same who had wired him the funds in Switzerland.

"Remarkably, this family friend was also a physicist, at the University of Pennsylvania, who introduced Pyotr Valerievich to another physicist at Princeton University, none other than Albert Einstein himself. With Einstein behind him, Pyotr Valerievich, now all of nineteen and a half years old, found himself with a train ticket bound for the state of New Mexico and the secret laboratories of the Manhattan Project. Once there, he was given a modest place to stay and begin his work. And, as they say, 'the rest is history.'"

"So," I began, "help me understand. A Russian came up with a practical design for a time machine. He defects from the *Rodina*, because he doesn't trust the it. He goes to the United States, and there, makes his dream come true. Doesn't that mean that the temporal device belongs to the Americans?"

With a broad and understanding smile, Colonel Piankoff replied.

"Remarkable, isn't it. And no, the Americans do not own the device, or its design, or even the *RUTI* that guides its proper use. If anything, it is our very own Academy of Sciences, along with the American's, that controls and administers the device in all of its aspects."

Now holding my head in my hands as if I had a vicious Vodka induced hangover, I said, "My head hurts. This just cannot be."

Again that familiar warm smile.

"Ah, but Vesna Borisevna, that is the total beauty of this. That a working, temporal device even exists is just too outrageous a fact to be true. But, nonetheless, it does exist. I can assert that because I was its first human guinea pig."

"So, where did you go?"

"Not where, Vesna Borisevna, *somewhen*. And while this detail might initially confuse you, Pyotr Valerievich's temporal device is a time machine only. It does not permit travel in space, just time. So to answer your question precisely, I went to Luxor and the Karnak Temple with a portable version of the device, and was deployed from there, within that temple's holy-of-holies, back into the *somewhen*.

"Now to answer your question. The *somewhen* that I first visited for the purpose of calibration was late Eighteenth Dynasty Egypt, during the reign of Amenhotep III, in the sixteenth year of his reign. At that time, his son Amenhotep IV, the later Akhenaten, was a mere boy. But later, the American and I returned several times, while Akhenaten was the Divine Horus."

I quietly moaned in recognition. "So that's why you cried at the museum, when I read that Amarna inscription."

"Indeed, for Nefer, as in Nefertiti, was a most beautiful woman, a kind and bright one as well, and a caring mother, while her husband was just as truly, a monster. And I can say that with some authority, as it was he who so injured my psyche, my mind. It was he, who caused my near stroke-like symptoms, symptoms that I am still recovering from. And, Vesna Borisevna, this was why you were suddenly sent to St. Petersburg, for I had just returned from the *somewhen* a very broken man. In fact, if it hadn't been for my American colleague, I seriously doubt that we would be having this conversation."

* * *

"You of course realize, that everything that I have just told you, cannot be retold to anyone."

"No kidding." I said with wide eyes.

"Then you also must be wondering, why did I do so?"

Wrinkling my brow with concern, I asked, "That did cross my mind several times. So, why did you?'

"Because Vesna Borisevna Gregorieva, I want you to be my successor."

"Successor? As in replacing you as the temporal field operative?"

Vesna! Stop and think for a moment! Is this mad conversation really happening? Or has your dear Sasha gone insane from a stroke and now is delusional? But if he isn't insane, then what? Then all of this must be, somehow, true!

"Yes."

"Why? Why me?"

"Because you possess many gifts that make you the perfect candidate. Physically, you could easily pass as an Egyptian. Additionally, you can easily withstand the strain of the temporal transit. Mentally, you are marvelously emotional, and yet strong and resilient. And philologically, you have embraced the ancient Egyptian language with an ease that is quite disarming. Put succinctly, you're a natural."

"But who will train me?"

"I will, of course. I have constructed a language training database that is quite good. And, my American assistant will no doubt do so as well."

"Your assistant?"

"Why yes, he's the American that I mentioned before, a man who shows great promise. He has saved my life twice already. Best of all, he is true of heart, clear of eye, and is as dangerous as a young lion."

"So?"

"So your training in the spoken version of the ancient Egyptian language can begin as soon as you are ready. And, as soon as you master my language lessons, then off you go to the United States to complete your curriculum, and meet your fellow colleagues."

What took place next was so impulsive that I am embarrassed to even admit it. I extended my hand across the table and shook his, and in so doing, the deep creases around his eyes softened. My Sasha had returned.

*   *   *

Several weeks later, I heard from several trusted medical sources within the Directorate that they could not believe the progress that Colonel Piankoff had made. One had even rather crudely wondered if the professional bachelor had recently gotten laid. But, as they were putting together their fitness report, Colonel Piankoff had made a firm request. He wished to meet with "the triad" as they were unofficially known. And when the medical staff had scoffed at such an idea, he then more forcefully made the request again, choosing to include that several rather damning items would be made known if they did not, and promptly.

Colonel Piankoff got his interview. Just where it took place, he would not tell me, only that it had taken place and that he had specifically requested the meeting to support my fitness as his successor. Beyond that, I can only offer my best surmise as to the conversation. Later in my career, I too was called before "the triad" within that musty old bunker, so I at least know the where of his historic meeting.

*   *   *

For a meeting of this sensitivity, "the triad" chose to meet within a secret bunker located deep within the Russian Academy of Sciences building. It was considered one of the most secure, while being one of the dreariest, even by Soviet standards. Despite the passage of time and the best efforts of the HVAC technicians, the air remained stagnant and tinged with the rank smell of acrid cigarette smoke.

At the room's center was a round table surrounded by five generously padded chairs. On this day three were occupied, as would be a fourth, shortly. Before one of "the triad" sat a thick, much-dog-eared, purple-colored file folder that indicated its ultra-level security status.

Vasily Feodorevich Ostrogorsky, the Director of Theoretical Biology for the Russian Academy of Sciences, regarded his two colleagues, his demeanor serious. "My dear colleagues," he said, his heavily callused hand resting on the thick folder for emphasis, "As you know, Colonel Alexander Andreovich Piankoff has requested a private interview with us. In some ways, his request is very timely, especially given his most recent adventures."

To this pronouncement, the first speaker received two grave nods and one hoarse comment delivered with as an Irish whisper. "No shit. We almost lost him again, if it wasn't for the American." said the second speaker, Karlov Gregorievich Drazinzka, the Head of the Special Projects Directorate.

"Excuse me, but, what are this young American's credentials?" quietly asked the youngest member of the trio, Stefan Nikolevich Rosovec, the new, green-as-grass Director of Advanced and Theoretical Technological Research for the Russian Academy of Sciences.

"My dear colleague," Karlov Gregorievich said, "he is the American's temporal field agent. His name is Joseph Richards. He is damnably remarkable and resourceful, and anyone who comes to the aid of my people, and in this case, twice no less, has credentials enough, and consequently, is worthy of my praise."

Rosovec nodded. His predecessor, Nikolai Alexandrevich Fedorov, an original member of the Hourglass Seminar and one with a wickedly mercurial temper, had recently retired to his Black Sea *dacha*, because of a minor brain embolism. That event had been caused by a fountain pen being rammed into the side of his expansive forehead by his esteemed colleague, Karlov Gregorievich.

"Excuse me, my dear colleagues," Ostrogorsky signaled, "but it seems that our guest has just arrived."

*   *   *

As Colonel Piankoff strode into the room, he noted how his crisp sounding footsteps had suddenly become muffled. Glancing to his right and left, he saw why.

Ah, it's the lighting fixtures. They are the aural dampers for this secure room.

Now, standing before his inquisitors, in an impeccably turned out uniform, with his formal parade ground issued hat placed under his left arm, he saluted crisply with the right.

"Alexander Andreovich, such formalities are not necessary among us," Karlov Gregorievich, his superior, quietly stated for the record. "Please, my good friend, sit."

Taking the leather chair opposite the other three, the soldier somehow managed to sit with his back straight at the front edge of the deep leather upholstery. No easy feat.

"Colonel Piankoff," Vasily Feodorevich also stated for the record, "We are gathered here at your personal request. Clearly, you have something on your mind, but before we get to that, how are you feeling? Do you believe you are fit for duty?"

"Academicians, I can assure you that I am ready for my next deployment."

Vasily Feodorevich challenged that self-diagnosis. "But Colonel, after all that you have suffered through, are you absolutely sure?"

"As sure as I can be, sir."

Now pressing further, Vasily Feodorevich added, "Colonel, and I realize that this may be an odd question, but still I must ask it. What was it like? What was this psychic encounter like with the alien life form?"

At the question, the colonel had unconsciously grimaced, a tell-tale that all three clearly saw, and his heart rate began to slowly elevate.

"'Encounter' would not have been my choice of

words, sir, but it will do," Colonel Piankoff said. "The experience began as a tingling feeling across my scalp, which quickly developed into warming sensation much like that of spring sunshine. Then, suddenly, we were in a complex non-verbal conversation, which proceeded at an incredibly rapid rate. Understandable, but one that cannot be put easily into something so clumsy as words. It all felt so intuitive, but then, just as suddenly, the rape began."

Piankoff's heart rate continues to climb with the retelling of that incredibly invasive event.

"Frankly, I was horribly helpless throughout the entire 'encounter' as you have so delicately put it. It literally rifled through my thoughts, my memories, my very being, as if my brain were a Rolodex. And, when it stumbled upon my mental blocks and psychic implants. It tried to circumvent them, even to the point of accessing the most primitive functions of my brain, all to break through, which it didn't. In the end, it was just greatly frustrated. Then, mercifully, it stopped. At that point, I was a sweating, highly disoriented, and befouled basket case. And just as remarkably, it then apologized to me for its impatience and heedless clumsiness. To this day, I will never forget the clinical way it expressed its sadness that we, as a species, are so fragile. It was as if I were a mere ant being studied under a magnifying glass."

Throughout this gripping account of Piankoff's telepathic "conversation" with the alien Akhenaten, the Russian officer had remained quite 'clinical', in spite of the fact that his respiration had nearly peaked.

Silence broke out, followed by several moments of quiet introspection, where an ear was scratched, a nose rubbed, and a throat was cleared. Finally, Karlov Gregorievich softly stated.

"So, my son, why have you requested this meeting?"

Wistfully smiling Colonel Piankoff said, "Because gentlemen, I have been trained to anticipate, to assess, and to decisively act. That said, I know that this old horse is nearing his end. I am honest enough to admit that I have lost a step. All the while my field craft has remained as sharp as ever. Nevertheless, we must admit to ourselves that I am no longer the equal of my stronger, American colleague, for twice now that fine young man has come to my aid. And in this business, this line of work, that is unacceptable. So, consequently, I wish to propose a candidate, who should be trained as my successor. Most fortunately, I have already identified that individual and she has already begun her language..."

"SHE!?!" Two of the triad said as one, with bulging eyes and flushed apoplectic complexions. Only the youngster, Stefan Nikolevich, Piankoff saw, had remained silent, no doubt fascinated by the events unfolding before him, and the genius of my proposed operational solution.

"Yes, gentlemen, 'she.' Her name is Vesna Borisevna Gregorieva. She is a rising star within the Directorate. And, believe it or not, she is the perfect candidate for the position, and here is why."

CHAPTER VI
Lioness

I was just getting used to the sing-song cadence of the language lessons, the subtle intonations, its many glottal stops and accents, when I was informed by my instructor that I should reapply myself to the task at hand. At the time, I must admit that I was completely enraged by the cheek of the man! As if I had been sleeping through the tapes! Here I was with an advanced degree in linguistics, and now nearly four and a half months of immersion devoted to Colonel Piankoff's vocalization drills of the ancient Egyptian language of the Eighteenth Dynasty.

I was so immersed in my studies that when I received the news, it was as if I had been hit by a thunderbolt. My Sasha had died, struck down by a common, third world, water-borne disease.

I was crushed, emotionally deflated, and grimly bitter as my mentor, sometimes friend, and yes, personal fantasy, had been so unfairly ripped away from me. But unlike the loss of my parents, this loss was different.

I heard whispers about the nature of Sasha's end, about the fact that there were some directly responsible for his untimely and tragic death. My beloved mentor had been admitted late on a Friday and those who could have saved him couldn't be bothered because they had had weekend plans.

And so, perhaps all too predictably, I reverted to my Directorate training. Systematically, I tracked the source of the medical malfeasance, and it was not hard, given the bureaucratic paper trail left behind. I discovered that there were indeed three men responsible. Each, I decided, would die in turn knowing what they had done, or more to the point, what they had so woefully failed to do.

All died by my hand, and I do not regret for one moment any of these acts. All three were supposedly model family men, but they were far from it. For each I had easily lured, and they were found in extremely compromising positions. All were found killed by a black, four inch spike heel, the sort of ankle breakers that only strippers wear, embedded in their left eye socket. Given the carefully seeded crime scenes, each was assumed to have run afoul of the highly profitable black market trade in hospital pharmaceuticals. Taken together, the three constituted an assumed drug ring by the authorities and provided the Moscow media several lurid and sensational news stories.

Indeed, the Directorate had trained me well.

*   *   *

Several weeks later the "triad" met again. This time, again in their secure location, their agenda was solely focused upon the fitness of the late and posthumously promoted Major General Alexander Andreovich Piankoff's proposed candidate, Vesna Borisevna Gregorieva. Stefan, to the total surprise of his colleagues, fully supported her candidacy, while Vasily Feodorevich could not bring himself to support Major General Piankoff's appeal.

Silent until the last, Karlov Gregorievich then queried, "Gentlemen, your opposing positions have been most clearly stated. For these I fully understand

and am most appreciative. However, Alexander Andreovich's judgment has never been once called into question. In fact, throughout his entire career, he has been a model of tactical logic and decisive strategic insight."

Now gently patting Gregorieva's purple file on the table before him, he continued, "So gentlemen, I ask you to dispassionately consider the following. Alexander Andreovich has already told us why Vesna Borisevna would be an excellent agent within the ancient Egyptians' cultural milieu. So, given that only he among us has been there, and as the Americans like to say, 'and done that,' why should we now not believe him? Why should we now question his impeccable judgment?

"Second, has either of you read about that triple drug murder that has flooded the Moscow newscasts lately? The 'Black Stiletto Murders?' Well, what if I told you that those three murder victims were the very physicians who were responsible for Alexander Andreovich's totally botched medical care? And what if I were to tell you that our very own Vesna Borisevna Gregorieva had a massive crush on our dear Alexander Andreovich? And, that the very same Vesna Borisevna Gregorieva, on her own, took the initiative and figured out the identity of the three physicians at fault for her beloved Sasha's death, and then actually did something about it? Something extremely primal, something very human."

Stunned silence followed the pronouncement.

"What are you saying Karlov Gregorievich?" Vasily quietly asked.

"What I am saying, my dear Vasily Feodorevich, is

that Vesna Borisevna Gregorieva is one highly trained and effective agent of the Directorate, one hand-picked by Alexander Andreovich, and one who is already trained in ancient Egyptian. More importantly, she is battle tested, three times no less, and three times left practically no trace whatsoever. In point of fact, this woman, this vixen, is capable of taking on much, much more than what Alexander Andreovich had ever imagined. She is truly a fierce lioness. Now, who in this room still thinks that she is no match for the American? Frankly, I pity the man," Karlov Gregorievich concluded.

More silence.

Then Vasily Feodorevich quietly asked, "My dear Karlov Gregorievich, you said 'practically no trace.' What did you mean by that?"

Grimly smiling, the head of the Directorate confided, "Our Vesna Borisevna got careless. My team discovered a trace amount of DNA on one of the four inch stilettos. This from a Directorate operative who has not been trained in field operations. She's just a watcher. Frankly, given her results, I personally find her performance all the more remarkable."

CHAPTER VII
Fast Track

Following the most unfortunate death of my mentor, the Directorate acted quickly and placed me on the fast track as his replacement. The language training continued at a break-neck pace to the point that I had memorized all of Sasha's lessons.

Then came further instruction in self-defense, which introduced me to an entirely new world – that of human destruction and mayhem. While no one had ever mentioned my extracurricular activities in connection with the death of the three physicians, it was more what was not said that clued me in, especially during the rigorous mat work, which my superiors had deemed necessary for my new career.

Then, finally, the day arrived, when I was informed by my new mentor, that Karlov Gregorievich Drazinzka himself, the grand old man and legendary head of the Special Projects Directorate, wished to see me. I must say that I was surprised, and then after some consideration, became worried that I was about to pay the hangman for my past misadventures.

I left early that day for my appointment with the Directorate. And it was well that I did, as just getting to his office door required passing several check points. They were not "check points" in the literal and former Soviet sense. Rather, I had to negotiate my way past no less than four bureaucrat's desks, each of which mindlessly checked my identification, asked a few innocuous questions, and then passed me on.

It was maddening, much like trying to make way in the heavy mud of a nightmare, or trying to quickly get at the Christmas candy hidden away in a set of wooden *matryoshka* dolls. But through it all, and in spite of them, I managed to arrive at his secretary's desk with several minutes to spare. And there I waited for what seemed an eternity, but in reality were only a few minutes. At the buzz of her phone, the grandmotherly secretary looked up at my expectant face, smiled, and simply nodded toward the heavy wooden door.

*   *   *

"Vesna Borisevna Gregorieva, I wish to thank you for agreeing to visit me today," began the elderly and white-haired Russian from behind his modest metal desk.

"I think that you should know that the late Major General Alexander Andreovich Piankoff personally met with me to argue for your candidacy. And, as I have always considered Alexander Andreovich as practically my own son, I carefully listened to his many interesting and cogent arguments."

At this point in the interview, I must admit that I had breathed an internal sigh of relief. We were not discussing my murderous dalliances.

"As for my colleagues, with whom I am obliged to discuss such weighty matters, they were, let us say, not keen on you becoming Alexander Andreovich's replacement. They thought that you, a mere woman, did not possess sufficient field experience, initiative, or creativity. They thought that you could not see your way through a complex situation. They even dared that you would not have the stomach to follow through on whatever might have to be done."

Pausing for effect, the man then continued.

"Frankly Vesna Borisevna, even with your exemplary familial pedigree, academic record, physical and combat skills, I too still had some lingering doubts about you."

At this last, I looked down at my carefully folded hands as I felt heat spread across my face, and the sickening feeling of rejection formed in my tightening stomach.

And then the old man dropped his bombshell. "However, in light of some truly sensational televised events, you have managed, in a rather imaginative and elegant way, to prove to me that you are, as the Americans like to say, 'the real deal.'"

I was stunned.

He knew.

Of course he knew.

But the real question was, now what would he do? Report me to the authorities?

Oh, my dear God!

"So, my dear, before we drop this minor side issue, I just wish to express to you my heartfelt thanks. I, too, was absolutely crushed at Alexander Andreovich's untimely passing. In my book, how you handled the situation was totally justified, even almost required. By the way, I particularly liked the way you left all of those tells at the three crime scenes. And because of that, you have convinced, no have proven to me, that you should follow in Alexander Andreovich's footsteps.

"As for my colleagues, well, they have been persuaded to come to the same conclusion. In fact,

Alexander Andreovich's choice of you as his successor has become strangely prescient of late. For it seems that the Americans specifically requested that we provide a woman to succeed him. So, within the month, expect to pack your bags for Chicago. Once there, they will test you, probe you, and test you again. And do not forget, that while Americans can be remarkably charming, may appear to be almost child-like, all of that is a ruse, for they are cunning actors."

Looking down at his heavily arthritic hands Karlov Gregorievich pursed his lips and said, "All we ask is that you do our Alexander Andreovich proud."

Then looking up into my face, he finished. "Can you do this?"

Apparently, my single tear was a sufficient answer.

*   *   *

The "triad" chose to briefly meet several days later. The specific agenda item that Karlov Gregorievich wanted to discuss with his colleagues was the status of his new temporal field agent, me. While the particulars of that discussion never made the light of day, a memo that encapsulated their thoughts did. Just how I got a copy of that internal memo those months later after my first deployment, I cannot say, but here is a redacted portion of it. I had been put on a short leash.

> [It has been decided that] Vesna Borisevna Gregorieva will succeed Major General Alexander Andreovich Piankoff, and in so doing, will take over all of his responsibilities and duties. In so doing, V. B. Gregorieva will undergo extensive debriefings after every deployment in order to

better determine her performance and provide any additional information about our colleagues that the board wishes. Further, the Special Projects Division under K. G. Drazinzka, will immediately begin the selection process and training of her successor, thereby ensuring that the candidate is more compliant to the goals of the board of advisors. If, however, in the unlikely event of her return after her first deployment to regular duty, and if her replacement is deemed fit and ready, then V. B. Gregorieva will be offered and encouraged at every opportunity to voluntarily retire. Irrespective of her performance in the field or accomplishments, at the board's sole discretion, and/or successful training of her replacement, V. B. Gregorieva will be forcibly and permanently retired from the service of the Directorate.

Chapter VIII
Chicago

I must admit that my first visit to the United States was quite an adventure. All of my handlers keep repeating the same mantra. Do not be deceived by their polite demeanor and open friendliness. They are not, under any circumstances, to be trusted. So I went with a lightly packed suitcase and a head stuffed full of suspicion.

But, quite frankly, nothing could have prepared me for that over flight of Chicago. At night it was simply breathtaking. The orange-colored grid of street lights stretched to the horizons. But the sudden appearance of the city's center, with all of its buildings up thrust like a crystal experiment gone mad, nothing in my experience could have prepared me for that vision.

In comparison, the most vertically dominating structures in Moscow were the university and the domes of St. Basil's. Here, quite clearly, financial and commercial structures held sway, bordered on one side by immense classical structures, parks, a brightly lit stadium, and even a Ferris wheel. And that's when I received my first revelation. Perhaps American capitalism wasn't so bad. After all, from this vantage point, look what it had done for this City of Big Shoulders.

Upon deplaning, my first smells of the U.S. included the reek of jet exhaust and the rubber of the Pirelli non-skid flooring. And from all appearances, my handlers were spot on in their warnings as I walked through the maze that is the O'Hare International arrival terminal. I could sense eyes upon me, electronic sensors, and perhaps even x-rays. Queuing up at the passport control with the rest of the passengers, I noted the crisp, cool, and professional way each and every passenger was scrutinized. And when my turn had come, even with my blouse undone to display my obvious charms, his appraising eyes had never once wavered from mine, a fact which I found to be particularly chilling.

Once beyond that test, I found that my baggage had already arrived and that it was undamaged. *So, they are efficient and courteous as well.* Having filled out the custom's declaration form in advance, and with nil to declare, I was whisked through that task and led out into a sea of greeting humanity. Some waited teary-eyed for their relatives, others in dark suits, held signs announcing who they were looking for.

And there, just as I had been told, stood a dark-haired man of medium height, athletic build, and a rugged look that screamed military. His placard said in large block letters: Ms. V.B. Gregorieva – Philology Annex. Presenting myself to him, he politely asked for my passport, confirmed that my face was a match, and warmly smiled. He took my bag and led me to his vehicle, a black one with four doors and heavily tinted windows. In comparison with a boxy Zil, this one was much sleeker looking.

He was a good driver, as he managed to smoothly navigate through all of the unruly airport traffic. But even more than that, the very smoothness of the highway was yet another revelation, as was the great width of them, and their clearly painted markings. It seemed that in mere moments we were traveling along at quite a high speed, in heavy traffic, where cars actually signaled their intentions. It was all such a visual blur, not to mention the tactile comfort of the vehicle's ride and its fragrant leather seats. As for my driver, I did catch him several times observing me with a frown. He then had the cheek to make me put on the provided seat belt!

Now at ground level, I got my first impressions of this vast American city. I noted the quality of the ground transportation to be less than that of European standards, the cars dark, dingy, and covered with graffiti. When it came to their cars, in all of their many colors and sizes, that I found to be stunning.

I saw sports cars everywhere, running this way and that, and most only carried one passenger. Leaving the highway, we passed through good and bad sectors. Excuse me, neighborhoods, and it seemed on purpose, as if the driver wanted me to know upfront that this urban metropolis had warts as well as flowers.

As we neared our destination, the driver explained that the Philology Annex was located on a major university campus. Many of the dedicated buildings that my driver mentioned had absolutely no analogues in Moscow. There, the university was basically one self-contained structure. But here, the norm was heavily treed boulevards and park-like grounds that separated one building from the next. And with that, I sensed an odd openness about this "campus" that I found unnerving.

As for the Philology Annex itself, I had expected something larger, something more grandiose than a simple three-storey brownstone walkup. As I now look back at those naïve first impressions, I can only smile, for that unremarkable building represented my doorway to personal liberation.

* * *

I'll not bore you with all the intellectual gaming, philology drills, and subtle psychological testing that occurred while I visited the Annex. The one item that truly did surprise me, however, was the extensive dental examination. I was told that if I passed my battery of tests, then all of my old silver fillings, which my father had paid so dearly for, would have to be removed and replaced with pretty new porcelain ones. When I asked why, the attending physician's answer chilled me to the bone.

"Two reasons, Ms. Gregorieva. One, we cannot have you laughing and showing off your wealth. Our kind of dentistry does not exist in ancient Egypt. But far more importantly, one cannot have any unshielded metal on their person. Take my word for it. Some very nasty things can happen, like total incineration."

For the most part, my handlers back in Moscow had been correct. While the Americans decided on my fitness to be Sasha's replacement, they had performed their role in the most sneaky and subtle of ways. Beginning with my driver, the dark-haired, rugged, military-looking man turned out to be none other than Joseph Richards, their temporal field operative, and the very one who had saved my Sasha on so many occasions. He possessed the most cool and calculating ego of the entire bunch. He did not like me at the start, and frankly, knowing what I know now, neither would have I. I was a insecure, complete, and total bitch.

On the night that I arrived, my circadian rhythm was so out of whack that I impulsively went out, in a strange city, in a strange neighborhood, for a run. For me, that meant two to three kilometers at least. After a while, I realized I was being followed by two other joggers, both male, and both extremely fit. I continued running, trying hard to burn off enough steam so that I could take a hot shower, and maybe, get some much needed sleep.

As much as my training had taught me to be on my guard, the two joggers surprised me by catching up and asking if I knew where I was going. That I was "cruising for a bruising" if I continued on in the direction that I was headed, and, that it might be wise to turn around and head back to my dorm.

They obviously didn't know who I was, so I raced them back to the Philology Annex. At the time I thought that I had smoked them, but as with so many things, I was completely wrong. They were Corporals Callahan and Sanchez, part of the Annex's security team. They had been awakened in the middle of the night to go out, follow me, and protect me in one of Chicago's worst neighborhoods. Again, I realized that I had a lot to learn. After all, this was Chicago, the hometown of Al Capone and the mafia: "Bang, bang!"

The fourth American that I met was the red-haired and fatherly Doctor Allen. I am very ashamed to say that I was true to form at our first encounter. In my defense, at least I was consistent. Yet, much like water running off a duck's back, he listened, remained supportive, and did not judge me to hell, and to this very day, I bless him for that.

As for Professor John Milson, right from the very start, he struck me as the most remarkable man of the Annex. During that brief first stay, in a strange sort of way, I came to love him much the same way I had my dear Sasha. What a kind man, so full of life, clearly an intellectual giant among lesser mortals. Yet, he had been so very injured by the passing of his beloved Alice. I just wanted to smother him in my arms.

CHAPTER IX
New Mexico

Yes, I passed the Americans' battery of tests, much to my pleasure and the outright surprise of some of my superiors. Yet, upon returning to Moscow, it was as if I had passed into a strangely foreign and gray world in comparison to that of Chicago. This disturbing impression, I kept entirely to myself. Frankly, at the time, I was one very conflicted individual. While my ancestral roots lay clearly with the *Rodina*, my American experience, brief though it was, had shaken me to my very core.

This psychic schism was only reinforced upon my return to the States for the rigorous training and acclimatization process in sunny New Mexico at their secret installation, called rather whimsically "Horizon Pass." First off, I was not used to the altitude nor such a cheerful desert environment of nearly constant sunshine and peerless blue sky. I initially wasn't fond of appeasing the god of the "all over tan" by jogging topless. And then there was the shaving off of my hair! My luxuriant black hair that I had worn long since childhood. That I found to be personally challenging. Not so much that it was gone, but confronting myself in the mirror. I no longer knew who the mirror's reflection was.

New to me as well were the local spicy foods that either caused stomach indigestion or painful runs, or for that matter, the thick German beers. Above all, I was not comfortable working with Richards, even though he was the most experienced temporal field operative.

Because he had worked with my Sasha, that brought sad memories to the surface.

And yes, I was resentful as well. For now an American, and not a Russian, was the acknowledged leader of the field team. I had serious issues with that.

On top of everything else, Richards was too damn serious and tightly wound. He insisted that we converse only in Egyptian while we were out on our daily runs. One thing that did startle me while Richards and I ran our circuit, were the long and painful looking scars that decorated his back from hip to shoulder. On our second day of training I finally got the courage to ask about them. "Oh those," Richards had replied. "When I was sixteen I dumped my Uncle Bill's motorcycle. It was his prize Indian. I really don't know who he was more concerned about, me or the bike."

Strangely, that brief window into Richards' soul had meant a lot to me. That and the patient talks that I had with Doc Allen really helped us, as a functional, operational team.

Yet, at the same time, there I was in the middle of a hauntingly beautiful scrub desert of brilliant sun rises and glorious sun sets. I conversed in a St. Petersburg dialect with Peter Borov, *the Peter Borov,* the creator of the temporal device, himself a defector from the *Rodina.* Borov was a man of immense depth and humanity, who suffered as a tragic loner both in life and nationality. Borov, who in time, would be like an elder brother to me. He was a much-need corrective, who could be firm one moment and with a wicked sense of humor the next.

In the end the New Mexican experience was a lot to handle, and at times, I really didn't know who I truly was as the days all too quickly ran into weeks. This was the American immersion process. Not surprisingly, I found myself asking a very seminal question.

Was I still Russian? Or, had I become an American? Or better, an ancient Egyptian?

*   *   *

After nine weeks of hard work, blood, sweat, some tears, and plenty of input from Doc Allen, Joey and I had become a team. It had taken a lot, but "we" were finally ready. It was time to deploy and we had a lot on our agenda. Specifically, I had to establish myself as Joey's sister and assistant in all things. That meant that I was a seer priestess, an oracle, if you will, of the god of the Great White Wall of Memphis, Ptah. And that meant that I had to choose an Egyptian name for myself. After much thought and research, and no end of help from Joey, I decided upon Maatkare, which in ancient Egyptian means, "the just soul of Re." Only three others carried this weighty name, two were the wives of high priests, but one was the female Pharaoh Hatshepsut herself, and I liked that – a lot.

Strangely, at nearly the same time Joey and I had made our peace, I had become aware. I began to notice more. The resources that the Americans had entrusted to Dr. Borov and placed at Horizon Pass' disposal were tremendous. On the one hand, the Philology Annex that provided the entire program's bureaucratic support and language training. Then there was the quiet linkage with the American military with its U.S. Army jump school training at Fort Bragg, the modified civilian jet and its U.S. Air Force crew, the use of the military fields at Chicago and Holloman bases, the USAF helicopters and their crews, and last but hardly least, the dedicated field security force. All things considered, the Horizon Pass' very existence depended upon the cooperation of many moving parts. And the crafter of this amazing arrangement was Dr. Borov, a refugee of the Second World War, long considered *persona non grata* by his native country.

When I realized the magnitude of this immense investment that was Horizon Pass, I deeply suspected that my superiors in Moscow did not realize the extent of the American commitment, or perhaps better, did not want to acknowledge it. And that realization was truly cause for pause, for everything I had heard previously suggested the entire opposite.

As for Horizon Pass itself, this secret installation is located out in the wild desert west of Alamogordo's Holloman AFB. Overland it's a couple of hours from the base, but by helicopter it only took about twenty minutes.

Imagine exiting a steep-sided canyon that led to an open plain with a two-fingered rock outcrop dominating the scene. That outcrop marks where Horizon Pass is, but *below* the surface. Right out of some cheesy James Bond movie, Horizon Pass was composed of starkly painted white tunnels that went in all directions, a temporal research laboratory, living quarters, a hospital, a gym, a mess hall, and is stocked with anything and everything else that you could possibly need.

Dr. Borov, ever the wit, playfully named all of these facilities: Tombstone, the Swamp, Rx, Venice Beach, Betty Crocker's, and Franks. The main passageways were similarly named, labeled in huge letters on their floors: Penny Lane, Yellow Brick Road, and the Appian Way, while their junctions were called Trafalgar and Time Square.

When I asked where all the concrete came from to build the complex, Dr. Borov said that it came from a nearby town with the outlandish name of Truth or Consequences. That the cement factory had been created from scratch specifically to build the complex, and now operated on its own.

As to who owned that concrete facility, Dr. Borov only smiled. Then when I asked where all the electrical power came from, he proudly said that he had it cabled in direct from the Hoover Dam. After that, I didn't ask many more questions as the sheer scale of the resources involved had boggled my imagination. And frankly, I did not want to know the story behind the Philology Annex, for during my testing there, I counted a minimum of three subterranean floors beneath it.

Last but not least, Dr. Borov had a nick-name for the temporal device as well. He named it the Soap Bubble, after the children's toy for blowing soap bubbles which it so closely resembled.

During Dr. Borov's guided tour of the central research facility within Horizon Pass, called Tombstone, which is contained within a naturally formed cavern located beneath the complex itself, I got introduced to the stationary version of the Soap Bubble. Dr. Borov even gave me a demonstration of this unbelievable device.

Imagine four black and narrow six foot pillars spaced equidistant from one another in a square. Mounted atop each is a bullhorn-like attachment that faces inward. Thick electrical cables power these four columns and their "horns."

But the truly sensational detail was a hoop or a ring about three feet wide. It hovered between the four pillars about five feet off of the ground, held firmly in position by the electromagnetic field created by the pillars. Then, once the entire is powered up, the gap within the ring disappeared and was replaced by a smooth, metallic gray, and ever so slightly shimmering effect. That, Dr. Borov had explained, was the temporal field itself. And then to prove that fact, he had an old rope noose, that was suspended from rigging in the ceiling, lowered toward the ring. Then, to my utter shock, first the noose and then the next two feet of rope disappeared into the field, but from my vantage point beneath the field, I saw not a ripple!

"Have you seen enough, Vesna Borisevna?" Dr. Borov had said with a smile.

"But, but…where did the rope go?" I blurted out.

"Well, let's see." He called to Mr. Mackey, "Would you please reel in the noose?"

As it was retrieved, I noticed that the rope and its noose were dripping wet. With a sharp electrical crack, the temporal field was gone with a reek of ozone. But the rope continued to drip, forming a small puddle beneath the still hovering ring. Forgetting myself, I went over and dipped several fingers into the ever growing slick of water. Smelling my fingers, and then tasting my fingers, I announced.

"It's seawater!"

"Yes, it is. But Vesna Borisevna, but it is Jurassic sea water," he said with a smile.

*　　*　　*

When we finally deployed to Egypt, we went in the custom Gulf Stream V commercial jet piloted by two of the U.S. Air Force's finest. I was assured by Joey that what you see is sometimes not what you expect, and during our trip home, I came to understand first-hand precisely what he meant.

Accompanying Joey and I were our nurse maids, our security team, led by a big and gruff Marine colonel named "Tuna" Cartwright. He and his "school" of sixteen were tasked to protect the portable temporal device, its power source, and us in the field. This last item, I learned from Dr. Borov, had been adapted from a NASA unit that had performed flawlessly on several of the U.S. moon landings. The power pack, mounted on a back pack and carried as such, was nuclear. So yes, the accommodations in the GSV were tight, but comfortable.

After two refueling stops en route, one at Gander, Newfoundland, and the other at Aeropuerto de Tenerife Sur, in the Canary Islands, we finally landed at the airport in Luxor, Egypt. At both of our refueling points, we got fresh airmen, and I was told that we would take an entirely different route home, just as a precaution.

As we arrived at night in Luxor, we taxied over to a private hanger, deplaned, and promptly loaded up into two rather broken down looking lorries. But once they were started, they didn't sound decrepit at all. In fact, their powerful engines were heavily muffled. So yet again, note to self, another detail to appreciate.

After about a half hour drive, we quietly arrived at the Karnak Temple's back door by way of a dusty dirt road. I was surprised to see a Sound and Light presentation in full swing that covered our arrival, the opening of the squeaky cyclone fence gate, and our passage into the back of the temple complex and our goal – the inner-most sanctum of the Great God Amen Re. It would be here that Joey and I would drop into the *somewhen*.

* * *

It was tradition that the field operatives themselves erected the temporal equipment and ran through it setup checklists. In many respects it made sense, much as the walk-around preflight drill that pilots perform on their airframes.

"If your life depends on it, then you better well check it!" Was the order of the day from Colonel Cartwright.

Joey told me that the portable Soap Bubble VI A was an improved and updated version. To me, at least, that meant reductions in size for the Little Beast II laptop computer, four superconducting towers and their ion cannons, the central drop ring, and the heavy-duty power cabling. But what really jazzed Joey was the new power pack. While it looked to me about the same size as an average backpack, but now was non-nuclear.

Listen to me! I sound like a bloody electrical engineer!

This drop, as with all the previous, would take place during the early morning hours. Our presence within the temple had been made possible by a special arrangement with certain individuals within the Egyptian Antiquities Service and the Egyptian Tourist Bureau. Again, note to self. Details, details, details.

Colonel Cartwright and his shadowy security force, which provided an airtight security cordon, tore down the Soap Bubble once our drop was completed. This same group would then re-erect it for the drop team's retrieval, again during the early morning hours, at two hundred hours. Cartwright's crew would fire up the device for thirty seconds. If nothing flew out of it, signaling our wish for retrieval, then the ritual would be repeated the following evening. While a tedious task, the exposure of the team and its priceless equipment was greatly reduced.

I almost forgot. Another important part of the temporal deployment setup was the erection of crude wooden scaffolding around the Soap Bubble equipment. This provided for us a platform to drop from. An old sailing rig, rope, and ancient pulley acted as our retrieval crane. These elements too had to be dismantled as well, at every drop or retrieval, and then secreted away from curious eyes. Again, note to self. There are so many moving parts that function together seamlessly.

CHAPTER X
Limbo

Following that first deployment, I would describe my return to Moscow as icy cool. I was right. The Directorate had not expected me to survive. Months later, however, I would have confirmation of that fact in the form of a leaked confidential memo that a friend within the Directorate had stumbled across.

But at the time, embarrassingly, I had nonetheless done so. After an intensive week of debriefing, they allowed me to return to my work at the university. And as the Americans like to say, I then "cooled my heels" for a solid six months of data entry, much to Konstantina Iosifeva's delight. As far as I was concerned, the database was finished. So I returned to my Sasha's tape library of the Egyptian language and began practicing anew. Language is like a muscle that must be kept in tone. So, I was toning.

Then, out of the blue, in late September, I received a call requesting me to meet with Dr. Rosovec, the Director of Advanced and Theoretical Technological Research for the Russian Academy of Sciences. Naturally curious, I complied.

My first impression of Dr. Stefan Nikolevich Rosovec was that he possessed dangerously youthful ambition mixed with a pretty face, and that meant only one thing: proceed with extreme caution. While he wasn't my superior, he was highly connected, possessed the appropriate security clearances, and so I remained politely respectful. During our brief meeting, he asked me to accompany him and his delegation of scholars to the States. I was flattered at the offer, and agreed.

*   *   *

It was only during the flight over to Chicago that I found out why Stefan Nikolevich wanted me at his side. I was to be his official tour guide. But that was not entirely true either, for the man was trying very hard, almost too hard, to understand everything about me. Clearly, he was curious about the entire temporal project, who was involved, the location of Horizon Pass, the entire lot. So, with some viciousness in my heart, I told him about the scope of the American investment in the project. I did not tell him, however, about the modified Gulf Stream V or Tuna's crack security team. He was duly impressed.

In return, I found out why we were going to the U.S. with three Russian scientists and their families. It turned out that the Americans had recovered something "rather important" and as a consequence had requested our technical support. As the granting of such "technical support" fell easily within Stefan Nikolevich's purview, he now wanted in on the action. His poker chips were the three scientists and their families. To him, it was a fair enough gamble given the potential technological windfall. He then confided that he did not expect any of them to return to Russia, which didn't surprise me in the least. But when I asked specifically what he meant by a "potential technological windfall," he just smiled and said.

"Patience, Vesna Borisevna. You'll soon see."

*   *   *

To my surprise, upon landing in Chicago and passing through customs, we transferred to another flight, this one domestic, to a place called Dayton, Ohio. Greatly disappointed, I tried not to show it, but apparently failed miserably.

"Patience, Vesna Borisevna," Stefan Nikolevich Rosovec commented. "We will be passing through Chicago on our return. Then, if you wish, we can make the rounds to visit your American friends. I promise."

Somewhat mollified, I pulled myself together and now became very curious about this Dayton place. What possibly could be there that would interest a man like Stefan Nikolevich? Much less, bargain away three of his scientists and their families? My questions were answered when I realized there was an U.S. air force base located in Dayton. A big one, Wright-Patterson.

Upon landing in Dayton, no less than four blue vans met our party and whisked us away. For me, this was just an opportunity to see another part of the States. For Stefan Nikolevich, this was his first glimpse, and much like my other countrymen, their heads were on a continuous swivel, all the while they excitedly noted this and that. As for the children, their faces, full of wonder and curiosity, were plastered to the glass of the windows. Seeing that, it made me smile and remember back to my first limo ride from O'Hare to the Philology Annex. Oh, how, I had grown. Yes indeed, Stefan Nikolevich did need a tour guide.

* * *

Upon our arrival at Wright-Patterson AFB, the three scientists were separated from their families, who were taken to scout out their new accommodations on the base. Meanwhile, Stefan Nikolevich and I took the scientists to a high-level meeting. From the very beginning, the level of security was startlingly obvious, causing me to wonder what we were not seeing, or even aware of.

As for the meeting itself, a rather officious bureaucrat with a British accent commenced it, and made the usual opening comments to a packed and windowless room of about thirty people. Rather quickly, he turned the proceedings over to a clearly scientific type, a man who was far more relaxed in his manner. This man, a Dr. Graves I believe, from MIT, then showed to the entire room slides of what he claimed was a recovered UFO, a craft that was found in Egypt of all places! At this point, I now understood what Stefan Nikolevich had meant by being patient, why he had gambled with his three colleagues, and precisely what he had meant by "a potential technological windfall." The people in this room were to take apart and analyze an alien space craft!

But there was more. Dr. Graves then relinquished the floor to a modest gentleman named Dr. Roy Allen Peters, who had been made, on the spot, the project's manager. All of this occurred within a matter of minutes, while the five of us sat stunned and huddled in the back of the room, trying unravel, but less follow the rapidly unfolding events. Without question, we had just witnessed a classic example of American project brain storming! Only in America!

*   *   *

Having left three families behind at Wright-Patterson with nothing but a stratospheric future before them, Stefan Nikolevich and I flew back to Chicago, and needless to say, we had a lot to discuss.

"I am jealous of them," Stefan Nikolevich gloomily stated.

"Why is that?" I said.

"Because those three just became members of perhaps the most exciting and exhilarating project of the century! And to do so in an atmosphere of such open candor. What is it with these Americans? Imagine Vesna Borisevna! Being invited to such a meeting, and then being told that you are now its project manager! It's simply unimaginable! Such a thing anywhere else would have been reason for justifiable murder and mayhem!" Stefan Nikolevich was practically sputtering.

"Dr. Rosovec," I confided. "Patience. Now doesn't that sound familiar? And trust me, if you can. But the Americans are just as human as we are. They breathe air, need to eat, and require sleep. But also remember this. Professor Milson, who we will be having dinner with this very evening, once explained to me that we Russians have been either fighting for, or defending our country, almost for our entire existence. As a result, he said that we, unlike the West, had never experienced an age of chivalry."

Stunned and thoughtful silence broke out for several moments as Stefan Nikolevich digested the implications of Milson's observation.

"Now my dear colleague," I continued, "imagine hearing that off-the-cuff historical analysis from an Egyptologist, of all things. This is precisely why the Americans are so unpredictably and surprisingly American. It is precisely because their psyche allows them to take leaps of *imagination*."

Silence, and then, "Vesna Borisevna, you are absolutely right. Thank you."

"But how would an age of chivalry have changed us Russians? Surely, it could not be as simple as that."

"No?" I said. "Well then consider for a moment what a civilizing effect chivalry had on Western Europe. First off, the most brutal aspect of that society acquired a thin veneer of civility, battlefield rules of conduct, a notion of what constituted honorable behavior, and perhaps even fairness, that was extended to the protection of non-combatants. Over time, such rules became laws, laws in which Christianity's influence played a tremendous role."

"For one so well qualified in the sciences, Vesna Borisevna, you sound far more like a philosopher."

"Why, thank you. I have been working on it," I cleverly said.

"And while we are discussing our barbaric Russian heritage, I think that you should know that I am not a man without a soul. My colleagues do not know that those three families are not meant to return. This, we must keep between the two of us."

"Of course."

"Also, Vesna Borisevna, it would not be wise to place too much trust in your superior, K.G. Drazinzka."

Oh really? I thought. How interesting to hear this from you of all people. This only further confirms the validity of that confidential memo.

"This I already know. Colonel Piankoff warned me about him, in his own way of course. But again, thank you."

So, what else are you going to counsel me on?

"An insightful man he was," Stefan Nikolevich

stated with a quiet certainty. "And just how insightful are you, Vesna Borisevna?"

"What are you now fishing for?"

"I am thinking ahead. Many of my colleagues are fast nearing their retirement. I will surely survive them all. As the most technically oriented of our cozy group, don't you find it curious that you report to K.G. Drazinzka and not to me?"

Ah ha! Stefan Nikolevich is empire building!

He paused for a moment, probably to let his words sink in, before changing the subject. "Such a fine man Alexander Piankoff was. I just wish that I had the opportunity to meet him."

"You just might." I said.

"How so?" Rosovec said with considerable surprise.

"Are we not having dinner with Professor Milson tonight?"

"Ah, yes. You are right! I had completely forgotten! He too is a very interesting man, and one that I have wanted to meet ever since I first heard of him. Although no one has said a word, my esteemed colleagues consider Milson to be quite a formidable opponent."

At Stefan Nikolevich's remark, I could not help but smile. "Oh, John indeed is."

"John?"

"Why yes. That is his first name."

"On a first name basis are you?"

"When in America, be American. And oh, by the way, I wouldn't mind becoming more technically minded either."

"You don't say?"

*　*　*

Just being in Chicago again was such a great joy! And John, being John, had thoughtfully sent a limo to O'Hare to pick us up. Sitting back in the deep leather seats again reminded me of my very first visit, and as a result, I watched Stefan Nikolevich carefully, noting his reactions, and answering his incredulous questions. As we came within view of the magnificent skyline, a look of pure wonder crossed his face. Frankly, now as tour guide, I just could not resist.

"My dear Stefan Nikolevich, welcome to the City of Big Shoulders."

"Why such a name?"

"Because the people here believe that they can do anything."

Now gazing at the towering architecture at even closer range, the bureaucrat said quietly, "I believe it."

*　*　*

We arrived at the restaurant where we were to meet John a few minutes early, which was something that I appreciated. I absolutely despise being late for an appointment, much less a dinner date with John. Entering the establishment, a warm glow hit me. It was perfect, just that kind of place with just that kind of atmosphere. Even the *maître d'* had been alerted about us and knew who we were. Unpretentiously polite and efficient, he guided us to a remarkably intimate location, with curtains, near a roaring fireplace. The table, set for three, was clothed in heavily starched table linens and gleaming formal silverware all just so. The crisp glassware simply sparkled in the candlelight. In short, John, as usual, had set the stage down to the very last detail.

At our approach, John, dressed in a subdued three-piece suit, stood and greeted us with open arms and his famously disarming smile. "Welcome, all, to Chicago!"

Seating me to his right, he then invited Rosovec to his left. Rubbing his hands together no doubt to burn off some nervous excitement, he began with his eyes all a-sparkling.

"First off, I would very much like to order for us as the chef is a personal friend. If that is agreeable, I need to know a few details. Like for example, do you like garlic? Do you like your steak bloody, warm, mildly cooked, or well done? Do you prefer soups or salads?"

And before we knew it, a waiter magically appeared and John placed each of our orders. Disappearing momentarily, the waiter returned with a bottle of wine.

"Folks," John enthused, "since we all are eating steaks, I took the liberty of ordering for us a marvelous red. It's an Argentine Malbec. One of my favorites. I certainly hope that you will like it as well."

I must say that John's taste in wine were indeed spot on, for it was delicious! Now that we were primed, so to speak, he got down to business and asked us how the Dayton meeting had gone. And so off we went with Rosovec launching into a rather long narrative about Dayton, and then he surprised me with his frank first impressions of America. Throughout this entire discourse, John listened carefully, no doubt dissecting every single one of Stefan Nikolevich's words.

I sensed a certain momentum and spontaneity taking place, which was noticeably accelerated with the arrival of the second bottle of wine that was accompanied by freshly baked breads and three steaming bowls of a thick potato soup, each of which had an individual shot of sherry on the side. By the time the main course arrived, we devoured it with gusto, and everything was delicious. And with this cheery glow, John then went on the offensive.

"Dr. Rosovec," he began as he pushed his clean plate aside.

"As you can see, I am an old man. By virtue of my life experiences, I have naturally developed along certain lines, certain tastes. This wine for instance. And as an old man, I have my opinions, goals, biases, and of course, prejudices. In many respects, my perspective on the world has been greatly shaken up by a colleague of mine, Dr. Joseph Richards. Clearly, there is a wide generational gap between us, perhaps even several. Hell, there's a technological gap as well. And yet, despite my age and my many prejudices, I have managed to learn quite a bit from him.

"And so there is a question that has been nagging at me for some time, a question that truly can only be asked face-to-face, and of course, under the right conditions. You see, Dr. Rosovec, at least from my point of view, your colleagues are easily as old as I am – perhaps even older. I have to believe that a generational gap probably exists between you and your colleagues in much the same way it does between Joseph and me. So, my friend, my question to you is this: have you ever discussed with your colleagues what their agendas, prejudices, biases and goals are? And by the same token, have they ever asked you for yours?"

Surprised by Milson's question and the candor in

which it was asked, Stefan Nikolevich responded with equal frankness.

"Dr. Milson," Stefan Nikolevich said while glancing significantly toward me, "it seems that today is indeed one filled with frank talk. And no, to your question, a discussion of those topics has yet to occur between me and my colleagues. I too dream of a day that may redefine old lines of thinking. Perhaps one day that may engender a warming of relations, the start of a renaissance where men of like mind can come together and speak freely.

"Professor Milson, John, allow me be frank, that possibility is one that I embrace. It is one that I can perhaps foster. However, such openness is not one that my colleagues would readily agree with. As you yourself have suggested, a generational gap does indeed exist, where I am the youngest. As you would expect, I am often the last to know what my esteemed colleagues are doing. Consequently, the establishment of such a utopian atmosphere will take time. But regardless, we must start somewhere. Yes? So why don't we begin that process this evening?"

Just what is Stefan Nikolevich doing? I thought with a furrowed brow. *More empire building?*

Then John said. "Time: what a marvelous concept! Isn't it ironic, given what both of our scientific communities are engaged in. We have a saying here in the States 'that time can heal all wounds.' I pray that that is so."

John, now silent, signaled to our ever-attentive waiter, who as if by magic, appeared with a frosted bottle of vodka in an ice bucket and three small glasses. Now grinning from ear to ear, John thanked the waiter with a wink, cracked open the bottle's seal with an expert twist, and began pouring.

"You know folks, and I hope that you don't mind, I selected this brand myself, just in case a moment like this might present itself."

Now raising his glass to us in near benediction, he warmly stated, "To friendship." Stefan Nikolevich then added, "And to progress, as well."

Definitely empire building!

CHAPTER XI
Changes

I first heard about the leadership shake up within the Directorate was while I was helping Konstantina Iosifeva reclassify a group of artifacts. It was one of those innocuous interdepartmental emails that have a block of names attached. For some reason, the shape of that block of names looked different, catching my eye, and sure enough, there were two new names where two others, far more familiar, used to be. And believe it or not, that is how I first learned that I had a new director for my department.

Four days later, I was "officially" informed via email that G.M. Popev and V.R. Sokolovska had just been made the Head of the Special Projects Directorate and Director of Theoretical Biology, respectively. Naturally, there were no further details. As far as I was concerned, my former boss, Karlov Gregorievich Drazinzka, had fallen off of the face of the earth. What was important now was to find out all I could about this Popev character.

Once again my Directorate training went into high gear. Popev, Gregorii Mikhailovich, was born 12 July 1960 in Dimitrovgrad, Ulyanovsk Oblast. He was a sensational junior hockey defenseman, who earned degrees in chemistry and mathematics. Later, he was a visiting research fellow at the *Max-Planck-Institut für Festkörperforschung*, Stuttgart, Germany. He wrote his PhD on the statistical basis of cryptographic systems. His father Mikhail was permanent faculty at the Federal

Nuclear Research Center (VNIIEF). His physical specifications matched his hockey position: height, two hundred centimeters; weight, one hundred and ten kilos; with a ruddy complexion add red hair.

So, my new superior was young for a position of this rank, clearly multilingual, a scientist, and was a big, big man, perhaps of Viking heritage. Well, that was a start. Now I wondered if I would ever get to meet him. Or, had Stefan Nikolevich managed to transfer me to his department?

Sometimes I simply wonder if one hand knows what the other is doing.

But regardless of these chess moves that were being made at the highest levels, my temporal career had once again been put on hold. Yes, I still practiced with my Sasha's tapes. Yes, I continued on with Konstantina Iosifeva's database work, but even that was fast coming to an end. So she had me putting together hieroglyphic translations for the major pieces at the Pushkin, with the idea of attracting more patrons to the museum.

Fortunately, there was always my running. That near daily cleansing kept my frustration levels down, somewhat, while I awaited news of my next deployment, or for that matter, news of any kind. About the only significant thing to mention during this time was that my hair had grown out and was at the point that I could comb it, yet not really do anything good with it. Fortunately, I was beyond that very awkward "concentration camp" look, that some of the youngsters seemed to like so much, which did not fit me at all.

* * *

While I was totally wrapped up in my little world, news of other changes arrived as well, but this time from the States. Tuna Cartwright had retired his field command of the security detail. Now, as I read between the lines, he was to be the all-seeing security mastermind from behind his desk. I had a hard time believing that.

In his place, Pat Callahan was promoted, now as a full lieutenant. I smile as I look back on that first early morning run in Chicago, when those two footballers had tracked me down, and then shooed me back to the Philology Annex, before I had gotten myself into some real trouble. Calli had been the taller of the two.

Dr. Borov, too, finally retired, now in his early nineties. Dr. Charles Naysmithe, his long-time protégé, now carried that vast burden that was the care and feeding of Horizon Pass. It was only later, when the two of us got to talking, that Dr. Naysmithe revealed what else his predecessor "had gifted him." For Dr. Borov had left poor Charlie to address two unfinished tasks. One was called CRYSTAL BALL. It was by far the thorniest and represented the initial reason that the American government had agreed to provide the seed funding for Dr. Borov's research and eventually Horizon Pass. In essence, it was a debt unpaid.

The other responsibility that was placed squarely upon Dr. Naysmithe was a strangely grim one: how to most effectively shut down Horizon Pass in the dire event of a hostile seizure of its facility, its temporal devices, or both. As to who would be doing the "seizing," Dr. Borov had remained mum. Charlie, however, had fully understood the gravity of the predecessor's concern. Little did I know that I would eventually be involved in both. All that I knew was that I had been curtly issued a plane ticket to Chicago. While I was overjoyed about that development, I again asked myself why my superior, whoever he was, had not informed me as to why I was going.

* * *

At first, it was all of bit of a mystery, as Joey and I sat in the empty conference room on the second subbasement level of the Philology Annex.

Damn he's looking ripped today! I wonder? What's he doing for lunch?

He with his hands folded in that patient school boy anticipation of his, me with my fresh Starbucks Grande, because I am not a morning person by design. Then an older woman appeared wearing a gray pinstriped pant suit. She walked briskly and crisply around us, and headed for the lectern at the opposite end of the conference table. Once there, she began to settle herself in by first removing two identical looking manila file folders, what looked like lecture notes, and then put on her reading glasses. With her half-glasses in position now atop the bridge of her nose and her hands clasped behind her back, the petit woman began.

"Good morning," she said. "I am Professor Mildred Hayes. I am a nuclear physicist by inclination and trade. But today I have been asked by your Dr. Peter Borov to be a historian of sorts. You see, there is a very good possibility that your next drop will take place in 1943, a time that I am quite well acquainted with."

While that statement was delivered, our lecturer had moved from behind the table's lectern to stand directly across from us.

"By the vacant looks on your faces, I can see that this is all news to you," Hayes stated with a wry smile as she handed each of us one of the identical manila folders.

"What I have just given you is something that I have been gathering over the past twenty-one years. If I were you, I would thoroughly familiarize myself with your folder's contents. So without any further ado, let us begin."

And begin she did, and what a story she told! In 1943, in the Philadelphia naval dockyards, a daring secret experiment, CRYSTAL BALL, had been conducted. The idea was to create an electromagnetic field around a naval warship so as to render it invisible. It was thought to represent the ultimate form of camouflage. And, as it turned out, the ship did indeed disappear, leaving only a hole in the water, where the ship's hull had displaced the surrounding sea water.

While the ship survived this experiment, the ship's crew had not, with some caught fire, others merged with the ship's superstructure, and the extreme disorientation of the field had caused a handful of men to jump ship and disappear altogether. Clearly, Professor Hayes explained, something had gone very wrong that day in 1943. And given the theoretical and technological similarity between the apparatus that was employed during the Philadelphia Experiment and that of the Soap Bubble, current thinking at the time believed that those who had jumped overboard had crossed over into a different time. The question then became, when, and if that could be ascertained, could we rescue them?

*   *   *

Frankly, neither Joey nor I knew where all the time had gone, for suddenly housekeeping arrived with lunch. *So much for my earlier idea!* Professor Mildred Hayes, now just Millie to us, had just held us spellbound for the past three and a half hours, pausing only occasionally to daintily sip some water from her plastic Mickey Mouse cup.

"So Millie," Joey asked, his mouth half full of a delicious Philly cheese steak sandwich. "The Navy covered up the entire experiment with a twin ship and crew with the same name? Did I get that right?"

"Indeed you did Joseph. And from what I have been able to divine, that bureaucratic trick itself was almost as difficult to orchestrate as was the experiment itself!"

Something tangential came to mind and so I asked. "You mentioned that while the experiment was underway, that there were reports of a greenish fog surrounding the ship's hull. Is that correct?"

"Indeed young lady, that is correct."

"Could it be the current that passed through the hull was strong enough to desalinize the surrounding layer of sea water, thereby producing a diluted form of chlorine gas?"

With a broad smile, Hayes answered, "Now that is a most interesting observation! And one, I might add, that I have not heard before. Excellent Vesna. I can see that you did not forget your college chemistry. But for your question, it's entirely possible."

Joey then asked, "Alright, if I get this straight, we are to drop into Philly, observe the experiment, and get back. Is that really it?"

Millie scrunched up her face in thought. "Initially Joseph, I suspect so. Confirmation that the event occurred is the primary goal. But once that has been made, there is a very strong desire within the Navy to see if you can retrieve the four lost seamen, who jumped overboard into the *somewhen.*"

"But how could we do that?" I broke in. "We don't know what the temporal calibration would be for a field as big as a ship, much less the power levels achieved."

With her eyes brightly twinkling at my insight, Millie said with considerable warmth, "Yes, yes indeed. Peter was right about you, Vesna. You truly do possess a keen scientific mind. But what would you say if I told you that you could somehow measure the field itself? What would that buy you?"

"I really don't know. I would have to first establish a baseline test with the Soap Bubble at Horizon Pass, and then correlate that against the Philadelphia field measurement."

"Precisely, my dear, precisely."

Joey's eyes widened. "Wait a minute here! You mean you want us to somehow measure that ship's field!"

"Yes young man, that's exactly what I want you to do."

"To do that we will need to get really close to the ship. What sort of equipment would we need to do a measurement like that? And then, what about the area's security? How do we get past that?"

After a brief pause to think, Millie just smiled that marvelous smile of hers and said, "You will do the measurements with a special probe that I was tasked to construct, while I was at Princeton."

"A probe!" Joey exclaimed, "Bringing that through the drop ring will be a major infraction of the *RUTI*. What if it gets lost or something? You'll never get authorization for that." He dismissively concluded with a wave of his hand.

"Joseph you are absolutely correct about the probe not going through the ring. But have you considered the possibility of the probe already being there? In essence, waiting for you, in the *somewhen*?"

Joey's jaw sagged.

Then I had another thought. "What really bothers me about all of this is getting so close to such a powerful field, and then penetrating it with a probe. Wouldn't we need some sort of insulation or grounding to protect us?"

"Indeed Vesna, insulation would be highly recommended, but a pair of rubber boots, gloves, and flash goggles should do the trick quite nicely."

Joey leaned forward. "Okay Millie. Come clean. Just where is this probe?"

"Well Joseph, I was wondering when you would come around to that issue. It's at Princeton."

"Princeton. As in Princeton, New Jersey?"

"Why yes."

"And how big is this 'probe thing?' Bigger or smaller than a bread box?"

Now taking a deep breath and looking down at her hands Millie answered. "Oh, very much bigger than a bread box. In fact Joseph, it looks very much like a fishing pole."

"How long is this fishing pole?"

"Six and one half feet in length." And then Millie

added for further clarification. "It weighs about five pounds total."

"So to summarize," Joey began. "We drop somewhere in Princeton. Next, we temporarily 'borrow' a fishing pole. We take the train to Philly. From the train station we take a taxi to the docks. We locate the secured area. We present our papers. We get in, somehow. We watch the experiment. We somehow get permission to probe the field. We note down the field strength. Then we catch a taxi from the docks back to the Philly train station, and from there catch a train back to Princeton. We return the 'borrowed' fishing pole. Then we are retrieved. Have I left out anything Dr. Hayes?" Joey concluded in disbelief, "And do you know just how nuts this all is?"

"Sadly, yes, Joseph." Millie said with a deep sigh. "I know that it is quite ambitious," and then took a dainty bite of her sandwich. Thereafter, we ate the rest of our lunches in silence, each deep in our own thoughts.

*   *   *

"Millie, I really don't know how to ask this, but I just have to. You said that you were 'tasked to construct' the Hayes Device, the probe. Did I hear that right?" Joey queried.

Again smiling with her eyes, Millie answered. "Why yes indeed Joseph. You did hear that right."

"Okay then, if that is indeed the case, then precisely who 'tasked' you to do so?"

"Now Joseph, what a penetrating question. It was Professor Einstein. Who else? He wanted to measure the strength of the Eldridge's field too, and then use that data to further his own research. I was initially slotted to perform that measurement, but in the end, at the last minute, I was not allowed to participate, and so the task was made merely optional. Boy was I peeved! As was Professor Einstein. Here I had built the probe, been briefed on all the experiment's particulars, its security measures, its passwords, and because I was not yet a PhD, I did not get my chance."

Now with wide eyes Joey continued. "Okay, fine. But Millie, why did you decide 'to hide' your device in the corner of an abandoned office of all places?"

Grinning ear-to-ear, the seasoned physicist answered. "Joseph, Joseph, such an inquisitive mind you have. You would have made such a fine scientist. But to answer your question, again it was Albert's idea. He has always been a big believer in hiding that which is secret in plain sight. But if I might anticipate your logical next question, the answer to it is demonstrably 'yes,' Albert and I did work together quite a bit and he openly shared with me his first and only true love – his unfinished Unified Field Theory, of which the Philadelphia Experiment was a direct, practical, although crude demonstration. But what neither of us could have anticipated was the intersection of that theory with dear Peter Borov's fine work. Little did either of us know that we would have a potential opportunity for a rescue effort."

Now sitting back in his chair, Joey, always the suspicious one, squinted his eyes and said. "Millie, what's really going on here?"

The smile on Millie's face faded and her eyes pooled with unshed tears. "Joseph. One of the lost

sailors was my big brother."
That statement broke my heart.

* * *

To place the drop within the Princeton University campus was brilliant. There were numerous locations on campus that had not changed one iota since 1943. In our case, we took advantage of a cover story that specified the sudden need for an architectural renovation to the University Chapel, a magnificent cruciform Tudor gothic structure, which closed it to the public for several days. Gaudy yellow construction tape Xs and saw horses decorated and blocked every entranceway. Callahan's troops further secured the interior and the university's own campus security patrolled the exterior.

A hastily constructed PVC scaffolding, platform, and boom with extraction rope and pulley were erected before the altar. The whole was then tented over in plastic sheeting to give the appearance of a construction project in progress.

As with our other deployments, we could not wear any metal during the drop. So, a canvas bag was used into which went Joey's military belt and buckle, his wristwatch, his fountain pen, his officer's hat, his slacks and his rolled up jacket with its brass buttons and medals. My contribution to the pre-drop bag included a wristwatch, purse, and my skirt with its zipper.

Since the drop was scheduled for 2:30 in the morning on Wednesday, October 27th, few thought that any would witness the event on the other side. But just to make sure that a penitential student would not be on the other side, Sergeant "Ozzy" Osgood first "peeked" by inserting his plastic optical device through the Soap Bubble's field. And, as expected, nothing was seen.

Taking up our usual positions on the platform of the scaffolding, almost on cue, I could feel the static charge cling to my stockings. With the ring in place floating about five feet above the sacristy's marble flooring, Osgood again did his visual check and gestured a "thumbs up" to Callahan.

"Okay Dr. Richards, you can drop the bag now."

And with that permission, the canvas bag disappeared into the silvery field.

Noting no abnormalities with the field, the ion cannons, or power pack, Callahan then said to me. "Okay, you're free to drop."

After about a twenty second pause, Joey followed me through.

* * *

Again that deliciously slippery feeling! Oh, how I wish that I could bottle it!

Landing clean and rolling on the smooth marble floor, Joey landed shortly thereafter, and with a thud, followed by an involuntary grunt.

"Jesus! Just once it would be nice to drop without all the purple haze."

"Shhh. Watch your manners." I hissed. "You shouldn't blaspheme in church." I teased him. I still could not control my concern about Joey's ongoing physiological reaction after a drop, and in this instance, it took him a full two minutes to uncross his eyes.

Still flat on his back, Joey looked into the darkness

and finally whispered. "Are we alone?"

"It appears to be so."

He sat up. "Good. Now let's find some pews, stretch out, and grab some sleep, as we're really gonna' need it tomorrow.

*   *   *

I sincerely tried to sleep on that wooden pew with its hard, unforgiving, and narrow surface. The best that I could do was curled up with my arm under my head. While that worked after a fashion, I couldn't endure Joey's snoring, or perhaps better, braying.

*   *   *

Before we caught the 7:28 train to Trenton with a change to Philadelphia, we had to make a visit to minor the Physics Department at Guyot Hall. Fortunately, it was located only a scant three blocks away down Washington Road from the chapel. Fortunately too, at 6:13 in the morning, few souls were out and about the castle-like façade of Guyot Hall.

Our goal was Room M27 on the Mezzanine Level. Ascending the red granite steps of the northern main entrance, we climbed to the next floor and quickly found the room. Like the main entrance door, it too was unlocked. In fact, its wooden door didn't even have a lock – just a simple door knob and an interior latch.

Within this dusty and cramped academic office, filled with a helter-skelter of boxes, we found it in the corner, just as Millie described it, a longish six foot cardboard tube about five inches in diameter. Grabbing it, we made our getaway back to Washington Road.

Now 6:20, we quickly settled into our long walk to the Princeton Junction Station. In retrospect, we may not have made our train, if it were not for a kindly milkman in his truck, who gave us a lift all the way to the station.

*　　*　　*

Ticket in hand and waiting on the platform on this early weekday morning, I quickly discovered that we were the only military personnel in this cigarette smoking crowd of commuters. Furthermore, we were the only ones on the platform with a six foot tube that could have been mistaken for a rocket canister. Not really used to being stared at, we stayed to ourselves, talking quietly, and wishing that the train would soon arrive. Nonetheless, eyes peered at us over folded morning newspapers. And given that all the commuters were male, my presence had been duly noted.

Blessedly, a few minutes later the train arrived.

*　　*　　*

The train ride to Trenton turned out to be a non-event. Once at Trenton, the transfer over to the Philadelphia connection went smoothly enough. Time just flew by and before I knew it we had arrived at Pennsylvania Station at 9:07. Now in Philly, we quickly blended in as the station was brimming with military personnel going here, there, and seemingly everywhere at once. But once again, there were few women among them. As for our Italian taxi driver, our naval uniforms did not impress him nor did he seem to care about our six foot tube.

With our feet once again on the ground, Joey led as we followed the directions that Millie had so insistently drilled into us. Now at the naval yard, we were lost within the hundreds of men and women who were employed there. But as we neared our goal, the crush of humanity had thinned out considerably.

The dock in question, Warehouse Dock 37, included the mooring of the destroyer escort USS Eldridge 173, had been cordoned off with two layers of cyclone fencing topped with barbed wire. Between the two fences, guards patrolled with German shepherds. Access to the secured area was through a dockside entrance. So we headed straight for it just as Millie had said. And sure enough, there stood two solidly built Marines at the warehouse's entrance. When we approached, the soldiers stiffened at seeing Joey's rank of commander, but their eyes widened in shock on seeing my lieutenant's bars.

The sergeant on the right requested.

"IDs if you please."

So we handed over our military identity cards. Receiving them back after a thorough examination, the sergeant next asked.

"Commander Richards, what's in the tube?"

Richards answered curtly, following Millie's careful and specific directions.

"That's classified Marine. But if you really want to know, we're here to do some fishing."

The sergeant, registering the coded words, nodded his head and opened the heavy metal door allowing us to pass through. Once inside we found ourselves in a long and narrow windowless hallway, that by the smell of it had just been freshly painted battleship gray.

At the other end of this security corridor was another door, another set of Marines, and another inspection of our papers. This time, however, Joey did open up the tube so its contents could be viewed and inspected. After resealing the tube, the Marine on the left, who had watched his partner put us through the drill, finally announced.

"Commander Richards, Lieutenant Gregg, you may proceed. However, as I do not recall having seen either of you at this facility before, I must inform you that you must first report to your respective cloak rooms, so that you can change into your protective gear before entering the secured area."

"Thank you Sergeant," Richards said with a short nod. I remained mum per Millie's direction.

As we moved off, each to our own changing rooms, I felt the eyes of the two Marines on me.

*　*　*

When we emerged from the cloak rooms, we both were clothed in white lab coats over our uniforms, rubber boots over our shoes, with heavy rubber laboratory gloves, and oversized flash goggles around our necks. Joey carried the probe without its protective tube. Cradling it horizontally in his arms, I reviewed in my mind Millie's carefully enunciated instructions.

"Joseph," she began, "the Hayes Device is just a probe. Think of it as just a heavily insulated lightning rod with a read out at the handle's end and the actual conductive rod, or probe, at the other. While the probe end is inserted directly into the outer boundary layer of the electromagnetic field, you must be holding it by its heavily insulated handle. What will be critical is the actual reading. The three position calibration toggle will help you to narrow the reading down.

"Remember too Joseph, we're measuring the intensity of the electromagnetic field in watts. So when you toggle on position one, the one on the far left, it reads as kilowatts, the middle position, as megawatts, and the one on the far right, as gigawatts. For example, the Soap Bubble puts out about fifty seven watts of energy. I also suspect that your initial reading may jump around at first, but then will settle out, and remain steady. And when it does settle, just remember that reading!"

*   *   *

We were directed by Marine personnel to a door that opened directly to Dock 37 and the moored destroyer escort, the USS Eldridge. Before it and along the water's edge were many people in white lab coats milling nervously about. We stood back from all of this activity, not only to not get into someone's way, but also to memorize every detail for our debriefs. For some odd reason, my attention was drawn to the sea gulls perched atop the communications array and I wondered what would become of them.

Then one of the lab coats broke that thought. Having seen Joey with the probe, he excitedly began to gesture to him, waving him over to the edge of the ship's bow.

"You there! Yes you! You're late! Get over here and take your damn reading already!"

As Joey quickly stepped forward he said, "Sorry. I

did not realize that the experiment had already begun."

Now with his hands on his hips, the imperious fuzz ball grunted. "It hasn't you idiot! I just want you to calibrate the Hayes' Device before we flip the switch. And just who the hell are you?"

"Commander Richards from Dr. Bush's office. And this is Lieutenant Gregg, my assistant," Richards deadpanned.

"Okay *Commander*, take your measurement and then just try to stay out of the way," he cracked as he simultaneously gave me a look of absolute disdain.

Managing to nod submissively, Joey extended the correct end of the probe to almost touching the hull, while he flipped through the toggle switches positions. Finishing, he flatly stated.

"I've got zero readings throughout the probe's spectrum."

The nervously expectant fuzzy-headed lab coat exclaimed, "Excellent! Just excellent! Now stand back as we begin the power up sequence. By the way, *Commander*, you got here just in the nick of time."

Again, obedient to this scientist's directions, Joey then almost robotically stepped back to rejoin me. "I wonder who that is?"

"I don't recognize him from any of Millie's photos, but I really want to level him," I gritted out between my teeth.

After the passage of nearly thirty-five minutes, the same exuberant lab coat began enumerating a rather long check list that I know meant absolutely nothing to Joey, but plenty to me, so I provided him with a whispered commentary.

"Our fuzzy haired friend has just ordered the

release of all electrical circuit safeguards…the generators aboard the ship are charging…apparently they have to reach some sort of a threshold before they throw the switch…hang on…can you feel all that static electricity in the air…okay, it's show time, they just threw the switch!"

*   *   *

The air first began to reek of ozone and then the ship just, suddenly, wasn't there. To say that the effect was jaw-dropping would have been an understatement. As the lab coats moved forward, several of them began pointing to the hole in the water, more a depression that was formed by the ship's hull. Then, after about ten seconds into the experiment Joey was again waved over by the fuzzy headed wonder to probe the field, which he did.

Millie was absolutely correct, the field's strength was not constant, but rather was oscillating over a broad range in the megawatt calibration setting. Now at Joey's side, I called out, "Thirty seconds."

After the passage of the first minute, the probe settled down between thirty and forty megawatts. Then I called out, "Sixty seconds."

At this point in the experiment, a greenish-yellow mist had begun to form at the bottom of the depression in the water. "Joey look!" I said excitedly. "The field is indeed desalinizing the water around the ship's hull. I knew it!"

"I read now a steady forty-one megawatts." Joey announced.

I then called out, "ninety seconds."

And then the inhuman screaming began.

*   *   *

As the experiment was planned to run a full fifteen minutes, the call for an emergency shutdown after only ninety seconds left the lab coats shocked and confused. The screams outright panicked them. At the two minute mark, the field was finally shut down by those onboard, but the bloodcurdling screams continued unabated. Then the agonized exhalations decreased in strength and volume, their meaning obvious to all.

Out of nowhere naval medics burdened with gear arrived and quite literally stormed the ship's lone zigzagging debarkation ramp. Along the dock, all was chaos. The lab coats were running all around, shouting this, and screaming that. Our fuzzy headed friend stood frozen like a statue before the ship's bow with his mouth open.

Taking in the scene, Joey said, "It's time to go." And I did not argue.

Stripping out of our protective gear, and with the probe again in its cardboard tube, we met at the second security station, and passed right through it.

The biggest challenge that we could have had at the dock yards was just finding a taxi for our getaway. But here my alluring wave and legs really came in handy.

*   *   *

Fortunately, the Princeton drop had gone without mishap, and Millie's details had been spot on throughout, not that the adventure didn't have a few tense moments. Joey indeed had held the probe during that gruesome experiment. After the post-drop analysis, the U.S.S. Eldridge's field had had calibrated out to

Monday, September 19th, 19,754 BC. In a true moment of deliberation and conscience, the membership of the Philology Annex voted against mounting a rescue for the lost seamen. It had been the physicist, Ernst Jung, who had turned that emotionally squeamish bunch of academics by quoting heavily from the *RUTI* and by posing a simple and cogent question.

"Okay, let's say we retrieve these men. Then what? Now what's going to kept them from talking? But even more importantly, as soon as we return them to their own rightful place in history, we promptly change our own. Do you want to do that?"

While the vote had been practically a unanimous one, none among the Annex membership were happy to shoulder the pressure of such a tough decision. All had tried to worm their way out of it, but in the end, the rescue had been nixed. As for Dr. Charlie Naysmithe, who had been dead against this adventure from the start, his worries had not gone away, as he still had an unpaid chit owed to Uncle Sam.

But perhaps the biggest surprise to come out of that deployment was that, for the first time, I felt as if I wasn't looking over my shoulder. Instead, Joey and I had blended into one, cohesive team. As I had never participated in any form of organized team sport as a child, I did not know what the feeling of such backup was like. I had been raised a loner, trained to be dependent upon none. And do you know what? I really liked it this thing called team.

*　　*　　*

On the very day of my return to Moscow, jet-lagged to the max, my lovely debriefing sessions began.

All too predictably, my interlocutor was the same, snide, sarcastic dolt, who had last quizzed me about the Egyptian drop. So, when I related everything that had occurred, he did not believe any of it, and instead, insisted that I must have run off to some sunny clime for a holiday, where in a rum-sodden stupor, I had totally invented what had taken place.

While I fully understood that my superiors wanted to know all of the particulars about what I was up to, relating those events in excruciating detail four and sometimes five times in a row really was quite tiresome. I kept thinking that surely, there must be some better way. But when you add that absolute moron and dullard to the equation, well, all I can say is, I finally snapped.

I think that it was midway through my fourth telling of the tale, that the maggot started laughing. It was right at the point, when I was relating what it was like hearing the American sailors spontaneously combusting on that wretched ship's decking. He had not heard their screams. I had. And so, I stood up and struck him with my chair across his head and shoulders. Before I could finish the slug off, several powerful sets of hands had unfortunately restrained me from doing so.

CHAPTER XII
Some Library Work

After the Princeton drop, it wasn't until the following June before I had heard any word about the potential for another. As to the where or when of this drop, I was not told. *As usual.* Regardless of that fact, I was overjoyed at the news as I had kept up with my language drills and my running. As for Konstantina Iosifeva and her department's needs, all of the museum translations had been completed and posted. And frankly, I could tell that she was beginning to scratch her head for things for me to do. We even discussed the possibility of me writing a thesis.

* * *

To my great pleasure, Joey met me at the international terminal in Chicago. *Damn was he looking good!* Per the usual Joey, he gave my hand a warm squeeze and then efficiently whisked me over to the military side of the airport, where a certain Gulf Stream V was waiting. Moments later we were in the air en route to Holloman AFB and Horizon Pass. As much as I was overjoyed at seeing Joey, after that first glass of champagne, I passed out in my seat and did not wake up until we had landed. And yes, there was that blacked-out helicopter waiting for us.

Upon landing and as we emerged from the blowing dust of the helicopter's backwash, a strong voice managed to reach us as the whoop, whoop, whoop of the craft began to fade into the distance.

"Welcome back to Horizon Pass!" greeted the

slender director of the facility, Dr. Charlie Naysmithe. Then with a slight frown on his face, he said.

"Let's get inside as our 'friends' are due to fly over in the next few minutes." This none too subtle reference was to a tasked and nosey Russian surveillance satellite.

Once beyond the entranceway hidden in the ramshackle hut, Dr. Naysmithe stopped before us and stated for the record, "Okay you two, you know the drill. Go get fed, showered, and hit the sack. You'll need every wink of sleep. Also, you'll find your daily schedules posted in your quarters. Read 'em and weep folks. Now off you go."

Well off we went, but not before spending a few cherished moments together.

*   *   *

The following day I finally learned about the deployment. Connected by a secured phone connection, Professor John Milson himself briefed us.

"Okay you two, here's the deal. And Joseph, this is your big chance, so don't blow it."

I quickly glanced at Joey and wondered what he was up to now.

And more precisely, why hadn't he mentioned anything either on the plane or last night! That little sneak!

"Joseph, you and Vesna are going to do some very low profile poking around into your favorite subject, the god Ptah." Milson said.

"What that means is that a brief social visit to Prince Horemheb may be in order, but isn't necessary. According to the date of your insertion, he will be still busy preparing for the return of the royal court to

Thebes.

"What you'll want to do, however, is to arrange for a meeting with Meryptah's successor, a high priest named Nebneteru. Keep your ears open. What you want is access to the archives of the Amen Re Temple.

"Vesna, do not be surprised if it is referred to as the *per ankh*, or the House of Life. Joseph will fill you in."

So this drop was Joey's idea? *And he managed to keep it entirely to himself? I must be slipping.*

"With luck, Joseph, you might find some clues to your mysterious Ptah. And you might have to make a side trip downriver to Memphis as well."

It definitely was his idea!

"For now, let's keep this insertion as discrete and as possible. In other words, no more than a week's time, relative. Do you have any questions?"

"I have just one, Professor Milson," I said. "I was under the impression that permission for a temporal drop was not easily granted. Yet, why are we endangering the current timeline, not to mention risking the rules of the *RUTI,* with such a seemingly casual sounding mission?"

While I thought the question was a valid one, especially in light of what had happened with the Princeton drop, Milson had not.

"Ms. Gregorieva," he answered, "this calculated drop is not a frivolous excursion. In fact, permission to undertake it was sanctioned by your superiors." While the response was polite, its cool delivery and firmness I had never before heard from the man. It had steel in it.

With that message delivered, I practically felt an intellectual slap in the face. My superiors did not want me to even know what this deployment was about, again, until I was on it! This had absolutely nothing to do with Joey's usual penchant for understatement and secretiveness. They, the trio, wanted me gone.

Then Milson noticeably softened his next words. "I well know, Vesna, that you have not been briefed on the details of this mission. That was intentionally done, believe it or not, because your superiors wished it so. Why, I do not know. That decision was not ours. At the very same time, I want to assure you that your role as Joseph's teammate has been in no way diminished. In fact, we are depending upon you to bring him back."

What!

Seeming to psychically read my rather turbulent emotional state across the thousands of miles that separated us, Milson pressed on. "You know, Vesna, despite what your superiors might think, you are an extremely observant, bright, and gifted woman. You know this. Joseph knows this. I know this. Quite frankly, you and Joseph, if you are to continue to work together, must be allowed the freedom to share your thoughts. Otherwise, your team's effectiveness and safety will be placed in great jeopardy.

"Now, as distasteful as the wishes of your superiors may seem, you must consider their point of view as well, no matter how paranoid or obtuse that point of view may appear. The fact remains you are an integral part of this deployment. Also, I strongly suspect that several very enlightening discussions will occur while you're away. I fully encourage this, as I do not want to jeopardize either the mission, or the trust that each of you have developed for one another.

"Joseph. Do you clearly understand what I am unofficially advocating?"

"Loud and clear."

* * *

Deployments, perforce, are serious undertakings. By their very nature, insertions threaten our current reality. So when we had finished with the conference call with John, I was expecting a short, succinct explanation for this one as well. Something like: assassinate a pharaoh, find a UFO, or rescue some sailors. Instead, Joey began sketching on a notepad, and when he was finished, he slid it over for me to see.

"Read that."

What I was looking at were only four hieroglyphs.

"Well, that's easy. This is the god Ptah's name."

"Yes, it is. Now, Vesna, I want you to look at only the first three glyphs and ignore the last, the determinative for a god. Now what do you see?"

"Well, I see a '*p*', a '*t*', and an aspirated '*h*'."

"Again, you're correct. Now does that triad of glyphs mean anything to you?"

I had to pause a moment, and then it came to me.

"Why yes, yes it does. That's the verb 'to create', or 'to make'."

"Bingo. Now, what are the characteristics of the god Ptah?"

"Well, he's the god of craftsmen...and...a creator god as well."

"Bingo again. And his theology is best expressed in a document called the 'Memphite Theology.' Have you ever run across it?"

"No, I haven't. Where are you going with this?"

"Patience, Vesna, that's all I am asking for. The

'Memphite Theology,' the creation myth as told to us by the god Ptah, is a very interesting one. In it the creation of a thing is first thought of, and then is created by enunciating it. In physical terms, then, mass is imagined and then created with the spoken word."

"Joey," I said. "Isn't that like the 'Logos Doctrine' in the *Book of Genesis*?"

"Indeed it is, except for the fact that the 'Memphite Theology' is several millennia older."

But before I could express my surprise, Joey relentlessly plowed on.

"Now, don't you find it a little odd that Ptah's own name, is based upon a glyphic stem that is the verb 'to make' or to create?'"

While I thought about this. *He's right. It is an odd coincidence.*

Then Joey continued. "Did you know that in the entire Egyptian language the only '*p*', '*t*', and '*ḥ*' combination is Ptah's name and that verb?"

I shook my head in negation, and with more than a bit of growing concern.

This is getting strange.

"Okay, now consider this. And I know that you have been exposed to this level of grammar because of your studies in St. Petersburg. Egyptian nouns have gender, male and female. The Egyptian signs of gender are '*p*' for masculine and '*t*' for feminine. Right?"

I nodded.

Joey now was covering over all the glyphs, except one, with his hands.

"Now Vesna, I want you to think like a scientist and not an Egyptian philologist. What does this '*ḥ*' glyph look like to you?"

"I don't know. It's a twisted rope, or a candle wick."

Then when I saw Joey's disapproving face, in exasperation I just quickly said. "I don't know. What do you see?"

"Vesna, what I see is a barely pronounceable name, based upon a hieroglyphic stem, which is used just once in the entire Egyptian language to express the verb 'to make' or 'to create'. But when we examine the three glyphs of the stem by themselves, the 'p', 't', and '$ḥ$', we get 'maleness', 'femaleness', and a twisted rope. Now do you see it?"

I clearly remember putting my hand over my mouth in total shock as I recognized just what Joey was getting at.

The twisted rope wasn't a twisted rope at all. It was a DNA strand!

"And Vesna, this is why we are investigating Ptah. And with any luck, we just might be able to meet the man."

*   *   *

We deployed direct from Holloman AFB in the "special," but plain-Jane looking, Gulf Stream V. This flight would be a long haul to Luxor, Egypt. As a consequence, I was not surprised to see that the plane had been outfitted with two external fuel tanks attached to places on the plane's wings. Frankly, although Joey thought them "cool," I thought that they stuck out like ugly eyesores. To my eye, the plane looked overweight with them.

Before we boarded, Joey gazed down the length of

the aircraft, while he supervised the loading of the Little Beast II and the portable Soap Bubble VI B. As he did so, Joey tried *again* to point out the plane's subtle lines and additions. He showed me the two shrouded fiberglass gun ports in the nose and the pregnant-looking bulge of the plane's belly, which had three parallel seams that hinted at the presence of doors.

As we walked around the plane, Joey told me again about its special tail and its powerful engines. Perhaps it's a guy thing, but I wasn't interested. But one thing I did find intriguing was the plane's paint and markings. Joey said that the copilot could, with a flip of a switch, trickle a low voltage charge throughout the plane's skin that allowed it to mimic its surroundings. In other words, the plane could camouflage itself! Even better, the same co-pilot could, at will, alter the lettering of the craft's registration markings using a key pad! It was so James Bond! Oddly, at the time, I never gave a thought as to *why* the plane needed such tomfoolery.

Upon entering the cabin, I could only shake my head and smile at the purely pure military seating and transport. Safe, secure, but butt ugly with olive green webbing, massive, but comfortable head and neck padding, and five-point harnesses for restraints. In all, sixteen such nests were arranged in two staggered rows around a common central aisle. We took the first two nearest the flight deck. The rest of the plane was empty as Callahan and his "school" had left ahead of us.

*   *   *

During the flight from New Mexico to Bangor, Maine, I read, but Joey mostly slept during the glass-smooth ride. The landing at Bangor's air base was glassy smooth, and Joey might have slept right through the turn around. But while the plane's tanks were being topped off and the new flight crew began their checklists, a third group opened up the plane's belly and began making lots of noise that resulted in several bumping and clanking noises. Then, Joey woke up.

" What the hell is all that racket?"

"I don't know." I replied evenly. "They have only been at it for about thirty seconds."

"Whose they?"

"I suppose your military."

"Whadda' ya' mean? We're on the ground?" Blurted out my still disoriented partner.

"Yes, we're on the ground, and, well, four men with a large object on wheels just rolled up to the belly of the plane and got to work."

Joey looked out one of the window ports.

"Did you see what it was?"

"You mean on the motorized racking?"

"Yeah, the dolly. It's called a dolly."

"No, I didn't. It had a tarp over it."

Joey frowned. "Huh."

"Did we get some new drivers?"

"Drivers?"

"Yeah, pilots."

"Why yes we did. They're settling into the flight deck right now."

I could tell Joey was not happy, so I asked him what was up.

"It's really quite simple. I'm getting the willies, because we have the newest version of the Soap Bubble aboard. This Bangor refueling stop wasn't necessary, but it's being done anyway. I suppose to top off the tanks. Now we have a fresh flight crew. On top of that, our bay is being modified. I don't like it. It smells like trouble."

CHAPTER XIII
Another Change

While Joey and I were en route to Luxor, Dr. Borov passed away, and we didn't hear about it until our return. What truly can you say about a man, who had devoted his entire life to research? Dr. Borov was a man who had never wed, yet who was much loved. He had never driven a car, yet had spent his entire life moving objects around beyond the speed of light. He was a man, who through his extraordinary intellectual brilliance and natural savvy, was able to move mountains, transform a solitary natural feature into the Horizon Pass facility, reroute energy from the Hoover Dam to power it, all to better understand and transit time itself. If there ever was a real "Dr. Who," it was Dr. Peter Valerievich Borov. If there ever was a time to affix the title "Legend" to a man, it was now.

Officially, or as best as anyone could tell, after some ninety-two years, four months, and seven days, Borov expired peacefully in his sleep. That he had intended to go for his traditional morning run was apparent to anyone as his shoes, jogging suit, socks and underwear were all neatly laid out and waiting. On that day his online day planner had him scheduled for an early morning meeting with Dr. Charlie Naysmithe to go over several proposed tweaks to the Soap Bubble's calibration programming, and three conference calls. A luncheon date with Doc Allen and Nurse Stewart was next to be followed with a post-meal nap, another meeting with Dr. Naysmithe about some nifty idea that Tuna Cartwright had cooked up, followed by some administrative paperwork, and finally, a perusal of his daily email to round out the day.

Always prepared, one of Borov's last wishes was to have his ashes scattered along the many jogging trails that wound around the neighborhood of Horizon Pass, to be followed by a "wild ass party," his very words, to take place at that research facility.

It was no secret. Borov liked his Coors cold and Jack neat. Another request was that a one-time, lump sum be deposited into the accounts of the children of Willard Libby, the inventor of the radiocarbon dating technique, the man who Borov had supported so early on during this research. Without Libby's crucial research in the dating of carbon-14, the calibration of the Soap Bubble might not have taken place.

To Colonel Charles Abraham "Tuna" Cartwright, retired, Dr. Borov left all of his much-beloved fly fishing gear, full knowing that that native of Louisiana would put them all too good use.

To Doc Allen, the Russian émigré bequeathed title to several acres of land located near the Colorado town of Rifle, complete with its own trout stream.

To his young colleague and successor, Dr. Charlie Naysmithe, the wily scientist willed him a framed, but still highly classified black and white picture of himself, grinning broadly, as he stuck a paper straw into the electromagnetic field of the Soap Bubble prototype. Affixed to the wooden frame was a brass plate with the words, "Charlie: I double-dog dare you to top this!"

CHAPTER XIV
Third Deployment

Despite Joey's radar being on full alert since our takeoff from Bangor, the second leg of the flight had gone smoothly. I finished my book and even got some sleep. The touchdown at Luxor was as silky smooth as any zoomie could have made it. However, what really bugged Joey was the lack of response from all of his attempts at chatting up the flight crew. What he did find out was that their drivers were professional U.S. Air Force, most likely fighter pilots. Their shoulder patches boldly said so: Maineiacs – 101st Air Wing.

These guys were all business.

This he read as another bad sign that something was up and someone far up the ladder was definitely concerned. That only meant that something had Cartwright's "witchy" radar a twitchin'.

*   *   *

Once again we were dropping into the *somewhen* of late Eighteenth Dynasty Egypt. In many respects, Joey could have easily done it alone, as the terrain and personalities involved were so well understood. But the *RUTI* was very clear on the point that solo drops were not wise ones, and so I got to tag along as his 'buddy'. And no, I'm not being snarky, just pleased that we developed into such a tightly knit team.

To my surprise, I learned that Joey had long instigated this deployment, all to do some library research on a god named Ptah. So we did just that. We visited the *per ankh* or House of Life housed within the Amen Re Temple complex. Finding little there, we journeyed north to Memphis and visited the high priest of the Temple of Ptah, a charming man named Ptahmesou, who was the brother of the late high priest of Amen Re, Meryptah, Joey's adopted father. Once there, we sought out what we could about their god, and that was when things got very interesting.

*　　*　　*

Invited to share the evening meal within the high priest's house, Ptahmesou asked.

"Now Mayneken, my nephew, the much-loved and adopted son of my eldest brother, the Osiris Meryptah, what caused you to travel all the way here from distant Thebes?"

Joey, with his mouth full of sweet bread, looked to me for help. Wondering where he put it all, I shook my head and firmly took hold of the reins.

"Noble Ptahmesou, as I see that my brother, ever the consummate ambassador, is currently fully engaged in negotiations with a honeyed sweet bread, may I answer that question for him? As we both seek the same."

"By all means most beautiful Maatkare!" The high priest encouraged, now pleased to legitimately focus upon me.

"We seek permission from you to visit the *per ankh* of the god Ptah, for we wish to study his wisdom, and if it is permitted, to even copy that which is needful to us. The why of this is clear. We find the creation myth of Amen Re to be, let us say, lacking in intellectual rigor, while we have heard that the theology of Ptah requires a certain discipline of thought, before it is put into words."

Ptahmesou sat spellbound during this brief and so cleverly constructed allusion to the hallowed "Memphite Theology" of creation. Blinking back into the here and now, the elderly high priest realized that while he had been enchanted by my beauty, he was now fascinated by my intellectual acumen.

Finding his tongue, "But of course, Maatkare! I freely grant you and Mayneken access to our most treasured *per ankh*. But from your words, it seems to my ears that you have already found what you seek."

Then catching himself, the high priest restated his answer. "But what is it that you two truly seek? Surely it is not wisdom alone, but perhaps something more?"

"My dear Ptahmesou," I said, "your instinct and insight are indeed honed to a very sharp edge! While I do not wish to sound blasphemous in the presence, in the house of the high priest of Ptah, truly 'He who is excellent in the execution of his handiwork,' we seek evidence of the *man* Ptah."

Without skipping a beat, Ptahmesou responded. "What you have said, Maatkare, has held my interest as well. This evening you and your brother will be my household guests. Tomorrow, I will share with you what I have found regarding this matter. I believe that you both will find it to be most interesting."

* * *

After the morning meal, Ptahmesou, true to his word, took us deep within the labyrinthine confines of the Great Temple of Ptah. After many confusing turns and passageways, we at last arrived before a simple cedar door that opened at the high priest's gentle pull. Before entering, the high priest bent down and took from within a small recess near the door jamb a palm-sized oil lamp that he promptly lit.

Once within the small, windowless chamber, the heady smell of papyrus greeted us. Much like the *per ankh* of Amen Re, this one also had its central copying tables, in this instance three arranged end to end with a small wicker basket at one end. Within it large, smooth river stones had been conveniently collected for use. At the opposite end of the chamber, stood a small table with several more of the diminutive oil lamps. Lighting two of them from the first, the high priest passed these on wordlessly to us. Now standing at the rear wall of the chamber, Ptahmesou then turned to face us.

"What is behind you is just one *per ankh* of this temple. As you can see, there are no classrooms nearby, and so this one it is seldom frequented. As to what it contains, that is so rarely consulted, are the ancient sun litanies that formerly were part of the *per ankh* at the Great Temple of Heliopolis, which regrettably is now in considerable disrepair due to recent, unfortunate events connected with the heretic's reign. It is sincerely hoped that the *next* pharaoh will restore that which has been lost to decay and the cruelty of common thieves."

Now in a more conversational tone, the high priest continued. "As I said, this is just one of our *per ankh*s, but in spite of its rather distastefully ignorant sun litanies, it is nonetheless the most important. I say this because there is only one way to it. In fact, I would estimate that it would take the two of you perhaps a full day to find your way back into the sunlight."

Now pausing for a moment Ptahmesou asked Joey with a surprisingly firm directness.

"Noble Mayneken, ambassador to Queen Nefertiti, adopted son of my own elder brother, and adopted brother of Prince Horemheb, how true is your heart?"

"Why, Great One, as true as one of Maat's own feathers."

"And you Maatkare, how true is your heart?"

Bowing my head slightly, I responded. "Great One, the very same as that of my brother."

Returning to the American and apparently satisfied with his answer, Ptahmesou now queried, "Noble Mayneken, what are the principle qualities of Ptah?"

No doubt feeling as if he was once before his PhD board, Joey replied. "Craftsmanship and creation. His thoughts, once so crafted, and then spoken, created all things."

Smiling with true satisfaction, Ptahmesou said. "So very well spoken Mayneken, for behold what Ptah has created."

With those words, the high priest handed his oil lamp to Joey, turned to face the blank wall that was behind him, gave it a gentle push, and a dark rectangular opening appeared!

To say that I was astonished by this development would be an understatement.

We now entered a dark and cramped passage, which by the flickering light of Ptahmesou's oil lamp indicated that he had already begun to descend a series of stone steps. After seventy-two steps, for I counted each of those treacherously worn surfaces, we passed through several layers of rock. At their end, we arrived at a small chamber filled with stale air slightly sweetened.

Joey confirmed, "Myrrh!"

"Indeed Mayneken. For this is the very tomb of Ptah himself!"

Stunned by the high priest's words, I began looking about. The burial chamber was formed as an elongated oval that was rough-cut into a fine limestone bedrock. Directly opposite the descending passage, an unadorned rectangular wooden coffin rested upon a raised pedestal, itself carved from the bedrock.

Examining it, Joey noted, "It is not constructed of cedar wood as is right and proper."

"Indeed Mayneken, your eyes are attentive. It is made of common tamarisk, the material of commoners, but note its clever design. Made of narrow planks as it is, it is both strong and light in weight."

"My uncle, just how do you know such details? How do you know that Ptah himself resides within?"

"Because my nephew, I too as a young man once asked the same question of my elders."

Shocked at the personal revelation, Joey blurted out, "Uncle! Please accept my deepest apology for my ignorant tongue. I meant no offense."

"Among us no offense was received. And besides, do you think that Ptah himself would have been offended by such a logical question? I think not. Now, Maatkare, come here and assist me. You of such delicate hands and fingers, so that I may prove to your doubting and muscle-bound brother that Ptah himself here resides."

Now indicating with the fingernail of his right little finger, Ptahmesou continued.

"Note here, Maatkare, the tiny square along the wood's edge? Yes, right there. Tease it out with your fingernail, no further than the width of your thumb."

I worked very carefully, and soon was rewarded as indeed a wooden plug slowly emerged from the coffin's upper edge. And as it did, my heart pounded with excitement.

"Excellent Maatkare! Now see here, here, and here along this edge? There are three more. Carefully, extract those as well, while I busy myself with the other side."

I must be dreaming. I am actually opening the coffin of a god!

After a few minutes of careful work, all eight of the camouflaged wooden locking pins had been pulled out to the width of a thumb.

"Now Maatkare, do you see where I have my hands positioned? Do likewise, but on your side. Good. Now very gently, lift."

And as one the wooden coffin lid rose about five inches, then ten, then fully to the height of my chest.

"Now Mayneken and Maatkare. Peer down into the face of Ptah."

As Joey stepped forward, I just peeked under the coffin lid, as the light of the high priest's oil lamp fell across an extremely old and fully intact mummy. Even with my background, this mummy's wrappings were performed in a most peculiar way, but one that was extremely precise. But the most curious aspect of the mummy were its hands, each expertly wrapped, each finger individually swaddled. Both hands held before the mummy a simple wooden staff that ended in a Y-shaped forked end.

Joey's jaw dropped. "By the gods, he is holding a common snake-stick!"

"Indeed again, my nephew, your powers of observation are most acute. My predecessor said that in Ptah's time there must have been a surfeit of snakes, so much so, that he was buried with his favorite staff, so that he could have use of it in the afterlife. In fact, it is so even today in certain districts, for during the harvest, a watchman with such a staff and ax guards over the field workers as they very often encounter cobras, sand vipers, and a dangerous snake that seems to spit a poisonous fire." He paused for a moment. "Are you now convinced Mayneken and Maatkare?" said the high priest.

"Yes my uncle. I now believe."

I just mutely nodded in response, stunned beyond all belief that I was actually seeing the mummy of a man, who had become a god.

"Good. Now Maatkare, you have been a fine assistant, help me reseal the god's coffin."

With considerable care, the high priest and I placed and then reinserted all eight of the wooden coffin lid's locking pins. Of the four, only one required some jiggling to seat it correctly back into its slot.

Meanwhile, Joey had been wandering about. He had found several lidded chests to the right, that I guessed held common domestic items. However, along the wall opposite wall stood wickerwork cabinetry made up of diamond-shaped spaces. All of these spaces were filled with rolls of papyrus, each roll wrapped in leather, and each bound in three places with twine. Affixed to the end of each roll, on a short bit of twine hung a ceramic label etched in archaic hieroglyphs.

Joey knelt before them, reading the labels with his oil lamp's radiance, "On Mending Wounds," "The Belly of Nut."

I nodded. In essence, "The stars of the sky."

Upon sampling another niche, Joey found, "On Writing."

Heedless to the thick dust that had accumulated on the tomb chamber's floor, Joey choked out next, "On The Heart and The Tongue."

And so Joey waddled on and on, examining each and every one of the papyri labels, reading them aloud to me. As I best recall, each niche contained treatises devoted to a general subject. Before us was Ptah's own writings on medicine and pharmacology, astronomy, grammar, philosophy, architecture, chemistry, metallurgy, and agriculture. Remarkably, I noted that not one was devoted to either of religion or magic. That was when I realized that Ptah was a true empiricist.

Then Joey announced, "I have seen sufficient. My head hurts."

Ptahmesou replied with a grunt, "As it should."

"And you, Maatkare? Have you too seen sufficient?"

"Indeed, Great One, I have, and perhaps have seen too much."

"Indeed, for I understand that sentiment. But my nephew, do you not want to read even one of Ptah's books?"

We then, in total shock we looked at one another and jointly blurted out, "But they are so old!"

Then Joey continued. "My uncle, just to touch one, much less attempt to unroll it, would turn it to dust!"

"Nonsense," said the elderly priest. "Each of these

is a mere copy, an exact copy I might add, of its predecessor. During my tenure as high priest, I have restored them all. That means that I have read them all as well, and I can say with some authority, that some indeed are quite interesting. So my nephew, I will ask you once again, which one would you like to read?"

Confronted with such a choice, I could tell that Joey felt trapped, much like a child with a dollar in his pocket peering into the window of a vast bakery. But after a moment's consideration, he gently lifted away the roll with the title: "On The Heart and The Tongue."

Ptahmesou, taking the roll and upon examining its label, just smiled as he handed it to me. "Maatkare, would you be so kind and gently carry this to the surface for your oafish brother?"

"I shall with honor."

So we then left the chamber and ascended the seventy-two steps, stopping once for Ptahmesou to catch his breath, and returned through the secret passageway into the seldom-used *per ankh*.

Upon closing the hidden passage's door, the high priest took the roll from my hands, carefully placed it on the end of the near table, untied it, and began to slowly unroll it, taking from the open wicker basket several of the smoothed stones to hold the papyrus down so as to prevent it from rolling up upon itself.

It wasn't long before the full length of the papyrus was exposed, nearly twelve feet of it. In all we counted thirteen panels of neatly brushed text, each about six inches wide by eight inches tall. Between each of the panels of text was a four inch space.

At this point, Ptahmesou pointed out to us a curious phrase located at the end of the text.

"Mayneken, Maatkare, note this cipher.

"It reads: '142nd Inundation.' Each of Ptah's books has one and each cipher is different. To my mind, I understand its meaning as: 'This roll was completed in my 142nd inundation.'"

"But Great One," I gasped, "is it even possible for one to live so old?"

Smiling up at my question, Ptahmesou replied. "Remember Maatkare, we are discussing a man, who has become a god. Anything is possible."

Now returning to the start of the roll, the high priest continued his commentary.

"Note that I have as accurately as possible copied what had been preserved on its predecessor. The characters are recognizable, but are very old ones nonetheless. The patterns of speech are curious, but with time and experience, they become understandable. To be perfectly honest Mayneken and Maatkare, when I copied my first roll, I was baffled as to its true meaning."

In the light of five oil lamps, the papyrus was fully illuminated and Joey's eagerness broke through. "My uncle, may I attempt reading it?"

"Absolutely my son," he said as he stepped away from the tables to give the American room.

At this point I knew exactly what Joey was attempting do: memorize the entire text character by character. And if he had to do so twice, or even thrice, then so be it. Joey can be thorough on the cusp of stubborn.

I was so very happy for him. So very proud. After all, he had brought the two of us here. And for me, that was enough.

*   *   *

Following his memorization of the text, Ptahmesou approached Joey with an interesting proposal.

"My dear nephew, as the adopted son of my elder brother, I hold you nearly in the same regard as I would my own son, if I had been so blessed.

"You have now seen the tomb of Ptah, gazed upon his visage, and even have read his very words. As I am an old man, would you consider taking my place, when that time comes? I am quite sure that my colleague Pahamneter would be in agreement with such a happy arrangement."

I could tell that Joey did not know how to respond. Yes, the family ties made sense. Yes, he had in essence gone through an initiation of sorts that every high priest of Ptah no doubt had to pass. But, a high priest of the god Ptah? Never before had I seen the American so conflicted, so unsure of himself.

"My uncle, your suggestion carries with it the burden of a great responsibility. I am speechless."

"As you should be my nephew. And your reference to responsibility is precisely why I made the suggestion. Think on it, noble Mayneken. That is all that this old man asks."

*   *   *

Our return to Thebes was uneventful, the temporal retrieval likewise. For myself, the impact of what I had just experienced was not as great as it had been for Joey. But what truly impressed me, was Joey's own reaction to Ptah's tomb. The words "stunned," "numb," and "flabbergasted" seemed to fall far short of the mark, but at least approximated what I had witnessed in my partner. For Joey, I can only imagine that he endlessly played and replayed back in his head the significance of all of the archaic hieroglyphic labels, even though upon leaving the crypt Ptahmesou had allowed him to make a careful list of them all. The vast corpus of knowledge that it represented was truly awe inspiring in the extreme.

Then there was that simply marvelous philosophical text "On the Heart and The Tongue," so filled with double meanings, especially when one considers that to the Egyptians the "heart" was the "mind" and the "tongue" was "speech." That treatise Joey memorized was the original version of the "Memphite Theology." And finally, there was Ptahmesou's offer to succeed him as one of the high priests of the god Ptah.

* * *

One more detail about this deployment must be mentioned. On our return flight we flew north toward Iceland en route to Gander, and in so doing quite literally hid ourselves amid the radar clutter of a heavily-traveled, commercial flight corridor. Kindly keep this fact in mind.

With all of us exhausted and securely strapped in for our safety, as Callahan had always insisted on nothing less, we and our security detail, which this time had accompanied us back, all slept the sleep of the dead, at least for awhile.

Then our world, quite literally, turned upside down. All personal gear that had not been properly stowed took flight. One unsecured helmet actually broke and badly bloodied the nose of one of Callahan's men. Now with his blood flying everywhere and the rest of us experiencing wrenching transitions between zero-gee and over five gee stresses, we then felt, more than saw, something detach itself from the Gulf Stream V with a roar. No, make that two roaring somethings.

Not surprisingly, I was disoriented having been violently dragged out of a very deep sleep, and consequently, I added to the general chaos with my own contribution: vomit. Needless to say, when our plane finally returned to level flight, the interior of our cabin was a sight to see, not to mention smell.

While I'm told that the total event only lasted some fourteen seconds, those disorienting seconds had seemed like an eternity. Our crack pilots evaded an attack by a hostile aircraft, and in retaliation, had fired two missiles of our own.

Callahan, who had gone to the flight deck after the encounter, returned, and raided from the galley a bag of wet wipes. As he began handing them out to all of us, he ordered me to the head to clean up, which I did. But while I was attending to my business, I distinctly heard through the thin partition of the bathroom's wall the lieutenant's rant.

"Okay gentlemen. Which one of you numbskulls' helmet struck Grimaldi? And Jonesy, get some gauze on that man's nose like pronto! He's bleeding like a stuck pig."

"Yes, sir!" The team's medic responded.

"It was mine, sir." A now very contrite Marine admitted.

"Okay Stoker. Guess what you inconsiderate fathead? You get to wipe down the entire roof of this cabin. And I want it spotless. Do you read me, Mister!"

"Crystal, sir."

"Alright, now the rest of you, excepting Grimaldi and Jonesy, police your area. I want clean. LIKE RIGHT NOW! Johnson. I'm putting you in charge of all the trash. Here's a bag to collect all the used up wipes in. Now let's move it!"

It took me a twenty minutes to clean myself and my borrowed USAF flight suit as I was a total mess. When I finally emerged from the head, my face was shiny clean and my suit dotted with damp spots. Stoker, God bless his soul, had already worked his way forward to near the flight deck's doorway. Johnson, with his bag already half full of used wipes, was generally policing the area and pointing out missed blobs of blood here and strings of vomit there. As for the smell, well, it was still there, but now was not quite so bad. Instead, the cabin now had the distinct smell of baby powder. And in that instant, I suddenly realized that I had something to do. So as I moved forward toward my forward seat webbing, I stopped and apologized to each and every one of those fine men for my lack of self control.

The rest of the flight back to New Mexico was a sober one. Clearly, someone had wanted us all dead, but had failed to do so, because of the many special improvements to the plane that Joey had tried several times to explain. Now, I wanted to know about each and every one of them. And Joey, being Joey, patiently told me about them all. The one that really amazed me was the vacuum seal on the heads toilet seat. I could only imagine what that might have been like!

*   *   *

On my return flight to Moscow, I grieved Peter Borov's passing. Upon landing, Callahan had told Joey and me that the fine man had died in his sleep. First a successful drop. Then a surprise air-to-air conflict. Now Borov's death. The words "emotional roller coaster" could not describe my wracked state of mind. Note to self: life can sometimes be a real bitch.

*   *   *

Once back in Moscow, I sucked it up and endured the debriefing process with the Directorate, but this time with a different interrogator. Apparently the former one had gotten the message.

"So, Ms. Gregorieva, allow me to summarize your last adventure. First, you visited the household of Prince Horemheb, who then introduced you and the American to the new high priest of Amen Re, whose name was, let's see now, Nebneteru. Do I have that right? Ah, good. Then this Nebneteru passed you off to his second named, ah, Merimaat, who then introduced you to the keeper of the *per ankh*, a man named Seshi. Is that correct?"

"No sir. It was Seti."

"Ah yes. Seti it is then. Splendid. Now once again, how many papyrus scrolls did you estimate that the *per ankh* of Amen Re contained?"

"Approximately 2700."

"You don't say…"

"Are you again implying that I miscount?"

"Oh no, Ms. Gregorieva. I just did not know that the ancients had that many things to write about. Perhaps your scroll count was more like 250, eh?"

"No you ignorant ass, I said 2700!"

"I see. Well splendid. To continue with your imaginative narrative, the American then skillfully enlisted, ah, Neshi's assistance, the keeper you say of the *per ankh*. To what end do you suppose?"

"The librarian's name was Seti! And I do not suppose anything you imbecile. Dr. Richards secured the name of the high priest of Ptah from him, a priest called Ptahmesou, who arranged for our admittance into their temple's *per ankh* in Memphis."

Yes, I was again a bit exercised during my debrief, but this time miraculously managed not to lay my hands on anyone.

*   *   *

The debriefing room, where Gregorieva and her persistent interrogator sat, had installed within it remote biosensors, hidden microphones, and a two-way mirror, through which a digital camera was recording the entire session.

"So," Rosovec said. "How long have they been at it?"

"Two days, sir," the technician responded.

"And do you have any preliminary impressions?" the bureaucrat asked.

"I do not know what you mean sir."

A bit thick this one is, Rosovec thought, and so he reworded his query.

"Do you have any gut sense as to whether Vesna Borisevna is telling us the truth, or, is she just telling us another one of her fairy tales?"

"Well sir, she has been consistent and unwavering in her story and its many interesting details. According to her body temperature and skin moisture levels, I would say that she thinks that she is being truthful. However, she is once again right on the edge, this time with Captain Ruskov. Her reactions to his well-honed talent for sarcasm have reached levels that I would have thought would have led to serious concern for his physical safety, as with the previous interrogator."

"You don't say," the bureaucrat said with a grin. "Well, so how is the previous chap doing?

"He sustained a broken clavicle and cracked skull."

"That's my lioness!"

CHAPTER XV
Farewell

Not long after the completion of the last marathon debrief, I received at my flat an intriguing telephone call.

"Hello?"

"Is this Vesna Borisevna Gregorieva?" the male voice said in impeccable Russian with a St. Petersburg accent.

"Da."

"I am a friend of a friend of Joey and John, and they would very much like you to make a quick visit."

"Oh?"

"Da. I am having a coffee right now at the Coffee Bean at Pushkinskaya 56. It's just the next block over from your flat. Do you know of it?"

"Da."

"Can you be here in fifteen minutes? I will buy you a coffee. You will find me on the second floor. I will be sitting in the corner booth."

Intrigued, I answered, *"Da,* fifteen minutes then. And, my friend of a friend of Joey and John, do you have a name?"

"Names right now are unimportant, but I know your face. In fifteen minutes."

So I agreed to meet a man and have a coffee. What could go wrong? Well, nearly everything and anything. With my background with the Directorate, this potentially could be a snatch and grab, with me disappearing...somewhere instead of *somewhen*. With the memory of that damn confidential memo still running through my head, I walked over to meet a man offering a coffee.

* * *

"Vesna Borisevna Gregorieva I presume?" said an elderly man dressed in a dark and slightly wrinkled suit.

I nodded.

"Frankly, your photo does not do you credit," his two twinkling blue eyes noted. Now reaching across the tiny coffee table and extending his open hand, the man added, "Vesna Borisevna, both Professors Milson and Richards send to you their very best."

Taking his offered hand, I noted that it was warm and dry. His sparsely populated pate was dry as well, just as was his cleanly shaven upper lip.

Absolutely no signs of stress, I thought. *Either he is very, very good or just sincere.*

"So Mr. Friend of a Friend of Joey and John, thank you for the coffee. What is this all about?"

Smiling warmly and in the process exposing to me his very Western cared for teeth, the man said, "Well, Vesna Borisevna, put simply, your friends are very concerned about your future. So much so, that they have asked their government to make you a one-time offer."

Now understanding the situation a little bit better, I almost dared to ask what that offer might be, but was preempted by the man.

"Do you have your papers with you?"

"Yes, always. Why?"

"I have been instructed to immediately escort you to Domodedovo Airport, where you will be processed as an American VIP. Shortly thereafter, you will board a very special airplane that I have been told that you know quite well. I am told that you have even lost your cookies on it."

My God this man is for real!

"Lost my cook…! Oh, yes, that did happen." I blushed bright red as I unconsciously moved my right hand to cover my mouth.

"Vesna Borisevna. To be blunt, the time is now for your decision. Upon landing, you will be granted asylum, a new identity, and will become a permanent member of the Philology Annex with a suitable salary. May I have your decision?" Then he rather pointedly looked at his watch.

"But what about…" I began.

"Vesna," the man quietly hissed while using the extremely informal address that a parent uses with their child, "your life is in jeopardy. Joey and John sent me to make this offer to you. I can only make this offer once. Now, what is your decision?"

"But I have to pack…" I began again.

"Vesna Borisevna Gregorieva," quietly interrupting and firmly all business, "I was told that you were stubborn, but they did not tell me that you were stupid as well. For the last time, what is your decision?"

"Do you have a car?"

"Now that's my girl!"

* * *

With my head in a whirl, we arrived at the airport twenty-seven minutes later. The elderly man then drove right past the passenger terminal. Seeing this, I felt my heart rate spike even higher than it had already been. Was this really all a ruse to test my loyalty to the Directorate? The man then made a hard right turn into a small unloading area that I saw was the entrance to the private terminal, frequented by heads of state, corporate heads, and the like.

Stopping at the curb before the set of sliding glass doors, the man now turned in his seat to face me. "Vesna Borisevna Gregorieva this is as far as I go. Now please walk through those doors. Once inside, go directly to the service desk that you can see from here, and request, in as haughty a manner as you can muster, the diplomatic envoy. Now Vesna Borisevna, off with you, and the best of luck."

For some reason I trusted the man's directions and so I was determined to follow them to the very letter. But before I exited his car, I turned and gave him a quick peck on his cheek. I don't know why I did that. Perhaps it was because he reminded me of my father.

I got out of his car, produced my very best runway model strut, and brazenly approached the service desk. Behind it I found a female receptionist. At my brisk approach, she just looked up with a smile.

"May I be of assistance?"

"Of course you can. I wish to see the diplomatic envoy, immediately!"

"And who may I say is making this request?"

"Gregorieva, Vesna Borisevna."

"Thank you Ms. Gregorieva. One moment please," the receptionist efficiently replied as she simultaneously pressed a button on her phone console.

Now looking up into my face, I could see that she was comparing my face to someone's description. Then she ended the connection. Removing her headset the receptionist then stood and said.

"Ms. Gregorieva, if you would be so kind and please follow me."

By my own count, once we had left the reception area, we walked through two doorways, one hallway, and directly into the cold interior of an aircraft hangar. There a very familiar looking white aircraft sat waiting with its door open and stairway extended. At the time I was so overwhelmed that I had failed to note the Swiss registration on the plane's tail: CH190.

Stopping at the bottom of the staircase, the receptionist smiled and wished me a pleasant journey. Quickly mounting the stairs, I entered the warmth of a familiar tan interior stripped of its civilian seats and interior. Now safely aboard, my good friend John Milson greeted me with open arms.

*   *   *

"I know, Vesna, all of this last minute 'cloak and dagger' stuff may have been a bit much, but it was deemed necessary, especially given recent events," Milson explained after their aircraft had leveled out.

"Recent events?"

"Indeed." Milson continued. "You see Vesna, you and Joseph, and the rest of the security detail, should not be alive today."

"Yes, I suspected as much. Joey and I had had a lot to talk about on our way home." I said. "But Callahan tried to explain it all away as some freak turbulence. Something about getting into another plane's wake."

"Well, this much I can confirm, what you

experienced was not turbulence." While pointing down at the airframe, Milson continued with a firm jaw line.

"This very plane was fired upon by an air-to-air missile from an unknown aircraft. What you experienced was the emergency evasive action of the two pilots, who by the way, are flying this plane right now."

"What! Who shot at us?"

"That, Vesna, is the real sixty-four dollar question. We do not know for sure, but we have some strong suspicions, and I think that you should know what those suspicions are.

"First off, the missile that was fired did not have a warhead. It was a dud, but a dud on purpose that was intended to cripple this aircraft by taking out one of its engines. In the process, the shrapnel from that kinetic impact would have killed nearly everyone in the cabin.

"Second, the aircraft, now crippled, was to land at a military airfield in Iceland, where other members of the plot were to kill the pilots and then steal the Soap Bubble. In short, the entire affair was about stealing the Soap Bubble. There were to be no survivors."

"But who..." My voice trailed off into a whisper.

Oh no...please no...

"Vesna, you are a very bright woman. Now consider: who even knows about the Soap Bubble outside of those at the Philology Annex and Horizon Pass? Who knew that you and Joseph were being deployed? And who knew roughly when you were returning?"

I felt my face transform from deep concentration, to suspicion, to absolute, flushed rage.

That damn confidential memo!

"Those bastards!"

"Yes. That is precisely what we thought too. And in a conference call two days ago, we told your former colleagues precisely what we thought. And so Vesna, here you are. We came to get you out."

*   *   *

Allow me to say here and now that John Milson is a wonderful human being. During the long flight back to Alamogordo, he presented me with my new self, an identity known as Valery Gregg, complete with a fresh U.S. passport, a New Mexico driver's license, a credit card, a fitness club pass, and a Social Security card as well. The importance and relationships of each, he carefully explained, and then pointed out, that my new address was located in a quiet condominium complex in Santa Fe. It even had its own pool.

"It's already furnished." He said. "The fridge has already been stocked. All you have to do is buy yourself some clothes, some incidentals, and move right in."

That was when I began to sob. With so much change in my life, this episode was just too much like my childhood move to Moscow. John's innocent comment about the fridge already being stocked had set me off, but after a minute or two, I dried my tears.

"Vesna, now that you are a U.S. citizen, you need a job. That job is working for the Philology Annex as its second temporal field agent. Are you okay with that arrangement?"

I just nodded as I continued to dab at my eyes.

"Now as our field agent, you must maintain yourself, hence the fitness membership card that is good in many cities throughout the U.S., including Chicago. It is also expected that you periodically visit us in Chicago for language refresher sessions, to attend meetings, and the like. Transportation to and from will be provided for. But in addition to those, I would like you to explore a second career in something that you truly enjoy. Think of it as your day job, versus your secret undercover job with the Annex. But above all, visit your colleagues at Horizon Pass. Believe it or not, there are many folks there that think the world of you. Who think of you as family."

CHAPTER XVI
Desert Dust Up

I was fast learning that no two deployments were ever quite the same. Pulling off a drop out in the open desert certainly qualified, in my book at least, as "a new challenge." Why the open desert and not the friendly confines of the Amen Re sanctuary? Well, because this drop was to take place near Memphis, but during the Egyptian Late Predynastic Period, a time when the Karnak Temple had yet to be built, Thebes a rude village.

The date selected was noon local, August 8th, 3200 BC. Never before had anyone dropped into the *somewhen* that long ago, much less in the open desert, and in broad daylight. But then I learned that someone else had dared an open desert drop, none other than my fearless Sasha, who back in the cowboy days of the Soap Bubble's calibration had done so four times! By current operational standards, however, such a ragged disregard of the *RUTI* principles was deemed unacceptable. But, it was argued, the currently available surveillance technology could successfully provide remote, pre-drop security for such a daylight, open desert drop.

In the end, the powers that be decided that the drop tests with the portable Soap Bubble VI B should be performed first within the walls of the Third Dynasty Step Pyramid Complex, which is located to the west of Memphis atop the Sakkara plateau. The appropriate permissions for both the tests and the use of the archaeological site were quickly processed by the

Director of Egyptian Antiquities, but with one lone caveat: that the tests were to occur during the first week of August, a time of notorious heat and low tourism.

What was not mentioned was the extreme pressure that such an open desert drop would place upon Callahan's security detail, even if we inserted at night. What we needed was someplace high up on the western plateau that overlooked the ancient Memphite area, but was sufficiently far enough away from any casual observation. No matter how you sliced it, such a location would be exposed and difficult to secure.

* * *

Just so you know Egypt in August is an insane time of oppressive heat and relentless sun. Modern Memphis, reduced to eye-searing glare and dusty haze, is a place where ill-fed and near feral dogs commandeer all available shade, family store fronts are shuttered, and the insufferable heat renders the concrete roadside security huts for the archaeological monuments uninhabitable.

True to form, Lieutenant Callahan, who had picked us up at the military side of Cairo International, just drove his rickety old Chevy truck through the sleepy village of Memphis all the way up to the tourist bus lot, right before the Step Pyramid itself.

Bringing his rig to a dusty halt, one of his security team appeared as if by magic out of a shadow carrying a stubby-shaped weapon. He appeared in full body armor and was wearing a goggle-eyed Darth Vader-like helmet. Striding forward, he handed through the passenger window ice cold plastic bottles of water.

Not saying a word, we all drank right then and there. Joey then opened his door with a creak and I got out of the sweltering cab. As the soldier returned to his post, I saw what looked like a shimmer, and then the soldier just, simply, disappeared. I'm not kidding!

Seeing our attentive stares, Callahan just whispered. "Adaptive camouflage."

Turning back to the truck, four other soldiers had "appeared" and were unloading the Soap Bubble's pylons. I grabbed our personal packs, while Joey beat Calli to the battery pack, which left him with only the Little Beast II computer laptop to tuck under his arm.

* * *

Testing began at nine that evening and from the desert a cooling breeze refreshed us. The first location was within the colonnaded entranceway of the Step Pyramid complex. With the four pylons and their ion cannons in position, Joey input the date of August 8th, 3200 BC, noon local, into the Little Beast. The portable battery pack gave off its subliminal hum and the ceramic drop ring rose to its operating height.

Once reached, Sgt. Glen "Ozzy" Osgood, looked to Joey, got an affirmative head nod, and then attempted to stick the plastic lens of his cobra-headed probe into the silvery sheen of the Mark VI's temporal field. The key word here is "attempted" as Ozzy could not penetrate the field no matter where he probed around the entire diameter of the drop ring.

"Zilch Lieutenant Callahan. Looks like solid rock. We need to try another location."

So it went that entire evening, and on into the early

morning hours. All the locations that we tested had encountered solid rock. The only conclusion that could be made was that the entire inner court of the Step Pyramids had been leveled. After some further thought, that leveling process probably provided the limestone for the Step Pyramid itself, its surrounding enclosure wall, if not for the inner courts' many structures.

"Okay, so we gotta' find somewhere that is not all rock," Joey concluded. Then focusing on the western side of the complex, he said, "You know Calli, and I'm quite certain that you will not like this, but we're going to have to go outside the walls, somewhere out west that-a-way into the open desert."

*   *   *

The following evening, we did just that. Calli, while not happy about the situation, scattered his men about as best he could. The drop point survey team hit pay dirt on their first try and to their great relief. As the fiber optic probe did its thing, "Ozzy" Osgood estimated that the surface on the other side was about four feet and so the drop into the *somewhen* really wasn't, it being more like a deep wade into the surf. That meant Joey and I would have to literally drop to our knees, and then crawl away from beneath the Soap Bubble's energized aperture.

The team marked the location of the pylons with pneumatically embedded surveyors' marks into the exposed bedrock, while the site's GPS location was recorded. The reports of the pneumatic gun noisily echoed forever off the Step Pyramid's western walls.

Then, rather suddenly, Callahan listened into his

headset. As one of the soldiers was about to embed yet another surveyor's mark, the lieutenant squatted down next to the man and showed him a fist, which instantly froze the soldier in place. Then Callahan told us in a quiet command voice.

"Kill the flashlights. Everybody get down. We have company."

Callahan and his three immediate soldiers dropped to their bellies, while Joey roughly pulled me to the ground. He then whispered into my right ear one word. "Don't you dare say a word."

Wide-eyed, I could just barely hear Callahan talking with the rest of his security squad through his helmet's radio.

"Sitrep. All report."

A longish pause occurred, while he listened to the status of his unit, he then turned to us and his nearby men.

"Okay, here's the drill. We, as a unit, are going to belly-crawl as quickly and quietly as we can west into the desert. Richards, you take the battery pack. Gregorieva, you take the laptop. Anderson, you have the hula hoop. We leave the pylons and cables in place as bait. Johnson and Emmett, you take point. Anderson and I'll follow with the civvies. Okay everybody, move out."

*　　*　　*

Crawling with a laptop was not easy. Crawling quietly was even harder. But when your life was on the line, it's amazing how you made do. So I imitated a lizard, as we put some distance between the abandoned pylons and whoever was out there in the darkness. While we were busy being lizards or snakes, Callahan was talking to the rest of his team. I later found out that they were repositioning themselves to form a kill sack with the pylons as bait. Callahan logic was impeccable, the intruders were after the technology, not the personnel.

At some point in our belly-crawling, Callahan stopped us, paired us with one of his men, and told us to quietly clear away shallow depression that we could slip our bodies into. While we did that, Callahan and Anderson disappeared into the darkness back toward the Step Pyramid.

At this point, I shivered and my teeth chattered. Not from the cooling desert, but out of fear. Here I was in this slit trench, not really protected, but out of view. The worse part, as always, was not knowing what was going on.

Then came the scary and helpless part, when the firefight started. I heard well-disciplined, three-shot sequences of suppressed gun fire. To me, it sounded like heavily muffled coughs, which were promptly answered with similarly suppressed returns. The fire fight did not last long. But who had won?

Then I heard Callahan's low voice in the darkness say to his men over the radio, "Move in."

Next, "Richards, Gregorieva. I gotta' go. Stay put until we come back to get you. Got that?"

For the next fifteen or so minutes, Joey and I lay there in the darkness, not knowing what was going on.

*　　*　　*

"So who were they?" we asked Callahan.

"Well, as best as I can figure they were Russians."

Them again!

"Several even carried *Spetsnatz* tattoos."

Special forces no less!

"By their tactical movements alone they were a professional team. Their silenced automatic weapons appear to be Czech in origin, with filed off serial numbers. They had night vision, communications, and GPS gear. By their kit alone, I would guess that they were some sort of governmental swat team."

Absolutely! They're the Directorate's men.

"So far no documents or IDs have been found. That fact alone makes them black ops. So that means we have to evac this area ASAP. I called up the Delta Force commander at Heliopolis for some helicopters. They should be here shortly."

Even as he spoke, we could already make out the distant sound of whoop, whoop, whoop carrying across the desert's clear, cool, night air.

CHAPTER XVII
Fourth Deployment

Following the desert "dust up" at Sakkara, my next deployment occurred during the middle of the following summer. Unspoken, but still very much on my mind, was the air-to-air encounter and now this nighttime fire fight. Men had been sent to their deaths, all because of the orders of others to acquire something that was not theirs to possess.

And along the way, if they can kill Joey and me, then they remove from the chess board the personnel as well. They're getting desperate. But who cooked up that mission? Rosovec or the other guy? The new guy, the Viking?

In the meantime, Callahan brought me up to speed on some improvements that he and Dr. Charlie Naysmithe had dreamed up. First on their laundry list were additional troops to backup the original team. Dr. Naysmithe, for his part, made sure that a very special geosynchronous satellite was positioned over the eastern Mediterranean. Well, actually, all that I could get out of that quiet and laid back genius from San Diego was something about a tightly focused, look-down targeting radar.

My question to him was, "Well that's just great. But what is it targeting for?"

Strangely, Dr. Naysmithe just gave me a strange and dreamy look and said. "No worries Vesna. That's my headache."

* * *

Given the exposed nature of this open desert evening operation, Callahan had both of his twelve-man squads scattered around our drop point, not that anyone could find them in their adaptive camouflage.

As for the drop point itself, it had taken on the look of a mini-Stonehenge, with the four pylons in position and the venerable wooden scaffolding erected around them. Despite the team's familiarity with the gear and its setup and the erection of the scaffolding, using red flashlights presented challenges on the uneven ground. In the end, only two pairs of donated socks were needed to steady the uprights.

At the appointed time, Sgt. Osgood keyed the power switches and the drop ring rose to its usual position. Joey and I waited, teetering upon the scaffolding's uppermost beam. My gymnastics experience came in handy sitting there in the dark. And as before, my wig's many tresses began to extend outwards as the static electricity built up.

"Now, don't giggle," Joey had whispered, which earned him an elbow in the ribs.

With the drop ring in place, Ozzy gave an affirmative nod and Corporal Cooper began to carefully probe the other side of the field with his fiber optic lens. While doing so he provided some useful commentary.

"Damn it's bright over there! From what I can see you guys have about a four to five foot drop max. Best of luck. And don't forget to duck!"

Looking now to Callahan for his thumbs up, Joey saw it, and dropped his leather money pouch through the silvery field. Then, after receiving the second thumbs up, I dropped through the field's lusciously silky smoothness.

*   *   *

Joey and I knew from the very start that this was going to be an interesting drop, principally because we had to land, and then stay as low as possible until the field closed. But beyond that, this was also our first daylight drop into the open desert. And Corporal Cooper had been right. It was really bright, especially having come from near total darkness.

I stayed low and rolled away just before Joey landed with a thump. He took a good two minutes to get his head screwed on straight.

"That was a most worthy hangover."

I then whispered in his ear, "Be silent my brother, for we have visitors."

When the temporal field's aperture snapped closed, we sat up back to back and found that we were the subject of considerable interest by three pairs of inquisitive eyes.

"They're jackals," Joey said, "desert scavengers."

I almost let out a laugh, as here we were, two humans surrounded by three sitting jackals with their heads cocked in pure curiosity.

Joey, with his senses fully available, slowly reached out and picked up a small stone. This action brought the three as one to their feet, their attention now on high alert. Their ears pitched with noses twitching.

"Watch this my sister!" Richards side-armed the rock at the nearest animal, not to hit it, but rather to fluster. In a flash the trio scattered and in moments disappeared over a neighboring rise.

"I thought so. Those jackals knew just what and

who we were, and that rock just proved it."

"My brother, how did you know that they wouldn't harm us?"

"Well, for one, we're not dead or seriously injured. For another, they are intelligent animals and know what a rock, once thrown, can do. And that means that we are not the first humans that they have encountered."

Now standing and brushing ourselves off as best we could, Joey began gathering stones.

"Help me, my sister. We must mark where we must return to."

When finished, we had constructed a small stone cairn that now marked the location of our drop point. Now it was time to find the late Predynastic village of Mennefer, as it could not be very far away.

Turning toward the vast expanse of the Nile Valley to our right, the faint trails of many cooking fires were easy enough to pick out, both before us, down slope, and also off into the distance on the opposite bank of the river.

Even to my eyes, the river valley looked nothing like its Eighteenth Dynasty version. What I saw was untamed and wild, everywhere its banks surrounded by thick and verdant vegetation. Only here and there could be seen areas of cultivation, literally hard fought pockets of space cut out of the surrounding wilderness.

We stood squarely at the edge of the Sakkaran escarpment that gave us a clear view of the junction of the southern Delta and the northern Nile Valley. This panoramic sight took my breath away in its scope and detail, as flocks of birds cast vast shadows across the river's surface, briefly startling a group of hippopotami cavorting in its currents.

Then I saw a rustic group of shelters built of woven and bundled grasses, along with farm animals that wandered, and children who noisily chased one another. But near this village of perhaps twenty such structures, one structure stood out from among the rest. This edifice, for that was precisely what it was, was built of smoothed, white washed mud brick. Its front porch roof was supported by two simple columns of bundled papyrus reeds. One would have naturally assumed that this was the village's central temple, as its location was just west of the village proper.

Looking down the sandy and rocky slope before us, the clear demarcation, between where the desert began and the furthest reach of the Nile's inundation reached, was unmistakable. Blinking, I could quite literally straddle that line with one foot squarely in the sand, while the other would sink deeply into the black, fertile mud.

Half sliding our way down that steep desert slope, we reached the vegetations' edge. Once there, Joey surprised me as he broke off a convenient tamarisk branch and began stripping it down to a single shaft that ended in a Y-shaped fork. I, hands on hips, quietly watched his industry with curiosity, and then with my usual impatience, finally asked, "Why does my brother have interest in such a flimsy tool, instead of fashioning a club?"

"Because my most beautiful sister, this field before us is swarming with dangerous snakes, and this is a snake stick."

Oh, that's right! Even the mummy of Ptah grasped such a stick!

On we continued, slowly making our way single-file through the muddy thickets toward the cleared area of the village, ever careful of our footing, and what might be indeed underfoot. And sure enough, after not thirty feet, Joey suddenly stabbed with his right arm. He pinned with his forked stick a horned viper about three and a half feet long. Swiftly crushing its head with the heel of his mud-caked sandal, he then draped the dead reptile around his neck and continued on. By the time we had reached the outskirts of the village, Joey had acquired no less than four deadly necklaces that surrounded his leather money pouch.

"My brother, why do you wear those frightful snakes?"

"To communicate a message, my sister."

Why does he always have to be so mysterious?

When we had reached within hailing distance of the prominent white washed structure, both of us were truly a frightful sight, since we were muddy from the knees down, sweat streaked, and covered with yellow and white pollens from the many plants that we had encountered. Additionally, Joey had chosen to take on a rather macabre look given the streams of snake blood and yellowish venom that had coursed down his chest and stomach to the waist of his once white kilt.

Now standing side by side one hundred feet from the white washed building, we encountered a curious and oddly fearful crowd that had gathered at our noisy approach. Women, children, and elders stood before us with their mouths' agape and their fingers pointing.

I noticed it first. "My brother, where are all the men?"

"Working in the fields, fishing, or hunting, I would suppose. Let's find out."

Slightly raising his head to better project his voice, Richards called out.

"We have traveled far. We seek a man named Ptah. Who among you is he?"

While all seemed to understand his simply constructed sentences, clearly Joey's accent was odd to their ears, from the gasps and giggles that it had caused. Nonetheless, we saw an old women whisper to a young girl, who then ran off toward the village.

And there we stood for the next fifteen or so minutes, neither side daring to move a muscle, or glance away.

*   *   *

"Did you see that old one instruct the girl?"

"Yes. Where do you think she went in such a hurry?"

"I don't know. But we'll know soon."

"But it's been almost a half an hour already!"

"Patience, my sister, we are the strangers here." Then Joey smiled. "Ah ha, my sister, I do believe that we have just hit pay dirt."

Joey's assessment was based upon the slow approach of the young messenger girl, who now respectfully followed in the shadow of a bald-headed man of modest proportions, who also walked with a forked staff. The front of his once clean kilt was stained and splattered in blood, much the same as was Joey's. Proof as to who this man was, was made manifest as the crowd wordlessly parted at his approach, and then closed formation at his passing.

Striding fearlessly toward us, the man stopped

about three paces away, and quietly announced.

"I am Ptah. Who beckons me?"

Before me stood a future god, but what does a god in the making look like? About five foot three, medium build, with an ever so slight paunch, round headed with a straight nose and expressive green eyes. The marked intelligence of his eyes definitely gave away that he was special in some way. Very special.

We, by agreement, had our mental screens firmly in place for this moment, fully in anticipation of what could happen. For me, the grand simplicity of the moment had brought me to tears.

Well, a god in the flesh!

Noting our odd silence, the tears of joy from me, and the reverence that emanated from Joey, when Ptah unconsciously attempted to probe our minds. I actually felt the feather-like brush of its sensation.

But since he had blocked our minds, Ptah was physically shocked to find that he could not read us.

I noted the sudden widening of Ptah's eyes, smiled in understanding, and said, "Great and Noble One. We have traveled far in search of you, just as you have traveled far in search of us."

This last turn of phrase caused a tilt to Ptah's head.

Bending down to kneel on his right leg, Joey carefully removed his rather gaudy and messy reptilian necklaces and placed them at the feet of Ptah, which brought a vocalized gasp from the crowd of villagers. His act was a clear sign of formalized "gift giving." And given Ptah's own forked staff, there was a meaning attributed to Joey's act that I could not quite get a handle on.

"We offer these harmful pests to you as a sign of

our faith, that we mean to make no harm, either to you, or your village."

For Ptah, I figured that his situation had become a bit more complicated. For one, he could not use his sixth sense on us and so was forced to verbalize what he wanted to say – a crude and inexact mode that he probably preferred not to use, especially given the current native vocabulary.

Second, the language dialect that he was hearing from us, while understandable, was in itself a potential barrier. I further presumed the older man understood Joey's act as a direct form of tribute, with an emphasis on "no harm."

Ptah looked truly fascinated. "The day has been a long one," he said. "Come. Refresh yourselves within my house, and dust your feet."

With that said, Ptah turned and led a Russian and an American to his house – the white washed edifice, much to the utter amazement of the villagers.

Both of us smiled at Ptah's 'dust your feet' phrase, for we were quite literally caked in mud.

*   *   *

The interior of the man's modest two room house was blessedly cool, and once within its shade, I nearly collapsed in thanksgiving. Seeing this, Ptah set about getting three cups, and with a beer jug under one arm.

Sitting on heavy reed mats with a low table between us, Ptah made a formal toast.

"May Ra rise tomorrow. May we rise tomorrow with him. May every thought worthy of the tongue bring forth that which is needful."

All drank deeply of the thick, cool, and refreshingly carbonated beer and so all three cups again were refilled, but before anyone had brought their cup to their lips, Joey offered a toast of his own and naturally their host was its object.

"There took form in the heart, there took shape on the tongue, the form of the god Atum. For the very great one is Ptah, he who gave essence to all the gods, through his heart and through his tongue."

Ptah eyes squinted. Then he formally began. "I am Ptah. You are guests of my house. I have offered you my hospitality and refreshment. Now who are you and from which village do you come?"

"I am Maatkare, Great One." I said with a slight bow of the head.

And in turn, "I am Mayneken, Great One. My sister and I have traveled far to meet you. And, we are indebted to your hospitality."

Facing me, again Ptah spoke directly. "Why Maatkare did tears come to your eyes when you first saw me?"

"Because Great One, you are, and will become in the hearts and minds of men, even greater than you can ever imagine."

"And you Mayneken, from where do you and your sister come that is so far away?"

"Noble One, before I answer that question, may I ask how old you truly are?"

Without pause Ptah answered. "One hundred and forty-six inundations."

"Now that is a very long time, Great One," Joey observed with a smile, "and yet you appear before us as man in the prime of life. But as to your question, how far I and my sister have traveled, to meet you, well, it is best expressed this way: 5,219 inundations."

With that answer, Ptah's startled eyes opened wide as both of us saw the understanding and the recognition in them.

"So that is why you speak so strangely, now I understand. But what I do not understand is why I cannot see your hearts?"

"Indeed," Richards began, "for in our many travels not everyone possesses such a gentleness of *sia*, of "divine understanding," as do you. In fact, some with such a gift have used it as a powerful and terrible weapon. So are we so protected."

Nodding in horror at the thought of misusing the mind, another question came to him. "But how Mayneken, can you speak of my own thoughts?"

"Great one, I do not, but I do know of your words. Words of wisdom that are difficult both to read and fully understand. But they are good words, full of deep meaning. Perhaps, one day, as we study your many papyrus scrolls, we will come to understand them more fully."

Surprised, the man asked, "So you have seen my scrolls as well?"

"Indeed Noble One. I counted fifty-six in all."

"Fifty-six you say? Perhaps I have written too much."

Now sitting back with his arms crossed in the unconscious body language of defense, Ptah looked up, sighed, and was about to say something, but Joey's damn stomach had gotten in the way as it rather noisily announced both its presence and its need.

Chuckling at the welcomed distraction, Ptah then

announced, "Enough talk. I will request that additional waters be brought so that we can properly dust our feet, and then, partake of an evening meal. But Mayneken, kindly take care not to lick yourself or rub your eyes as the poison of the *fy*-snake is all over you!"

*   *   *

The evening meal had been extremely tasty and filling, much to Ptah's pleasure and that of the villagers, who had so kindly provided it. Roast duck and fresh fish comprised the main course with baked onions, garlic, and bread. Settling in and mildly drunk by all the beer that had been forced upon us, and now in the midst of a food coma as well, Joey decided to ask.

"So Noble One, now that you know from *when* we come, from *where* do you come?"

The smiling Ptah truly enjoyed the word games that we liked to play. "I could frankly answer that question with several possible answers, and all of them would be truthful, in all respects. But noble Mayneken and beautiful Maatkare, just as beer may loosen my tongue, so also does beer loosen one's grasp, one's control of the mind. And now that I am fully seeing your heart, I will truthfully answer your question the way that you wish me to."

Oops! We simultaneously thought.

"As you yourself have said, I have traveled far."

To which I responded, "Indeed Noble One, you probably have, but is it true that you are one of the Old Ones?"

Now smiling even more broadly than before, the man called Ptah answered. "Ah, now that is a name that

I have not heard for a long, long time. In fact, I think that it was my brother Thoth, who had last used the term. From whom or where did you hear of this term, 'the Old Ones?'"

To that question I said, "Noble One, we discovered its mention in the writings of another visitor to this land, who remarkably, was also seeking evidence of your passing, but who had failed to do so."

Now with his interest piqued, Ptah asked, "Now that is remarkable. Tell me about this other visitor."

What followed was a somewhat abridged version of the encounter with the being called Akhenaten, his attempt to improve the human gene pool through his offspring, and his agenda to philosophically influence the course of human history.

Listening throughout the telling of this tale, Ptah then shook his head, "Such crass interference with the natural course of the body and mind is an abomination! For there is far too much that can happen that is not wished for. This Akhenaten was doing wrongful things. But the teaching of ideas is another. And you say this Akhenaten left behind a book of his many journeys?"

"Indeed Noble One," Joey said, "for he and his kin had journeyed very far before he had stumbled upon our land."

Then the man named Ptah chose to add something that almost seemed out of character.

"To traverse the cold darkness of the stars is a lonely and solitary task, my dear Maatkare and Mayneken. It is one that tests the balance, the very *maat* of the mind. In some ways, I understand the desire of this Akhenaten to make many improvements. But to understand is one thing, to undertake is another."

Now spreading his arms wide in a gesture that seemed to encompass the entire village, but upon reflection, perhaps the entire globe, he said, "Yet, here, in this beautiful and virgin place, there is no cold darkness, only life, a wonderful abundance of life. And, in its own way, there is a peacefulness, a sublime *maat* that must be respected. The man named Akhenaten did not respected *maat*, and as a consequence, I seriously doubt that he even understood it."

And with that heady pronouncement a brief pause fell upon the conversation. Then Joey concluded. "So, Noble Oone, if we understand you, you arrived at this place after being in the cold darkness of the stars for a time?"

"Indeed that is so."

"And then what is your purpose for being here, living among these people?"

Again the man named Ptah smiled, but this time a deeply satisfying one that beamed almost with a kind of rich emotional release.

"Noble Mayneken, most beautiful Maatkare, do not you already see? My purpose is complete, for your very presence is the proof of it."

Moved, and at the same time stunned, by the elegant simplicity of the statement, we both nodded in understanding and acknowledgment.

But the man named Ptah was not yet finished. "And while I rejoice at the proof of your physical presence before me, I am troubled Mayneken, that you will pay a very high price for this privilege. Even though I have yet to lay my hands upon your body, I can nonetheless see your troubled *ka*. Mayneken, you must be vigilant, and shortly attend to this sickness.

And for this judgment I truly am sorry."

Then turning to me, he said, "As for you Maatkare, truly a worthy name, your *ka* is not sick, but instead is bright and vibrant, and for this judgment I am most pleased."

At this point in the evening, the man named Ptah began to gently rub the sides of his temples as if to relieve a tension headache, sighed deeply, and simply stated, "I must now sleep on this."

As he levered himself up, Ptah pointed to the two raised bed frames that the villagers had thoughtfully provided. He then staggered off to the back of his house and lay down.

Joey looking at me, then quietly said, "And what was all that about sick and healthy *ka*s?"

I shrugged in confusion at Ptah's words as well, "Perhaps we should consult our physician once we are safely home."

* * *

Just as sleep came quickly, so did the sunrise of the following day. Awakening remarkably refreshed and none the worse except for a few insect bites, we found ourselves alone. The man named Ptah was absent, perhaps out and about, as some fresh bread, onions, and cheese were waiting for us on the table, wrapped in a finely woven linen cloth.

Reaching for the bread in order to tear it in half so that I could share it with Joey, I commented, "Mayneken, we have just missed him. This bread is still warm."

With our first meal finished and our bed coverings

folded, we went exploring to find our kind host, pay our respects, and bid him farewell. But as we passed through the door way, we were stopped by a little girl, with red eyes. As I bent down to her, tears again began to flow anew.

"What troubles you so, little one?" I protectively asked as I unconsciously began to stroke her head.

With a sniffle came the answer.

"The Noble Ptah has left our village!"

"What do you mean?"

"Last night, while you were asleep, he came to me with one of his scrolls as a gift, and said goodbye." Sniff.

"Oh come now," I crooned. "He's just gone for a walk, or perhaps to bathe in the river."

"No! He left our village! I saw!"

Now Joey squatted down and asked. "Little one, what is your name?"

"Mekbet."

"So little Mekbet, can you tell us what you saw?"

Nodding like a bobble-head doll, the little girl said, "I followed the Noble One into the desert, there."

We looked in the direction of her rigidly extended arm and finger.

Again Joey gently asked, "And when you followed the Noble One into the desert, what did you see?"

"A bright light, like Re."

I prodded. "And then what did the Noble Ptah do in the desert?"

"He went into the bright light, and then the bright light flew across Nut's tummy, and became a star."

*   *   *

191

After hearing little Mekbet's account of the Noble Ptah's departure, we left the village and made our way toward the desert in order to make our high noon departure. Joey, ever mindful, had brought along his snake stick, had killed two more horned vipers, before we reached the steep sloped base of the Sakkaran escarpment.

While trudging up the sandy and rocky slope I swore that I heard someone behind us, but when I turned, there was no one there.

After reaching the top of the escarpment, we made our way into the desert and after a bit of searching, found our stone cairn marker unmolested. Sitting down next to it, Joey enunciated what he had been ruminating on during the entire hike.

"You know my sister, he told us that he was leaving. Do you remember the comment that he made about us being proof of his purpose?"

Thinking a bit before I answered.

"I think you're right. Still, I cannot get over that I actually spoke to an alien, drank beer with one, and even slept under his roof. It's all so very strange. And then all that talk about sick and healthy *ka*s. That frankly scared me."

"As it did me. I wonder if he was referring to the Post Drop Syndrome?"

And at that moment, above our heads, a second sun disk had begun to form.

*　　*　　*

Little Mekbet could not believe her eyes. From her vantage point in the rocks, the friendly strangers were just sitting in the desert next to a pile of stones as if they were speaking to it.

Then, a bright light appeared above them!

And then, they disappeared into it!

And then, the bright light went away!

Curiosity not being one of Mekbet's weaknesses, she got up and investigated the pile of stones after the kind strangers had left. She found nothing, but a snake stick. This she took it back to the village as evidence of what she had witnessed.

In the fullness of time, the village's recollections about the departure of Ptah and his visitors would blur, but his practical use of a snake stick would not. So became Richards' discarded tool a much-revered early totem of Ptah, one that would even be buried with one of his early priests, along with some other items, only later to be discovered by an Austrian archaeologist.

* * *

There was a strangely odd somberness among the security detail, and especially with Callahan, at their retrieval.

Once all the gear had been taken down and just before their departure, Joey and I took the big Irishman aside and stared into his eyes.

"Okay lieutenant," Joey said, "I have never before gotten such a vibe from you. What's up?"

First looking down at his boots, and then finally meeting our gaze directly, it was then that we saw the tightness in his eyes.

"It's Professor Milson, isn't it," Joey said.

"Yes sir, it is. I am truly sorry."

During the short helicopter ride back to Heliopolis' military airport, blessedly the surprising level of emotional grief that I expressed provided Joey some cover for his own. With my sobbing head buried in his chest, he held me as my father once had, gently rocking me back and forth, all the while oblivious to the passage of time.

Eventually, we learned that Milson's passing had been a peaceful one that had occurred during his sleep. His last day had been a full one, just like his life. Joey, his own handpicked successor, was away having just successfully dropped into the distant *somewhen*, the purpose of which was to interview an Egyptian god no less. He was happy beyond words that their joint struggle to understand the archaic version of "The Memphite Theology" was about to be cracked.

A widower since the death of his beloved wife Alice, the discovery of his situation had taken two full days. Fortunately, his documentation that stipulated his final requests had been in the hands of Paul Young for the past four years, ever since the onset of Milson's nasty encounter with cancer.

While Milson's papers did not mention any provision of memorial service, his colleague Young, a devote Anglican, went into high gear in its planning. A date was chosen. The university's chapel was booked as were two full floors at the Student Union's hotel for all of the expected out-of-town guests. The announcements and arrangements were sent worldwide. The only potential fly in the ointment, that could foul all of these machinations, would be a hitch in our safe return.

* * *

The memorial service for Professor Emeritus John Allen Milson took place within the gothic grandeur of the university chapel. The edifice was packed to the gills. There were even bodies crammed in up in the choir loft.

Even before the remembrance ceremony had begun, I spied to my everlasting shock, that my retired superior from the Directorate had attended, Karlov Gregorievich Drazinzka! He was accompanied by one other, probably a friend, and my God, did they look old. *Look at the way the pair support one another.* And then a truly odd thought came to me. *This was probably their first time in a Christian church.*

After that, I almost drifted off into a dreamy state, but when I saw the bastard Rosovec had actually dared to show his face. Suddenly, I was on fire, and Joey, seeing my reaction, casually put one of his powerful arms around me, encircling me, protecting me, and yes, in the process, protecting Rosovec.

*　　*　　*

After Milson's public memorial ceremony had been concluded, a far more private farewell took place at the mortuary. It was in fact a highly emotional Irish wake. With an open bar, Joey and I, Young and Jung, Cartwright and the military, Drazinzka and his colleague a retired biologist named Ostrogorsky, and Rosovec, somehow managed to empty two full bottles of the house's best Vodka. (As for myself, I twice almost strangled Stefan, that two-faced, rat bastard! But in total deference to John, I remained a total lady.) As the vodka had been kept nearly frozen, I blame John for that thoughtful detail, and the hangover that was guaranteed to greet me the following day.

Damn you John!

Two full trash cans were filled to the brim with empty Silver Bullets, a goodly portion of which had been Joey's own doing, with ample assistance from Cartwright, Callahan, and four other soldiers of the security detail.

While toasts abounded and endless stories were told, that great man became a legend. It was Joey's farewell speech that took the prize, and as they say in Chicago, "nary a dry eye could be found in the house."

In the end, and after the rest of the hangers-on had left, a small cadre of the inner circle still remained. These included all of us Russians, Richards, Naysmithe, Cartwright, Jung, and of course Dean Young.

To this close group, Joey announced, "Folks, I wish to thank you all for waiting this out, but I think that John would truly appreciate this one last farewell gift."

Stepping up to the cremation niche, which now contained the remains of Alice and John, Joey placed within it a small papyrus scroll bound with three Egyptian blue lengths of yarn. Then, Joey closed his eyes and raised his arms forming a U-shape with his palms facing forward. When he took that priestly pose, only then did its significance hit me squarely between the eyes.

His arms formed the glyph for the Egyptian ka*!*

And then in a long dead language, Joey delivered a beautiful chant to the rhythm of a plain song.

I open your mouth, so that you may speak,

I open your eyes, so that you may see Re,

I open your ears, so that you may hear of your glorification,

And I grant movement to your legs, arms, and heart so that you can repulse your enemies.

Long may you live most righteous John Milson.

The effect on those present was profound. Drazinzka, Ostrogorsky, and Rosovec, I later was told, had all already witnessed this same ceremony at the burial of my dear Sasha beneath Lenin's Tomb. This time, however, I freely translated Joey's words into Russian for them. Cartwright, with considerable pride, actually managed to understand most of it. Only Naysmithe, Jung, and Young were left in the dark, but the streaming tears of the others expressed well the gist of what had just taken place.

CHAPTER XVIII
Break In

I wasn't there at that mandatory meeting at the Philology Annex, when Dr. Naysmithe had dropped his bombshell. Given all that had happened, all the attempts to either outright steal the Soap Bubble or kill those associated with it, Naysmithe voiced a logical premise. To wit: that perhaps Horizon Pass, the Philology Annex, the entire project, might have to be shut down. Its technology had become a liability. And if it was stolen, then what?

I had later overheard some of the inner membership saying that they thought Naysmithe had cracked under all the pressure.

Those poor simpering, limp-wristed academics! What do they know about pressure and stress?

While I never once doubted the man, little did I know just how prescient Dr. Naysmithe's proposal would become.

*　*　*

I was working out at the spa in Santa Fe when my cell phone rang with a specific tone, a tone that I had attached to the telephone numbers, emails, and texts of a very select number of individuals. Looking down with concern, I saw a short text from Dr. Naysmithe. While the message looked innocuous, its import was anything but.

Oh shit! This just begins to cover it.

Moments later and sitting in my car still dripping with sweat from the treadmill, I called a specific number.

After entering my six-digit password, the recorded message said,

ALL STAFF

RETURN TO NEST IMMEDIATELY

THIS IS NOT A DRILL

*   *   *

Three and a half hours later, I and my white VW, smeared with bugs, pulled into the parking lot of a warehousing outfit in Alamogordo. There, a tan Jeep Cherokee driven by a security officer was waiting to take me to Horizon Pass. Grabbing my compact travel bag containing a snatch-and-run bundle, I jumped into the front passenger seat and off we went down Highway 54 past Holloman AFB. Then at mile marker 32, we turned right onto a desert track heading directly into the rapidly setting sun. Forty-five minutes later we arrived.

*   *   *

Dr. Naysmithe himself greeted me at the airlock entrance of the underground facility. And much to my surprise, the man actually hugged me.

Frankly, I was surprised by how good that felt. Well, I know how it felt, but at the time just didn't realize it. I was welcomed home.

"Thank God you're finally here." He said. "Follow me."

Rather unnecessarily I said, "I got here as quickly as I could. Probably breaking in the process several land speed records in a Volkswagen."

The physicist smiled briefly. "Yeah, I know. Curtis told me that he had arrived at the warehouse moments before you arrived. You have a lead foot lady!"

*   *   *

Dr. Naysmithe took me directly to Tombstone, the refurbished and expanded natural cavern that had formed beneath the twin red sandstone outcrops that towered above the complex. Within its confines were housed the facility's control room and electrical junction, adjoined to it stood the permanent laboratory bench version of the Soap Bubble temporal device, and nearby, the IT Department. Entering the latter, I saw three people huddled around the central conference table with a complex-looking, multi-colored schemata unrolled.

"Excuse me folks, but Gregorieva has just arrived."

Only one face rose, a female's, looked up and nodded in my direction, and then returned to studying the document on the table top.

"Well, I suppose it is to be expected." Dr. Naysmithe said as he turned to me. "Gregorieva, in short, we've been hacked and they're trying to figure out how it took place."

"When?" I asked.

"It was discovered about five hours ago."

"Who?"

"We don't have a clue right now."

"What?"

"All of our schematics to the Soap Bubble, the calibration software, and some historical documentation on the device as well. In other words, you and Richards' finalized debriefs."

"Oh boy!"

My heart sank beneath my feet at that news.

"Now, as to why you are here. Vesna, you are a highly trained field operative, and I might say, a damn good one. But you are also Directorate trained. So, henceforth, you are my in-house spook. I want you to peek and probe, think 'spooky', and in general comment as appropriate on everything and anything dealing with our security. And of late, we have been getting some unexpected visitors, so I am going to clue you in with Lieutenant Sanders. He's our facility's security commander. Pick his mind and report back to me with whatever you find."

And before he left me, his gentle hand squeezed my shoulder.

Yep! I'm home.

*   *   *

When it comes to computers, their temp files, and the Internet, trust me when I say that every transaction leaves a foot print, no matter how savvy you are. There will be a trace. And I am not talking about cookies, either. So when the IT team figured out that the hack originated in Tehran, I was not at all surprised. But what did surprise me was that the Iranians had broken into and copied all of Joey's emails directly from his university's server. That breech alone was unforgiveable, but based on Joey's correspondence, several Horizon Pass emails had been sorted out, and then exploited. And now that the damage had been done, the IT team was furiously at work shoring up the facility's cyber defenses.

Meanwhile, we assumed that eventually the Iranians would build their own temporal device, with a mind to deploy it, and no doubt, to tamper with our current reality. Temporal terrorism was now a reality. The only question was where and *somewhen* would they deploy. And then, whether we would be able to stop them in their tracks. Consequently, Joey and I, the only fully trained temporal field operatives, were put on a permanent alert status. Where we might be deployed next was anyone's guess.

* * *

"Dr. Naysmithe, as you probably know, I have long been trained not to accept coincidence," I said, "and I am finding evidence of such nearly everywhere I look. But from my point-of-view, I see basically one operator, who is running multiple investigations on Horizon Pass and the Philology Annex, just from several different angles.

"To begin at the beginning, in a discussion with Joey, he told me that about four months ago a very select group of the Egyptian Antiquities Service guards had been called out for an intense interview by an imam with a Farsi accent. In the midst of this, Joey, sporting an Egyptian mustache, inserted himself into this interviewing process, confirmed the imam's Farsi accent, and the real point of his thirty-odd interviews: any odd goings on within the Karnak Temple.

"Apparently, the imam was not satisfied with those interviews, so then a former high level Egyptian Antiquities official was kidnapped, interrogated, and then released in a much drugged state at a local clinic. But it gets even better. Most recently, Joey and Cartwright practically grabbed the current Director of the National Museum off the street, at her own request, as she too feared for her life because of what she knew. So at this point, the common thread was that all of these Egyptians had contact with us and our temporal activities. And on top of that, both of these high Egyptian antiquity officials had been in contact with Joey via e-mail."

Dr. Naysmithe, his head in his hands, just shook his head in utter bewilderment. "You mean to tell me that they actually grabbed and interrogated Dr. Moussa senior?"

"Yes sir. Then during my discussions with Lieutenant Sanders, he told me that there had been several recent attempts over the past six months at covert reconnaissance in the Horizon Pass' neighborhood. Those 'unexpected visitors' that I remembered you had first mentioned. One of those intruders had been captured, a Mr. Blackfeather, ultimately leading to a Native American couple, who were his handlers. They in turn led to a certain Mr. Roots, who was really Jahan Manu Rabiei, a member of the Iranian embassy staff in Washington, DC. Clearly by all accounts, his actions label him as a member of their secret service, the SAVAMA. Doc Allen then told me that he had planted in the man a RFID tracking device prior to his deportation back to Tehran. That was very, very clever.

"As for the hack itself, or perhaps better stated, hacks, for there were at least two of them: the first was directed at a low security asset, the university email server at Joey's institution. That hack, and what it gathered, guided the second hack against two email addresses here, at Horizon Pass.

"So, in conclusion, it is my belief that a single operator, an Iranian, somehow got wind of our activities, and just like with a loose thread from a carpet, he began to tease away at it, looking for leads, looking for information. He began first with low level interrogations of the Egyptian Antiquities guards to build his case. Seeing that those interviews were promising, he then went to the daring act of kidnapping an Egyptian official and then interrogating him with drugs. That probably confirmed the initial interviews and provided actual names, places, and dates. But this guy wanted more, and just missed grabbing Ms. Moussa off the street."

"Daring, aren't they."

"Very much sir. Now with perhaps only one name, he went to the Internet, found Joey, and hacked his email server. Now he has over four years worth of correspondence to pick through and God only knows what this Iranian found there. But one thing is certain. This guy attacked two emails here at Horizon Pass, a place that he could not locate on the ground. But it's the subtle level of the second hack, reduced to a slow trickle of information that the IT team would not notice.

"Dr. Naysmithe. This guy is good. That's the bottom line. When he gets the Soap Bubble up and running, then we have to be able to rapidly respond, otherwise, a much-changed reality may not allow us."

Naysmithe, his head still in his hands, groaned. "Okay Vesna. Anything else?"

"Yes. We need some way to detect when their temporal device is up and running."

"That's it?"

"Ah, no. I am very sorry, sir, but there is just one other thing. We need to be able to anticipate what the Iranians would want a temporal device for. In other words, where and *somewhen* they would want to use it."

*   *   *

The next day, Dr. Naysmithe flew me into Chicago as he wanted me to be his eyes and ears. Five nationally accredited scholars of Islamic History were contacted on the scientist's behalf by Paul Young, the Dean of Humanities, to inquire on their near immediate availability for a Saturday afternoon conference at the Philology Annex. To quell any possible no shows, the invitation included first class airfare, a five-star suite in downtown Chicago, all meals and ground transportation, and an honorarium of $25,000.

"It's truly remarkable," Young had commiserated with me in his office, "four of the five responded positively. Do you think that the 25K had had anything to do with that?"

*   *   *

The four experts represented a historical brain-trust. One was from the East Coast, one from the West Coast, one from Canada, and the fourth was a local resource. As one might expect with such academic luminaries, they had egos to match. But what Young, Joey, and I were counting on were two things: the sheer breadth of coverage that these men represented, and the fact that two of them were the former students of the Canadian. It was hoped that the latter fact would help put a damper on things if anyone's ego flared.

This gathering of eagles met on the second floor of the Near Eastern Institute, Joey's own department, amid the heavy oak tables and fragrant shelving full of old books. The room itself, more the attic of a barn in size, enjoyed plentiful daylight from its gothic spear-shaped windows. Being a Saturday, the closing off of such a cozy reference area had been readily accomplished. Still, unknown to the four guest scholars, two of Callahan's men in plain clothes were stationed outside its door to discourage any interruptions to the proceedings taking place within.

Seated around a single table, with Young at one end and myself at the other, the conference began promptly at one. As usual, Young chaired the proceedings.

"Ladies and gentlemen, thank you for coming and fitting this brief conference into your busy schedules, and on such short notice. Have you all received an envelope from my secretary?"

Nods all around.

"Good, now for some housekeeping issues. The bathrooms are available to the right and down the hallway. In one hour's time, we will take a ten minute break and some light refreshments will be brought in. I think that that about does it for me at the moment. Ms. Gregorieva?"

"Yes. Thank you Dr. Young. What I am now

passing out to all of you is a simple, one page Confidentiality Agreement. Before we can begin, kindly read it, and then sign it."

It was clear to me that several of these individuals had never before seen such a document, one clearly bridled at even touching it, and another just smiled a very knowing smile.

"Thank you all. Now, as you can probably imagine, a flash gathering of such intellectual horsepower must have a reason. That reason is top secret. However, we can still move forward if we approach the situation with a working hypothesis. And that hypothesis is precisely this: If the current government of Iran could change the course of history at any point, which would be the most advantageous to its future?"

I had to work very hard at keeping my face impassive as I saw the looks of disbelief from the scholars gathered.

"What kind of crap is this anyway?" was the first vocalization expressed by the youngish, bearded, West Coast scholar.

"A very serious one," I said stony-faced. "As in very serious crap, as you so delicately put it."

Not used to being so directly put in his place, my look alone silenced any more smart-assed comments.

Pause.

"So," began the older face with gray hair from the local resource, "what you are asking us is to provide you with x-number of historically significant events?"

"Precisely." I answered.

"So," again stated the older face, "we are looking to identify macro-historical events that if somehow changed, would greatly benefit modern day Iran."

A nod of encouragement from me. "Yes, precisely."

Now began the ear pulling, nose scratching, and the face rubbing. Unconsciously, I began tapping my pencil on my yellow legal pad, and in the silence of the room, it sounded like a bass drum, so I stopped.

"Well, for starters," posited the scholar from the East Coast, "we could start with damn critical battles, battles that history itself seemed to pivot itself upon..."

"Absolutely not!" the West Coaster firmly stated. "Socio-religious shifts are the way to go."

The Canadian, silent to this moment, finally spoke with a distinctly paternal tone.

"Now Todd, you know better than that. What Jeremy here has suggested has legs. What do you have? Theory? By the looks on these folks' faces, and the check that is now securely in your pocket, I really don't think that they are about to buy your half-baked, nice and fuzzy, PC theories on the development of Shi'a Islam."

Now turning slightly to his right and patently ignoring West Coast Todd, the Canadian continued. "Now, Jeremy, just what did you have in mind?"

Now pinching his lower lip, East Coast Jeremy considered.

"Let's just imagine what might have happened if the Battle of Tours had gone all wrong. The macro-historical figure, Charles Martel, killed. Who's to say that the rest of Western Europe would not have fallen to the Caliphate? Who's to say that the Mediterranean would not have become Allah's Own Sea? And, with the death of Martel, where would that leave the Carolingian Dynasty? The very foundation stone of

Western Europe? Much less of Charlemagne, who was his grandson? However you look at the situation, without Charles Martel, the entire course of Western Civilization changes, radically, toward Islam's favor."

While other worthy "macro-historical" situations were discussed, even one critical Islamic philosophical shift, the group always seemed to gravitate back to the lynch pin, that pivot point, which was the Battle of Tours.

In my mind, that had to be it, and it had the advantage of being operationally simple. Send in a one-way assassination squad to take out Charles Martel. Then let the rest of history just fall into Iran's lap.

CHAPTER XIX
Detection

I have always marveled at how different my recorded voice sounds. This same sort of introspection occurred at Horizon Pass, when Dr. Naysmithe began his detection analysis of the Soap Bubble's electromagnetic energy signatures. He was amazed at the spectrum and amplitudes expressed, just as with one's own recorded voice. Even when he flew a drone over the facility, the temporal device's signature was clearly detectable through all of the facilities concrete, rebar, and sandstone, when using purely off-the-shelf energy detectors at one thousand feet.

But then I really popped his bubble when I asked.

"Okay, but can you calibrate a specific date on the basis of the temporal device's energy signature alone?"

Blinking once, twice, he then said, "We have to be able to do that, don't we?"

"Yes we do, that is, if you want Joey and me to stop whatever the Iranians might be up to."

*　*　*

While I really do not know how it was all arranged, somehow Dr. Naysmithe got a geosynchronous satellite, with an appropriate electromagnetic detector, placed above Tehran within a month of the hack at Horizon Pass. As you can probably appreciate, this was an exceptionally impressive exercise of engineering clout, which came with an equally impressive price, as the much-hurried launch was with a privately-held organization, who had to bump several of its faithful customers out of the way, one of which was NASA. Regardless, almost five weeks to the day after the hack on our servers at Horizon Pass, that dedicated satellite logged a brief, but very specific electromagnetic energy bloom within the Tehran city limits. Then over the next several weeks, six more emissions were recorded, of various strengths and amplitudes. Clearly, the Iranians were progressing fast. And as their device became better tuned, for lack of a better word, the location of where that event was happening became far more precise as well. In fact, the location was NRI, the Niroo Research Institute, a high-energy think-tank, located at the western end of Shahid Dadman Boulevard in Tehran's northwestern quadrant. Coincidentally, the NRI had been the source of the hack on Joey's email. Also, and as a result of the Saturday conference, Dr. Naysmithe had a similarly equipped satellite parked over western France.

* * *

As soon as the last energy bloom had been detected in Tehran, Joey and I were informed that a deployment was now just a matter of time. What had been very instructive was that the bloom's intensity, as it was calibrated to the eighth century. The Battle of Tours was beginning to look more and more like a sure bet, and so Joey and I began to prepare for that eventuality.

* * *

Perhaps it was just inevitable, but eight weeks later the satellite over western France began to scream its head off at precisely four o'clock in the morning, while the weekend skeleton crew was on duty. The location of the event was highly significant, a point some twenty kilometers northeast of Poitiers near the village of Vouneuil-sur-Vienne. The precise location seemed to be just west of the village about a quarter mile along the D 15 Highway. The local time was high noon. And as for the electromagnetic field frequency reading of the event, it calibrated to 12:03 pm, October 2nd, AD 732. Apparently, the Iranians decided to arrive early as the actual battle took place on Monday, October 10th. Then, rather suddenly, the field's frequency violently spiked and winked out altogether.

CHAPTER XX
Becoming a Weapon

It is not like the Directorate had put me out on the street as a defenseless little girl. Quite the contrary, I had been trained to defend myself from the very start. And of course, there was my seamy episode with the three derelict physicians. That truly had been a creative act, but had been a terrible waste of three imported sets of pumps. Nonetheless, it had been made abundantly clear that western France in the eighth century was nothing like ancient Egypt. It was, generally speaking, a brutish, rough-in-tumble place full of ignorance and filth.

So, while Joey was off being a knightly gentleman, learning how to ride a horse and shoot a bow, I, a diminutive and disarmingly beautiful and graceful dancer, was training how to become a fearsome weapon. I was to learn how best to gut, maim, bash, and dismember my opponent with my bare hands as quickly as possible. After all, if I was to properly support Joey on this deployment, then such deadly skills were deemed needful, if not necessary.

But before I took on this quest for new heights in mayhem, I wanted to know just who Karl the Hammer was, a prominent name in the history of the battle. So I talked to Joey about it, and he said that he had just asked the very same thing of one of his colleagues.

"Well, Professor Richards," the colleague had told him, "all I can tell you for sure about Karl the Hammer is that he was a battle-hardened Frank, a brilliant strategist and field tactician, and a damn good administrator as well. As for his appearance, well, that I'll leave alone, as nobody really knows, but I'll wager that he was better than average in height and was built like a brick shit house."

Joey had then asked him, "You mean that we have no coins with his image? No depictions of him in manuscripts? No statues? Nothing?"

"Professor Richards, that's right. Karl was a disowned bastard of a king's concubine, who rather brilliantly turned that pedigree into a strength. He was a soldier first and administrator second, first and always. He represented the hidden power behind the throne, while never taking it directly. So, no, there are no reliable images of the man that I can place before you, no text that physically describes him in a reliable manner.

"But given his life and his many battles, you can bet the house that his nose was broken countless times, that he wore his helmet so long that he was balding, and I wouldn't be the least bit surprised if his face was scared many times too, just like a hockey player's. A scar on the face during that period was a trophy that proved that you didn't run in the heat of battle. And that was Karl to the max.

"What many will not tell you was that Karl's first battle was a rout. He was woefully unprepared, and he never, ever forgot that lesson. So Karl henceforth was always the prepared one, even while most of the time outmanned. Without question, he always, always was unpredictable, did things that were not supposed to happen, arrived early, attacked from an unexpected direction, or performed some tactical maneuver never before seen. He vexed his opponents and purposefully got into their heads. In short, he was a master of medieval psy-ops, as he outright owned, through his fierce reputation and force-of-will, the battlefield. Needless to say, his regular troops would follow him anywhere, at any time, even to the very gates of Hell, if so commanded."

*   *   *

My challenge was now to find who could teach me the dark arts of close medieval combat, complete with all the dirty tricks. Clearly, no one modern soldier could, but I turned to Tuna Cartwright nonetheless, seeking his aid and advice in this matter. And wouldn't you know, right off the top of his head, he identified no less than six candidates that could potentially fill the bill.

Ever the wise one of these things, the first words out of his mouth was a clear warning. "You realize that this next deployment is not back *somewhen* to Egypt, but rather into the wilds of medieval Gaul. From everything that I have read and have been briefed on, you will not enjoy the many freedoms that you did in Egypt."

"Yes, so I have been told," I answered.

"In fact, Ms. Gregorieva, because of that fact, I have arranged for you to train with no less than five experts, each a specialist in their own particular field, all to prepare you for the medieval environment. So, are you still interested?"

"Is Joey going?"

"Yes, he is. In fact, he is in training right this moment."

"Well then," I said with a smile, "I guess that I will

have to go as well. Gods only know what kind of trouble he will get himself into."

*   *   *

My personal training curriculum, as Tuna Cartwright so antiseptically put it, included some very intriguing and blood curdling subjects: anti-rape maneuvers; knife fighting; short sword training; garroting and nerve physiology; and the best for last, soft tissue penetration. Clearly the former Marine colonel wanted me prepared for everything and anything, or as he had so quaintly put it, "the truly awful unknown." The truth is that the Directorate had given me some anti-rape training and some basic personal defense, but nothing like what I was about to learn. I was now going to graduate school in mayhem.

*   *   *

I began with anti-rape training with a Ms. Marlene Carter, which I thought was a bit odd. A former Marine and now a security consultant, Mar was a stocky, ham fisted, and a determined Latina woman. Her flat nose had been broken God only knows how many times, and she regarded me as a lost cause and said as much.

"Well, pretty girl, prepare for an ass-whipping!"

And with that rather eloquent greeting, we began our mat work. "Listen carefully sweetie, there are three targets and three targets only: the guy's eyes and his balls. Get any one of those, and your lover boy will lose interest fast. If not, then go for his throat. One sharp blow, delivered correctly, will collapse his windpipe."

After five days of bruises, Mar had me reacting

without thinking, delivering lightning-like strikes. The last two days, she wore body armor and a full helmet with protected eye sockets for me to spar against. And so I attacked her with a vengeance that I didn't know that I possessed. The last day, graduation day, she had me practicing gouging out pig eyes, because they were the closest thing to a human's. The realism of that exercise was memorable.

*　　*　　*

My session on knife fighting began two days later, while I was still sore and bruised. Jack Matthews was one very scary man and could have easily been a cut-throat pirate in another place and time. Short and wiry of build, Jack "the knife" was blazingly quick with both of his hands, and in actual fact, that is how we began, slapping each other and blocking the blows. By the end of second day, both of my forearms were black and blue and one cheek bone was more than slightly swollen.

For the next couple of days, now accustomed to hand fighting at extremely close range, Jack introduced me to two wooden blades, complete with metal hilts. And now the hand slapping became stabs, slashes, faints, blocks, and counter blocks. As a result, I gained a new respect for a knife's hilt and what it was used for. I learned how to watch an opponent's feet and hips with my peripheral vision, as those two would first signal any move or attack.

After three days of wood, Jack moved on to the real thing, but now we both wore heavily padded chainmail armor on our torsos and arms. While the additional weight and bulk slowed our movements somewhat, I slowly began to improve, get stronger, and faster.

Defense I could do all day, but my offense was still a bit lame, that is, until Jack began with his trash talk. While funny at first, it got really personal all too quickly, and so I reacted, just as Jack had hoped. And, I surprised him. Using some of my mental training from Doc Allen, I imagined myself as a patient cobra, focused, waiting for that perfect opening. Jack came at me. Block. Block. Block. Then I flicked my tongue out at him, and in that moment, he froze, and I struck, hard, twice. He'll never forgive me for that move.

* * *

Again, after only two days rest, I was on to my next session, this time short swords, with a red haired and ruddy skinned Scotsman named James Crowfoot. A true gentleman, Jim and his ever drooping ginger moustache, taught me to use both hands, as Jack had.

"Now lassie, you never know which hand will be free. So's you must learn to use both of 'em."

Apparently, Jack "the knife" and Gentleman Jim had had words, so that this session turned out to be a continuation of what Jack had begun. And how did I figure that out? Well because our first day began with two wooden swords apiece and the padded chainmail corsets for protection. And then Jim said, "And lassie, there will be none of that tongue flicking with me."

And then he charged.

In a former life Jim must have been either a Viking or a mad Pict! But I survived. Jack's knife blocks worked here too. And if the blocks worked, then why not try the stabs, slashes, and faints. The only real difference was one of space. For I found that my reach had been expanded, and conversely, my footwork had to be quick enough to account for Jim's reach as well. All of that peripheral work with Jack held true here.

At the end of day one, Jim announced.

"Lassie, ain't you the plucky one. But when I git through with you, you'll be a survivor, you will."

*   *   *

John Black was my next instructor. Medium build, fit, dark haired, and with a face that was totally unremarkable in a crowd. He could have been an insurance salesman as easily as a mortician. But when he opened his mouth, John had a voice, a command voice that was strangely enticing, almost soothing in its delivery. I could listen to him all day, and so we began with a physiology discussion, and one of those hanging plastic skeletons that you usually see in a biology laboratory.

"Nerves, Ms. Gregorieva, allow us to think, move, and feel. If you deny someone any one of those functions, then you have a decisive advantage. Now on this skeleton, note all the red dots that I have placed along the neck and shoulder regions. You are to memorize these, as they are the basic pressure points that will incapacitate your opponent. And just for the record, none of these constitute a Vulcan neck pinch. That's pure Hollywood. But if I pinch this skeleton's neck here, it will cause the mouth to open involuntarily. That can be handy if you are pouring Drano down someone's throat."

Frankly, John's all too clinical and bloodless discussions and demonstrations of nerve pinches and garroting were very unsettling. The man clearly knew what he was talking about, but I soon decided that John was a real ghoul, and a very sick one.

The one lone highlight from his sessions was practicing what John called the double-handed rip move on a melon. I was amazed at how a thin wire, lamp cord, computer cable, whatever, could so easily cleave that fruit in two!

*   *   *

The final self-defense training session was with an enigmatic Asian woman named Sun Zung. Frankly, I never did figure out which was her first name. But when it came to soft tissue penetration, she knew her stuff. And in her own way, was as frightening a personality as was John Black.

From the start, we began with full scale ballistic gel torsos, necks, and heads that had embedded bone to provide realistic resistance and strategically placed bladders of red dye. And as with the anti-rape training and knife fighting, this form of close-in fighting was immensely personal. Ripping out throats, eyes, tearing off ears, and thrusting your hand up and into your opponent's diaphragm tends to be extremely messy.

In many respects, Sun Zung's choice to include the many bladder packets during my training was purposeful. The sight of gushing blood tends to sicken most, causing them to allow their conscience to take hold and stop the assault, when your opponent is so vulnerable. Instead, this diminutive ball of energy encouraged me to take that immediate second blow in order to mercifully finish the opponent. What she didn't say, but I did notice, was that blood is a lubricant, one that actually allows fingers, thumbs, and hands to be transformed in virtual blades of steel. And I found that my longish finger nails now had a far more practical purpose.

CHAPTER XXI
My Fifth Deployment

Now trained in ways that would have alternately fascinated and disgusted my Directorate self-defense trainers, Joey and I took up residence in the quaint French town of Poitiers and awaited further orders. Only some thirteen and a half miles from where the battle was to take place on October 10th, AD 732, all agreed that this course was the most prudent. In the meantime, Joey allowed his hair to become shaggy and let his beard grow out, while I, swallowing hard again, allowed my hair to be cut in a more medieval manner – a shoulder length page boy cut. My transformation from the sultry to the impish Joey found amazing. I nearly gagged.

Also deployed to Poitiers were Callahan, his security troops, Horizon Pass' only portable temporal device, and a Gerry-rigged PVC drop and retrieval tower. Some snickered at the location as a "really tough duty station," but the cagey Tuna Cartwright figured that if and when the Iranians dropped into the neighborhood, he wanted his people in position and ready to go within one hour's time. Fortunately for us, he had negotiated a secure location for our deployment and much hoped for retrieval point within the fourth century Baptistery of St. Jean. As of our arrival, the much revered location had been closed to the public due to recently discovered structural issues. How convenient.

* * *

During the weeks-long wait for the Iranian deployment, we made it our business to discover every interesting nook and cranny on our daily runs through the town of Poitiers. Initially, the motivation was to keep fit and to acquaint ourselves with the town's layout. Then the daily runs became more of a scavenger hunt for the odd and curious.

Always starting at the Romanesque Baptistery of St. Jean, we familiarized ourselves with the oldest parts of town, which we believed would become useful landmarks for us once deployed. Then, as the runs extended and became more like mini-marathons, specific locations to stop and rest became favored, above all, ancient wells and spring heads. We reasoned, "You always need water."

Entwined between the runs, we tried to remain sharp on our new skills as well. For Joey, it was the long bow. For me, I basically picked a fight with one of Callahan's men on nearly a daily basis. While the retrieval of errant arrows was not much fun, Joey's skill was steadily improving. And after seven day's worth of sparing, the security force flat out refused to mess with me anymore, so Joey began teaching me how to shoot the bow, more to keep me out of their hair than anything else.

Sheer boredom, both for the drop team and the security force was the main obstacle to our operational preparedness, and only so many cultural tours, books, games, and videos could fill the void. With such sharply honed personnel, waiting quickly became a unique torture of its own.

One day, during a pleasant lunch of salad, bread, and cheese, we learned of the Iranian deployment.

Without having to say a word, we both got up and changed into our threadbare medieval attire of coarse linen shirts, vest-like jackets, and leather belted woolen pants. To save us from any undo scratchiness, all of the woolen garments had been carefully lined with cotton material. For shoes, we donned heavy leather moccasin-like foot coverings that laced to a degree.

Once so attired, we boldly walked the two blocks from our flat to the baptistery. Joey carried over his shoulder his long bow and a quiver of period authentic arrows. As for me, I had three hidden leather sheaths with knives. We both also carried over our shoulders a small burlap sack with one loaf of fresh bread and a tiny pouch of silver coins, most of which were late Roman in origin. Only four people witnessed this brazen display of period attire and only one of them even bothered to turn his head in curiosity. It was the baker.

Once within the natural coolness of the baptistery, we were greeted by Callahan and four of his men. The rest, armed to the teeth, were sprinkled around the environs, all in their signature adaptive camouflage that allowed them to quite literally disappear into the shadows.

Erected in the central nave, the engineers had set up the Soap Bubble's pylons, along with the incongruous looking PVC platform standing next to it. Upon entering, there was a tangible buzz in the air as the charging up of the drop ring was in progress.

"Well folks," Callahan began, "per usual procedures, we will power up the Bubble every midnight local time for thirty seconds. If you don't throw anything through to signal us for a retrieval, then we'll just shut down for the next day.

"Any questions?"

Getting none, the lieutenant turned away and began barking out orders for the drop sequence. With the ring hovering at its nominal height above the floor, confirmation was made with Corporal Brown as to the temporal coordinates and time for the drop: October 2rd, AD 732, at twelve hundred hours. Next, Corporal Small inserted a non-metallic, low light fiber optic lens and cable into the still metallic gray surface of the temporal field. After several moments of perusal, Small reported that the surface on the other side was also about a five foot drop and that the coast was clear.

Mounting the platform, Joey reminded me to bend my knees, drop, and roll. Smiling nervously back at him, I said, "Just don't pass out on me again."

In a serious tone, Callahan said, "Okay, Robin Hood and Maid Marian, Cartwright and the rest of your merry men send their best. Now get out of here."

First Joey, and then I, dropped our arms and personal sacks through the ring's field. Then, just as wordlessly, we each stepped out, and one by one, soundlessly disappeared.

*   *   *

Landing clean and rolling out of the way, I awaited Joey's arrival. And as so many times before, he landed like a bag of potatoes.

"Willahelm. Willahelm. Wake up damn you!" I hissed into his ear. "Get your damn fat ass moving!" I creatively composed in my newly acquired Latin tongue, courtesy of the Annex's language lab.

Grunting his way back into the here and now, Joey had to brace himself on his elbow against the cool stone flooring. Then, just as fast as it came, his nausea left him.

"Damn salts." Willahelm commented. "How long have I been out Veer?" He asked in perfect Latin.

"Almost two minutes. You had me worried – again!"

"Understood. Now, let's get out of here."

* * *

Having collected our gear, we left the tomb-like quiet of the baptistery and its faint smell of sacred incense. Out of its relative protection, our senses were suddenly assaulted by the bright sunlight, a blue cloudless sky, and the reek of the vile open sewers that served as the streets of eighth century Poitiers. Holding our hands over our noses and mouths, we barely choked the bile back down our throats.

Looking quickly around to orient ourselves, we made our way down slope toward the town's southeastern gate. Our goal was to reach the bridge that went across the River Clain, which surrounded and protected the town to the east, while the River Boivre, a tributary of the Clain, completed the circuit around the town to the west.

To our utter amazement, the town gate stood wide open as the rural population, with their carts and animals, flooded in, no doubt to get behind the protective shadow of the town's ancient walls. All the while the gate's two seated and yawning guards carefully monitored the situation. With the fragments of their lunch still decorating the fronts of their tunics, we passed them through the hustle and bustle, made for the old Roman bridge, crossed it, and turned left on an equally ancient stone pavement. It was the Roman road that led north toward Tours, where we hoped to find the main Frankish army.

After having taken only fifty paces on the road, an old man, carrying all of his life's possessions in a sack over his shoulder, stopped us.

"My son, do you not know that Saracens frequent this very road, as if it was their very own?"

"I do sir," replied Joey, "but we are making way to join the Frankish army. We were told that this is the way."

Shaking his head, the ancient one murmured. "Indeed it is my son, but armed with only that old bow, your quest is madness, utter madness."

With those words of encouragement, we continued on walking in a direction that no one else was taking, all the time receiving over the shoulder glances mixed with worry and disbelief at our chosen direction.

After about an hour's trek, we found that while we were making excellent time, we also were alone and dangerously out in the open. As the road gently rose and fell following the natural contours of the land, our sightlines were not always the best, and the distinct possibility of a surprise encounter loomed as a real possibility. Yet, for the moment, that was not the case. Nonetheless, our heavy garments were warm in the sunshine and from our excursions, which meant that a water source had to be found. Instead, we encountered a short marble pillar that stood alongside the road. Joey read it aloud.

"Now that was a rather a long-winded declaration just to say that he fixed this section of the highway." I quipped.

Joey smiled. "Actually, the stone mason was probably paid by the word. But we still need to find some water, and soon."

*   *   *

While we trudged north toward Tours, we had no idea where the Iranian team was, but it had to be somewhere ahead of us. Per our briefing, their task was to not only to kill Karl, but also to ensure that the same did not happen to the governor of al-Andalus, 'Abdul Rahman Al Ghafiqi. His survival was key as he, and he alone, held the Caliph's *fatwa* to command his vast army, which was nothing more than a wild collection of Berber tribesman, Moors, Libyans, Egyptians, and Arabs. This is why we believed that the Iranians would be near Al Ghafiqi, for he was the glue to that circus of an army. Al Ghafiqi had to survive, and if he did, then history would be rewritten.

*   *   *

With that verbose milestone a good hour behind us, we next came upon a low walled ruin. More a scatter of stone blocks and broken orange ceramic roof tiles, it was overgrown with prickly holly bushes and a riot of colorful wild flowers. More importantly, we spied what allowed for such vegetative abundance – a stone trough bubbling over with clear water. After having filled ourselves to the brim with its cool deliciousness, Joey lectured.

"This structure was once part of this Roman road system. It's called a staging house for the change and watering of horses. That must mean we are at least halfway to Tours."

I frowned. "How can you be so sure?"

"Because that's the way the Romans did things."

As soon as he had finished saying that, and before I could argue with him about it, we distinctly heard the approach of horses. Lots of them. Frantically glancing around, we made for the ruins' low walls and burrowed beneath the holly bushes, which concealed us, and just in the nick-of-time. For over the northern rise of the road galloped forty heavily armored Islamic warriors.

They were resplendent in their flowing red capes and domed helmets, with chain-mail from their necks to their knees, carrying broad shields, spears, and curved scimitars in ornate scabbards that hung from thick belts on their left hips. From the look of them, they had been in a recent fight as fresh gashes marked their shields, and blood splatter was everywhere. Those who had been wounded, heavily sagging in their framed saddles, practically were falling off despite their stirrups. But even in their dire physical need, their horses were watered first, and they did so greedily. Only then did their riders dismount with many grunts, drink their fill, and tend to their wounds.

We lay motionless, silent, fearful, and listened. Because of his contemporary Egyptian Arabic, Joey managed to pick up quite a bit of their conversation, which he whispered into my ear.

"They are a raiding party, who just received a bloody nose by the Franks.

"The big one over there is in charge.

"There are four wounded.

"All they want to do is get back to camp with their booty.

"The big one doubts that two of the wounded can even make it back.

"He's decided that they're leaving soon.

"That one keeps babbling his wife's name. He must be in bad shape."

After a half hour's respite, true to Joey's prediction, the forty rode off heading south on the road that we had just walked. Clearly, the old man's warning had been justified.

Extricating ourselves from our hiding place took a good ten minutes of extremely colorful and linguistically mixed swearing. Even so, just as darkness began to fall, we both looked like we had been in a cat fight, where the cat won. With our scratches washed and stomachs again filled with water, we pressed on north toward Tours, occasionally munching on our bread ration.

*   *   *

We reached Tours around midnight, and since the gates had been long closed and bolted, a nearby hay stack served as our hotel, where we burrowed in, ate some more of our bread, and huddled together for warmth. Not knowing whether this was our last day, we found a great comfort in joining as only two desperate humans might. Arm in arm, entangled, moaning in pleasure, we forgot ourselves in the moment. Finally, we managed some restful sleep.

CHAPTER XXII
Iranian Melt Down

While we were in the process of deploying in Poitiers, I later learned from Callahan what one of his squads had found and what we were up against.

He had dispatched a six-man to track down, capture, and destroy the Iranian temporal device. This wasn't a blind hunt, since their whereabouts had been supplied by the dedicated satellite overhead. The electromagnetic energy bloom indicated a point twenty kilometers northeast of Poitiers near the village of Vouneuil-sur-Vienne. The location was just west of the village about a quarter mile along the D 15 Highway at its intersection with Fonbrede Road. As for the specifics of the event, the Iranian's electromagnetic field violently spiked and winked out altogether at 12:04 local.

When the squad arrived in their white panel van about forty minutes after the event, they were not alone, for the local fire department had beaten them there. A Mercedes truck was ablaze and billowing dark clouds of smoke. In its flatbed were four large electrical generators. What the French firemen ignored for the moment were the four sets of heavy cables that extended from the truck around to the back of the two-story stone house.

Racing around the house, Calli's squad found the melted remains of four pylons, a shattered drop ring with a portion of a rifle barrel fused to it, a wooden step ladder, a laptop, and the grotesque body of a man, who was nearly split in half. Seeing that their job had already been done, they quickly photographed the scene, scooped up the laptop, collected the fragments of the drop ring, and then made themselves scarce.

*   *   *

Back at Poitiers, Callahan was aghast at what his men reported and brought back. The drop ring fragment with the fused rifle barrel told him more than he wanted to know. The real bitch was there was no way Calli could warn us that we were going to a gun fight with a long bow and some knives. Not good. Not good at all. Then more news arrived.

"Excuse me sir," said McCormick, the team's sniper, "I know this barrel."

"What is it corporal?" Callahan asked.

"It's from a Barrett XM500, sir. That's a fifty caliber sniper rifle. Best damn sniper weapon know to man. You can snuff a prairie dog at fifteen hundred meters with that weapon."

Callahan thought hard about that last tidbit of information. "Corporal, how long is that sniper rifle?"

Without blinking an eye, McCormick answered.

"Forty-six inches sir. It's a big son-of-a-bitch. All told some twenty-six pounds of lethal, God-like firepower."

"Thank you, corporal."

Callahan considered the facts. This would explain the sudden energy spike the satellite picked up! Some idiot grounded that long rifle in the drop field! That explains the flatbed fire, the ruined temporal device, and even the grotesque corpse. I'll just bet that the rifle was loaded, it discharged in the field, and killed that Iranian, who was probably handing it through.

That means that the Iranians do not have their long rifle on the other side, as it and their operator have been incinerated. That's about the best spin that I can put on this. Got to tell Dr. Naysmithe about this.

CHAPTER XXIII
Preliminaries

During our deployment briefs, I remembered that a lot of topographical inference was offered about the battlefield and what we might expect. And what came out of that was that the battle did not take place at either Poitiers or Tours, but rather, somewhere in between at the fork of two rivers to the southwest of Tours. Here, in a hilly and treed area, the Franks dug in with their backs against the water and with a thin tree line before them. The Franks hoped that those trees would blunt the savage charge of the Muslim heavy cavalry.

Another misconception is that the battle took place on 10 October, AD 732. The actual fact was that as the main Islamic force slowly ground its way toward Tours, six days of low grade skirmishing, plundering, and raiding had been taking place in anticipation of taking the far greater prize, Tours itself.

Tours, like so many towns in Europe, began as a first century Roman fort. Its strategic importance was its bridgehead that spanned the Loire River. This crossing point allowed trade to flourish. Whoever was master of the bridge controlled the town's future. By the fourth century the fort, now a thriving trading depot, had become a full blown Late Roman city.

As Tours grew it became more important. With such recognition, came wealth and even its own amphitheatre. With Christianity's spread, St. Martin became the city's patron saint and as a result placed Tours on the great pilgrimage route through Europe. With the rise of Clovis as the first Frankish king, his lavish largess benefited the city and the Abbey of St. Martin. In short, by AD 732, Tours was a ripe and irresistible plum, which the raiders of Islam dearly wanted to pick.

When I had piped up and asked why the Muslim forces were even in France, our professor of medieval history said their presence could be attributed to two main themes: religion and greed. A main tenet of Islam is the conversion of the Infidel. Since the conversion process itself is a simple one, where one orally submits to Allah and acknowledges Mohammed as his prophet, this fact explains in large part why the conversion and conquest of North Africa resembled a prairie fire before a stiff wind.

Christian Spain, however, was a far different story, as its conquest was a hard-earned one, but one that was very profitable. So was whetted the Muslim's greed, for beyond the Pyrenees' range lay even vaster resources, there for the taking. In fact, the main reason for the sluggish, if not near-glacial, progress of the main Muslim force as it inched toward Tours, was because of its baggage train of loot taken from the sack of Bordeaux. They left it a burned out shell of a city.

As for the battle itself, the historical accounts differ, but perhaps the best source, whether Latin or Arabic, is the *Chronicle of 754*, written in Latin by a chronicler in Muslim-held Spain. This is the critical passage that Joey and I were given to read.

While Abd ar-Rahman was pursuing Odo, he decided to despoil Tours by destroying its palaces and burning its churches. There he confronted the consul of Austrasia by the name of Karl, a man who, having proved himself to be a warrior from his youth and an expert in things military, had been summoned by Odo. After each side had tormented the other with raids for almost seven days, they finally prepared their battle lines and fought fiercely. The northern peoples remained as immobile as a wall, holding together like a glacier in the cold regions. In the blink of an eye, they annihilated the Arabs with the sword. The people of Austrasia, greater in number of soldiers and formidably armed, killed the king, Abd ar-Rahman, when they found him, striking him on the chest. But suddenly, within sight of the countless tents of the Arabs, the Franks despicably sheathed their swords, postponing the fight until the next day, since night had fallen during the battle. Rising from their own camp at dawn, the Europeans saw the tents and canopies of the Arabs all arranged just as they had appeared the day before. Not knowing that they were empty and thinking that inside them there were Saracen forces ready for battle, they sent officers to reconnoiter and discovered that all the Ishmaelite troops had left. They had indeed fled silently by night in tight formation, returning to their own country.

"So," I remember having said, "on the basis of this account, there is no mention whatsoever of a battle between Muslim cavalry and Frankish infantry. Only that the Franks, having killed Abd ar-Rahman, took a break from the fighting until the following day. Did I read this correctly?"

Our historical expert said that I was correct, but then noted that allowing the Saracens to retreat was probably the wisest course of all.

*   *   *

Having spent that huddled night in the hay stack, we awoke at dawn to the clatter of marching men banging their swords against their shields. Rousing ourselves, I beheld about one thousand of the most tough and battle-hardened human beings that I had ever seen. Their massive bodies swayed in cadence as they marched toward the now open gates of Tours, as its inhabitants waved in greeting from atop the city's walls.

"Who are they?" I asked.

"By the looks of them, veterans," Joey surmised. "Germans to be sure. I see a lot of blue eyes and blond hair beneath all of that dried blood, sweat, and filth."

After the last of the horde had passed, we dared to fall in. And while we had gained entrance to Tours, our next challenge was to make contact with Karl, the Mayor of the Palace. Logic suggested that following the soldiers would get us at least into the mayor's vicinity.

The interior of Tours was an odd mix of stone Romanesque architecture, massively built on a grand scale, and hovels built of mud and straw brickwork with sooty, thatched roofs. Again, as in Poitiers, the unmistakably rank smell of the open sewer assaulted our nostrils, as these streets too were precisely that. But here a narrow stone notch ran down the center to encourage the flow of the effluence. How nice.

In the center of the town, before the twin doors of a large stone edifice, we learned the palace of the archbishop of Tours, the soldiers gathered as one, and stood in silence. But not for long, as a broad shouldered figure appeared, dressed as they were, in full battle armor, but lacking in only a helmet and shield. Accompanying the sound of one thousand swords being drawn as one, a shout was unleashed as those same swords were raised high in the air.

"Lord Mayor! We are here!"

As the echo of that call faded off the building's facade, the figure smiled, extended his arms wide as if to encompass the entire one thousand, and said, "My brothers. I see that you are well-bled by the look of you! Woe onto the Saracen devils!"

And again came that roar as one, "Lord Mayor! We are here!"

*　*　*

As the troops began to noisily disburse after their acknowledgment by Karl, and he of them, we decided to make for the double doors of the archbishop's palace. While we threaded our way through the milling crowd, we were noticed, but were immediately forgotten, as calls for celebratory wine and mead were being made.

Mounting the palace's stone steps, Joey brazenly pushed against one of the door leaves, which gave way to his pressure. Once inside the cool, low ambient light of the building, we sensed, more than saw, that we were surrounded within a large space. Stopping and standing stock still, Joey firmly called into the gloom.

"I am Willahelm the True, and this is my wife Veer. We wish audience with the Mayor of the Palace."

Only then did we hear the shuffling of booted feet, and indeed, we were surrounded.

"And just what might your business be with the lord mayor?" challenged a strong voice from directly behind us.

Holding his open hands up for their inspection, which I copied, Joey answered. "I offer my bow and my knowledge of the ways of battle. As for my wife, I offer her cunning ways with a blade and an even sharper tongue."

This last caused several chuckles and one rather lewd remark that told us where all the guards stood.

"Careful friend," Willahelm softly said, "my wife is not one to be trifled with. Trust me. I'm her husband."

More guffaws broke out, but the one guard behind us just couldn't resist the temptation and so made the colossal mistake of grabbing me.

What happened, happened so fast, that it was quite literally over before it began. In spite of what a modern physicist might have to say about the validity of such a statement.

I threw the man over my right shoulder, put him on his back, and held him there immobilized with a single hand holding a painfully twisted wrist. The more the man squirmed, the farther I bent back his wrist, until he struggled no more.

"My good men, now you can see what I have to put up with on a daily basis."

Several appreciative grunts were voiced.

"Veer, my sweet, let go of the man. For he was only doing what his lord and master asked of him."

With a grunt, the fallen man got to his feet, rubbed

the back of his head, and then attended to his wrist.

"Indeed!" Boomed a voice filled with command. "Alberic *was* doing precisely what he was told. But he deserves his discomfort for not heeding a husband's own warning. Bring them to my chamber, as I wish to speak to them."

*   *   *

Entering through a peaked key-stoned doorway, we stood before a pacing giant of a man. To say that Karl was big would be one thing, but to stand near him, was another. Imposing. I guessed him to be around two hundred and sixty pounds, all muscle and bone on a barrel-chested frame of six-two. But I also saw the facial worry lines, the beginnings of gray at the temples, the intelligent brown eyes, and slab-like hands of pure callus.

Bowing his head, Joey stated, "Lord Mayor, I am Willahelm the True, and this is…"

"Yes, yes, I know, your 'ever faithful wife Veer.' What do you want? Do you have a grievance? If so, see your local bishop about it, as I have a war to wage."

The big man waved dismissively as he continued his pacing.

To this Joey smiled that vexing little smile of his. "And what you want most of all is the most advantageous place to do battle, perhaps a hilly spot, between two converging rivers to protect your flanks, and with trees before it to bedevil the Saracen cavalry. How am I doing so far Lord Mayor?"

Joey knew for a fact that he was doing well as the nobleman stopped his incessant pacing, but his raised eyebrows betrayed him.

"Lord Mayor, what I and my wife want, is to join your army. I can offer you stratagems and my long bow. My wife is a superb scout, and a silent, deadly raider.

"You, Lord Mayor, have a disciplined veteran army that the Saracens have yet to encounter and will not expect. Meanwhile, the Saracen army is a haphazard collection of many tribes and nations. The Saracen leader struggles to manage them, as their only true god is plunder. So they come for Tours, to pillage its wealth.

"Lord Mayor, if during the battle, Veer, and a select number of your men were to attack their camp, placing it in serious jeopardy, then who would truly command the battlefield?"

A grunt.

"For a man called 'the True,' I would wager that you are more wizard or witch, as only I have considered such things, never have they reached my lips. Willahelm 'the True,' do you have any more ideas about how I should make battle?"

Again with that slight smile, Joey suggested. "Lord Mayor, I have two suggestions. One is an old ruse. It is called 'The field of pots.' This stratagem causes the defender to dig holes, put empty pots or wicker baskets in them, and then cover them up with a light layer of soil. These holes should be dug between the trees where horses might find easy passage. As the Saracen cavalry gallop between the trees, their horses' hooves will find those holes, which will trip the horses, making them fall, and breaking their legs. After all, Lord Mayor, what good is a Saracen rider without his horse?"

With a deeply furrowed and intent stare, Willahelm

could see that Charles was seriously considering this.

"As for my second suggestion, I wish to remain at your side throughout the battle."

"But you are so puny, Willahelm the True. What can you possibly do to protect me that my own hand-picked band of friends and relatives cannot?"

Now smiling broadly, Joey set the hook.

"Lord Mayor, who in your army is an archer? Who in your army can kill a man from over two hundred paces? Lord Mayor, I and my hunting bow represent an advantage that the Saracens have never tasted. If my puniness can hide me in the center of your formation, I can wait until I see when their leader is within two hundred paces. Then I will slay him. And once that comes to pass, what will happen to his army of many tribes and nations? What will happen when this army sees the smoke in the sky from their burning tents? That their camp is being plundered? Their gold taken. Their women ravaged."

* * *

"Joey," I later asked, "what is this field of pots? I don't remember anything about that during the briefing back at the Philology Annex?"

Again that damnable smile. "That's because it wasn't in it. I just thought that I would help the Franks by causing some low tech chaos. But the idea is not mine. It's actually quite ancient. The Greek historian Herodotus recorded in his *Histories* that the Phocians had used the stratagem against the Thessalian cavalry. So why not use it here as well?"

"You know Joey this idea of yours is quite creative, devilishly so. But my only question is this:

will you have enough time to dig enough holes to make a difference before the battle begins?"

"Good point. I only hope to God that we do."

CHAPTER XXIV
The Battle

According to Joey's recollections, by the time the forward elements of the Saracen horde had reached full gallop, they had reached the tree line. With their lances at the ready and their war flags flying, he described the charge as something out of Hollywood's *Wind and the Lion*, or *Lawrence of Arabia*, but real. Men with gritted teeth, leaned forward in their saddle racking, urged on their much-beloved mounts through the gaps in the tree line. Up the subtly rising slope they went, racing headlong to either victory or paradise, come what may. They sounded like thunder. Joey said that he felt their approach. Their passage quaked the earth.

Then, within the tree line, something odd began to happen. Here and there horses began to topple, fall, and scream as their forelegs were broken. Their riders, thrown, fell awkwardly; some even cart wheeled to an instant death. The cries of the stricken horses distracted others. Horses began to shy as they came upon those who had fallen. Collisions began to occur among the trees. Both horses and men were trampled by the continuous pressure of the Saracen surge. The many fallen had begun to slow and then clog the Saracen momentum. Those riders, who successfully got through, now had to charge, uphill, against the massed Frankish formation, which they did not expect. And the Franks were eagerly waiting for them.

*   *   *

A mere hundred paces beyond the tree line, Karl and fifteen thousand grizzled veterans waited in a tight rectangular formation with their heavy shields grounded, their spears facing out like a prickly porcupine. After their initial slowing to get through the trees, the Saracen cavalry now had scant time or the real estate to recover, organize, and then muster a full force charge against the Frankish formation. Joey's stratagem of the field of pots had seriously degraded their surge. And not knowing how to attack such a mass of men, the riders just flung themselves and their mounts upon the phalanx, fully thinking that they would give way before their charge.

They were wrong. The Frankish line held and the truly grim business of close-in battle ensued. What the Saracen cavalry did not understand was for each mount that came into contact with the square, there were at a minimum four spears waiting for them. At impact, the front line subliminally and subtly dimpled, creating a momentary pocket, where the Saracen horse and its rider were briefly surrounded on three sides. There they were hacked to pieces.

*　*　*

During the early dark hours of the morning, prior to the battle, I, and a group of raiders, all handpicked by Karl, ventured out a hidden postern gate of the city's walls. Our task: take the Saracen camp. Avoiding all roads and byways, my raiding party, with our faces covered with black ash, wordlessly moved as one, in an almost snake-like formation, along a game trail near the river's bank. Moving in a southerly direction, we reached a point that was equidistant to and not far from the still sleeping Saracen camp. For the moment, we settled in to wait in the high grass, forty-one warriors strong.

On my belly and peering at the camp at dawn's first light, I could not believe my eyes. The central collection of tents alone seemed to cover more than two acres, while surrounding them were hundreds, no thousands, of sleeping horses with their masters. I wished for a Gatling gun, as from my position I would have made quick work of the area. Instead, I had four period-piece knives, and I knew how to use them. They had been my training tools.

A slight rustle in the grass announced that another had joined me on point. It was none other than Alberic, one of Karl's personal guards, and the one that I had bested at the palace.

"A truly intimidating sight to behold. All those tents, horses, and men."

Smiling, I whispered, "Think not on that, my friend, but instead on all the gold we will find."

Truly pleased with the tone of my answer, Alberic continued.

"Do you really think that we will find some?"

"Without question. I can smell it. But before we think of riches, think on this. Somewhere among those tents are men who are dressed strangely. They bear strange and powerful weapons. If we encounter them, avoid them, or you will surely die. Let the rest of the men know this."

"But who then will kill them, if we all avoid them?"

"Trust in *me*, my strong friend, I will personally kill them all."

"Why such a dangerous and foolhardy plan?"

"Because this is personal. This is about *Wehrgeld* –
'man-money', and I intend to collect it, all of it."

Alberic was momentarily breathless. "Are you
always so fearsome?"

I smiled, bared my teeth for emphasis, and then
creativity lied. Well, only half lied.

"My husband is Willahelm the True. I am called
Veer the Bloody. I killed my mother in childbirth and
was born in much blood. I fought beside my husband at
Bordeaux and we barely escaped with our lives. We
both lost our families to the strange men in that camp. I
claim them as mine. Now do you understand?"

"Indeed. I will pass the word."

*   *   *

It was not long after dawn's true break that the
slumbering camp came alive.

"It's like the stirring of an ant hill," Alberic
whispered in awe. "There are so many of them."

"Worry not." I said. "That camp will soon be far
fewer once they mount their horses for battle. Then, my
strong friend, fire will become our greatest ally," as I
took measure of the direction of the breezes across the
field's long grasses.

And within the hour, my observations proved true
in every respect, as hundreds upon hundreds moved off
toward the north, organizing themselves under their
colorful war banners.

After the passing of another hour, only a thin force
seemed to mill about the central tented area, and then I
finally saw what I had been looking for. A shaggy
headed figure wearing green BDUs had appeared from

one of the myriad tents to relieve himself.

"Alberic!" I hissed. "Spy that one? In the green? He is one of the strangers that I told you about. He and his kind are mine, all mine."

"Yes. I will pass the word of this as well."

*   *   *

"Alberic, see how far the tall grass grows?" I whispered.

"Yes. It looks to extend about thirty paces from here."

"Tell the men to slowly, quietly, crawl to the point where it thins and then wait for my signal."

*   *   *

Putting two fingers to my lips, I let out a loud and clear whistle, and out of the tall grasses, as if by magic, forty Franks appeared and ran toward the nearest tents. All but one failed to reach their shade, as Alberic's own brother was impaled on a thrown Saracen spear.

Finding unattended and smoldering heating coals and cooking fires, the firing of the tents began, which were accompanied with the screams of women and children and the grunting sounds of hand-to-hand fighting.

While all of this raged around, I stalked the Iranians, and in the process surprised many a Saracen, who had taken me too lightly. Then, I heard gun fire, undisciplined gun fire, which made me smile.

Go ahead, waste your ammo. I'm still coming for you! I snarled as I vectored in on the reports.

The first Iranian that I encountered, I could see had

killed six of my raiding party. So I distracted him with a knife throw. When he stupidly looked down at the hilt that was buried deep in his left thigh, I took him with a vicious slash across his throat that almost decapitated him. Now with my face and chest painted in blood, I stripped the fallen carcass of its ammo, AK47, and its two handguns, which I strapped to my thighs.

Looking down, "Angelia Jolie, eat your heart out." I said as I slapped in a fresh magazine and charged the rifle's receiver.

* * *

Joey saw the smoke first and pointed it out to Karl. Over the tree line the Mayor of the Palace indeed saw the smoke and then heard the distinct sounds of thunder in short, repeated, claps.

He shouted. "My brothers, we have taken their camp! Look toward the south. It burns."

The men responded to his words with a roaring cheer, and with their spirits so renewed, the force of their blows redoubled.

* * *

At this point I had literally taken the lead, as I hunted down the rest of the Iranians. Any Saracens unlucky enough to cross my path were efficiently shot twice to knock them down. Alberic and the others then finished off whoever was still alive.

"All of them." I ordered. "Make sure that you slay all of them. I do not wish to be surprised from behind." I bellowed, as we grimly went about our business.

Then, I came across a tent that contained three full

military backpacks, which were leaning together at its center. Bending down, I ransacked them all looking for ammunition, which was not there. Emptying them of their personal affects, I tossed one to Alberic, and the others to two to his men.

"Remember to fill these with any gold that you find. That will be our offering to St. Martin for ensuring our victory."

*　*　*

As the smoke from the burning camp filled the sky, even 'Abdul Rahman Al Ghafiqi could not ignore it, as he could see that his composite army was faltering, their allegiances torn between fighting an unexpectedly tough and formidable force, and the threat to their plundered fortunes. Seeing this, the governor called for yet another charge against the Frankish formation. And for the first time during the battle, with that impulsive act, 'Abdul Rahman Al Ghafiqi had placed himself in harm's way, fully expecting his forces to follow.

*　*　*

I saw the second Iranian walking about as if in a trance, firing indiscriminately at anything that moved, even his eighth century compatriots. I made short work of him, stripping him of his ammunition and weapons. So far we had yet to find any treasure, but the raiding party, now only twenty-one strong, naturally followed along behind me in a broad V-shaped formation. With me at its point, I slaughtered wantonly all who came in my path. It was extermination, pure and simple, and that fact was not lost on my comrades.

"Alberic!" said Grote, "she is most formidable with that thunderous weapon! It is like taking trout in a dammed stream."

The last Iranian, who had heard the approach of the disciplined shots, thought that one of his own team was fighting his way toward him. He was greatly mistaken, as I removed his face with two rounds.

Now with three rifles and the same number of holsters slung over my left shoulder, I called to Alberic for assistance.

"My strong friend, I need your assistance. Carry these for me as I cannot." I piled twelve loaded magazines and two handguns into his backpack. Then I slung two rifles over his shoulder.

"What are these, Veer the Bloody?"

"Flying death for the Saracens. Now, let's go."

To my great displeasure, I encountered no more Iranians, so we began the slaughter of the first returning Saracen cavalry, which caused them to turn away back toward the Frankish formation beyond the tree line. I well realize now just how lost I was in the moment, but I just kept seeing, imagining, how brutally my parents had died in the train station. Somehow I knew, at some point, that my bloodlust would end, would be satisfied. But now was not that time.

*　*　*

Joey recounted to me that fateful last Saracen charge. With about fifty men and horses, it was a feeble act. Once again the Frankish formation readied itself for impact. Karl, seeing the Saracen leader, called to Joey to ready his bow. This he did, but then found he could not see over the men before him to judge the shot.

"Lord Mayor! I am too puny! I cannot see over your men!"

Laughing, Karl called out to the front line. "Kneel and ground your shields! Willahelm the Puny needs to see over you."

Sharing the humor of their lord mayor, while the Saracen charge was underway, the line knelt as one and suddenly all was clear. And what a sight it must have been, for Joey saw three men dressed in modern military garb, and carrying rifles!

The Iranians!

Quickly drawing his bow and kissing its string, Joey briefly paused to settle himself, and loosed the arrow. Without giving a second thought, the second arrow was away just before the first struck a horse full in the face, toppling it and its rider, much to the cheers of the Frankish front line.

The second arrow struck one of the Iranians square in the chest, and because the man wore no body armor, only the arrow's feathers could be seen as he had been pierced clean through. Another cheer erupted.

The third struck another horse, which clearly faltered at the blow. The fourth hit the second Iranian full in the face and the cheers reignited.

The fifth imbedded itself in the shield of 'Abdul Rahman Al Ghafiqi himself, striking the muscle of his forearm, causing extreme pain, which caused his shield to drop. That was a fatal mistake.

Joey's sixth buried itself in the crest of the Saracen governor's armored chest, causing him to sag like a rag doll, supported only by his saddle's racking. And at that, the roar of the Franks had become deafening.

At this, the last remaining Iranian went berserk,

after witnessing the slaying of both his men and the mortal wounding of 'Abdul Rahman Al Ghafiqi. Flicking his rifle to full automatic, the Iranian goaded his horse into a full charge at the Frankish formation and literally began to carve out a space in its front line for his horse to pass directly toward Karl.

As soon as Joey heard the automatic rifle fire, he flung himself at the Lord Mayor, tackling him to the ground, as three of his surrounding body guards were being felled by twenty-first century technology. In so doing, Joey felt the searing sting of a bullet graze along his upper left thigh. Ignoring it, he rolled over to one knee. And while shielding the Lord Mayor's person with his own, he loosed his seventh arrow squarely into the chest of the bloodthirsty Iranian, who fell from his horse into the middle of the square.

Going to him, Joey grabbed the dying man by his shoulders and looked deeply into his eyes.

Speaking to him in Egyptian Arabic, he said, "Look into my eyes evil one. You know me. You spoke to me in Cairo."

The expiring, fluttering eyes of the Iranian widened with recognition and disbelief.

"Yes, it is I, and I am an American. It was my emails that you hacked. I am Joseph Richards. Remember this, as you slowly burn in hell's fires. Remember also, that you failed. Miserably."

Then Joey slit the man's throat from ear to ear.

*   *   *

With their governor dead, the charge lost its energy, failed, and soon evaporated like an early morning mist over a still pond. Still, the reports of my gun fire could be heard, and heard advancing. Realizing what this meant, Joey whirled to Karl, who had regained his feet.

"Lord Mayor! We must advance, as the raiding party is trying to reach us!"

Accepting this assessment of the situation, the formation rose and began to advance in good order, ruthlessly dispatching here and there the occasional Saracen. Along the way, Joey retrieved all the Iranian weapons and their ammo. Upon seeing him, he looked more like a clanking surplus weapons' armory than an archer.

* * *

With the Saracen camp gutted and with Alberic leading fifteen men and fourteen horses straining beneath their golden burdens, the hopelessly fragmented Saracen coalition beat a hasty retreat from the battlefield and eventually France itself.

Upon linking up with the main infantry formation, I was quite a sight to behold as I presented myself to my husband. The two of us, dropping our weapons load, ran to each other. I leaped into his strong arms as he lifted me high from the ground. Joey whispered in my ear, somehow ignoring all the dirt, sweat, blood and gore in my hair.

"I am most pleased, my wife, that you have survived."

"As am I for you, my most brave archer," I whispered back.

* * *

On the short march back to Tours, long after the fallen enemy had been plundered, the many bone fires had set afire, the abandoned Saracen camp picked over, and the wounded carried away, Joey asked Karl if he knew of a good blacksmith. To this Karl chuckled, and indicated that there were several. My Joey asked which one the Lord Mayor preferred. Having received a reply, Joey then suggested to Karl that the Saracen saddles should be gathered up as well.

"Why?" The Mayor of the Palace asked.

"Because," Joey hinted, "the next time the Saracens come, you, Lord Mayor, will want to field your own cavalry against them."

*   *   *

To say that the next three days of celebration and feasting were epic seems, well, somewhat redundant. One tenth of the plunder from the Saracen camp now filled the coffers of St. Martin's treasury in pious thanksgiving for the good saint's intervention – albeit acknowledged after the fact.

A portion of what was left went to Karl's veterans as did a portion to the local archbishop, who initially had funded the standing army. The Mayor of the Palace had mended his fences, proving that even during the Early Middle Ages money does make the world go round.

During all the merriment and carousing, I learned in surprising detail from Joey of just what had taken place, and when, on the battlefield that day. How Karl and he worried that the raid would not turn the tide. In the process, I was afforded a front row seat on how myth and legend were created. I heard of how Joey's field of pots tactic had worked so masterfully at slowing the Saracen cavalry charge. I listened with great interest as how the Frankish square had withstood so many determined assaults, mostly provided by the near superhuman deeds of the heroic dead, which were related in extraordinarily reverent and gruesome detail.

What really stood out for me were all the Frankish warriors, who tried so mightily to narrate Joey's archery shots, all the while taking much delight in the flight of a particular arrow, not to mention the effect of each and every one upon the enemy. But perhaps the best was of Joey's own self-deprecating humor, the command given by their beloved Lord Mayor to kneel so that Willahelm "the Puny" could see over their shields.

Then Joey was regaled with stories and already embellished tales of my fearsome leadership, cunning, and above all, bloodthirsty ruthlessness. It was Alberic himself, with considerable respect, who had so generously sprinkled his version of the facts with "Veer the Bloody." Something that today I am not proud of, but given the situation and environment, was most necessary.

But elsewhere in Tours, a blacksmith was hard at work. Seven promised gold pieces helped mightily with his motivation during such a celebratory time as this, as he stoked his fire to the highest temperature possible, all to melt six rifles and seven side arms into one, molten state. The blacksmith, a true craftsman, possessed many useful molds and into one, he poured the molten river of fire. Several hours later, he had completed his sweaty labors, now seven gold pieces richer.

* * *

It was on the third day of these near marathon celebrations that we presented Karl with a battle trophy at a feast attended by his veterans. The trophy was a battle hammer, affixed to a stout oak handle wrapped in leather, complete with a heavy leather thong for the wrist.

"Karl, Lord Mayor of the Palace of Austrasia!" Joey bellowed, while standing atop a table in order to get the full attention of the rowdy audience.

"I, Willahelm the Puny, and my wife, Veer the Bloody, present you this battle trophy, this war hammer of Donar, forged from the captured thunder weapons. Henceforth, you, Karl, shall be known as Karl the Hammer!"

To this, a deafening explosion of boisterous cheers erupted, partly because of Joey's bravado had again made fun of himself, and partly because the Germanic veterans fully appreciated the pagan reference to Donar and what it symbolized – the Romanized Hercules and Nordic Thor. And before they were finished toasting and boasting to their victorious mayor, we had begun our journey back to a certain baptistery in Poitiers.

* * *

While our retrieval went without a hitch, our appearance and smell were duly noted by Callahan's men, and one, the newbie Blackfeather, actually voiced what everyone else was thinking.

"Those two smell damn rank!" But after a hot shower and a good delousing, just to make sure, we were judged fit for transport back to the States for the usual post-drop debrief at Horizon Pass. After a detailed personal account of the deployment delivered directly to Naysmithe, Callahan, and Cartwright, we got a physical examination by Doc Allen.

Joey, excepting a mildly infected thigh from a bullet graze, various lice and insect bites, and a bunch of beautiful bruises, passed with flying colors. His post-drop syndrome, however, remained very vexing and worrisome, as I estimated in my written report that this latest blackout lasted some two to three minutes.

As for me, besides some bruising, I was physically fit and ready to go. During Joey's report, I had received only glowing praise for my ingenuity and combat leadership. But, as for my wellbeing and demeanor, Doc Allen noted that I was noticeably calmer, more "together," than he had ever seen me before. Gone was the chip on my shoulder, which was replaced with a calm that was markedly new.

When I was asked why I "was cool, calm, and collected," the physician Allen recorded that I just shrugged and said, "My dear Dr. Allen, you know me so well. I am now at peace. I can live my life knowing that I have struck back at the monsters of my childhood, who had so brutally killed my parents during the First Chechen War. Doctor, you may not know this, but Iran greatly aided that Chechen uprising, much to my country's displeasure, and my personal pain. And so, with my actions during this last deployment, I had my revenge on those animals, and on my own terms. But to be perfectly honest with you, I now am disgusted with myself. I went too far. Yes, I survived. But I went too far. I, in essence, became one of them. And that, I am ashamed of."

These words Dr. Allen recorded and added to my medical file.

It seems that whatever demons used to bedevil her soul, they have been banished. What has replaced them is a far surer sense of self. Does she have regrets? Yes she does, plenty of them. What sane person wouldn't? But in the final analysis, this gal has been purged and the dark side has lost. Thank God for her, and for that matter, the rest of us as well.

CHAPTER XXV
Hell's Own Fire

The Iranian actions were so wrong and on so many levels. Yes, they had been thwarted, but for how long? Then the real question became, when would they try again? After all, in a matter of months, they could construct a new temporal device and deploy yet another temporal terrorism squad. Could Time survive two insertions? So how should they be dealt with? Something swift, decisive, and direct was required. That something would require deft creativity and zero second thoughts. But what sort of action? And perhaps even more importantly, by whom? This is when my eyes were opened to what a small group of motivated people could accomplish if they put their heads together.

*   *   *

The germ of an idea to address the Iranian temporal indiscretion, not to mention all the preliminaries, was formulated in the second subbasement of the Philology Annex. There, a gathering of select individuals discussed, to poorly paraphrase V.I. Lenin, "what must be done."

"Usually," Tuna Cartwright began without preamble, "Dr. Young is the fine gentleman who convenes such confabs as this one, but he has deferred that custom for today, for what will become clear in a few moments. So," as Cartwright rubbed his hands together, "what do we know, people? Let's get it all on the table."

Buddy McGuire, the head of the IT group at Horizon Pass, discovered that his hand had involuntarily shot into the air.

Acknowledging it, Cartwright encouraged. "Thank you, Mr. McGuire, for getting the ball rolling. What do you have for us?"

Nervous, Buddy looked down on his yellow legal notepad for security. "Actually, Commander Cartwright, I have several things. First off, our discovery of Iran's interest in us was purely accidental. As part of Marla von Epping's interview screening, we had her hack the email server of the NRI, the Niroo Research Institute in Tehran. Partly because it had already been the target of a well advertised hack by a Brit, partly as a pure prank, partly to test Marla under stress. But to our surprise, when we looked at Marla's take, we discovered a whole bunch of emails that specifically mentioned us. So in a sense, we have been under the microscope for an unknown period of time.

"Second, and I freely admit perhaps in response, the NRI initiated an extremely crude hack of this university's email server, specifically to copy all of Professor Richards' emails. This tells me that somehow, Richards was placed on the Iranian's radar as a person of interest. But regardless, they must have had a field day with all the emails' address lines, not to mention their content.

"Finally, and now I am talking specifically about the hack that was done to Horizon Pass. They broke in using a very elegant and sophisticated worm that was attached to several of our email addresses, addresses that they got from the Richards' email hack. Tracing back this hack did not led us to NRI, but to a dead end somewhere in Tehran. So I suspect that the Iranian Secret Service, SAVAMA, was involved in this second hack. Yes, it is also possible that the Iranian Cyber Police and Communications Regulatory Authority might have been in on it as well, but my chips will stay with SAVAMA."

"Thank you Mr. McGuire. Well said. Anyone else?"

Next, Callahan spoke up. "Well, recently we have been very busy out at the ranch. I would say that for the past several months, someone had been trying very hard to get an eyes-on look at our New Mexico facility. To date, our security measures have prevented that. We even captured one of them, who turned out to be a down on his luck veteran. He is now one of us. But because of that capture, we cracked the cell itself, sending two folks on their way to prison and deporting their handler, who was, believe it or not, a for real employee of the Iranian government in Washington, DC!

"Now for what is really hilarious. Wily Doc Allen secretly inserted a military RFID chip into the Iranian perp during a routine blood draw prior to his expulsion from this country! So, with that chip, we can now track the guy from fifty thousand feet. And if he is SAVAMA, which I totally buy, then we can figure out where he works. That means we have a target, people, either a SAVAMA location, or maybe even, SAVAMA central itself."

"Fine report Calli," Cartwright said with some pride. Rubbing his hands again together, he added, "Now, anyone else?"

Joey raised his hand. "Well commander, it is very possible that we have a face to go with all of this. As you already know, I was interviewed in Cairo by a shady imam with a Farsi accent. As a favor to our friends in the Egyptian Antiquities Service, I agreed to pose as an antiquities guard, as all of the guards that we have been associated with in the field were being interviewed by this creep. And it was a good thing that I did. He wanted to know about all the odd things going on at the Karnak Temple. While I cannot prove it, it's even money that he was the one behind the kidnapping of Sharil Moussa's father and probably was responsible for that risky sodium pentothal interrogation. And, this is, by the way, the same dude that I killed in France. While we burned and melted down all evidence of their passing, the people that he worked for must pay."

"Anyone else want to get something off of their chest?" Cartwright prodded.

Then I spoke. "As the newest member of this group, I believe that I must speak for Major General Piankoff. What would he do? I suspect he would call for the physical destruction of the NRI and SAVAMA facilities to ensure the obliteration of their computers. They must not be allowed to construct another temporal device. So, something swift and total, something memorable, something permanent. My Sasha would want this, as I do."

"Anyone else have something to say?"

Now it was Dr. Naysmithe's turn. Sitting with his arms folded across his chest, he quietly stated, "I want to hurt SAVAMA. I as am convinced that they are behind all of this: the interviews, the hacks, the abduction of Dr. Moussa, the build of their temporal device, even the deployment of a temporal team. And, I agree with Vesna. We have to turn both the Niroo and SAVAMA facilities into craters."

Only one had remained silent to this point, the aging physicist, Ernst Jung. Gray haired and slightly stooped in posture, complete with his tweed jacket and leather elbow patches. So Cartwright prompted, "Do you have anything to say, Professor?"

"Thank you Commander. Yes, I do indeed. I think that we should respond to SAVAMA and the NRI in several ways. Some we can do. Others, I'm afraid to say, will require some outside help. So, kindly consider the following suggestions. And by the way, Ms. Gregorieva, I do like your straight-forward and aggressive suggestion.

Bless you professor!

"First of all, both of these institutions can be seriously hurt by a well planned cyber attack. We ourselves possess people who can execute such wanton destruction.

"Second, any and all damaging information that we glean from the cyber attack, we publish on the Internet. While Iran tries mightily to control all access to it through their various governmental agencies, their population remains ever creative in circumventing these controls. So, we broadcast what we find. And who knows, we might spark a revolution. But allow me to be clear, I am not speaking of the dissemination of misinformation, I refer only to the truth.

"Now Iran does not play by the rules. They do not think like we do. Consequently, they are not as constrained operationally as we are. Their leadership would think nothing of sacrificing ten million of their own people in a nuclear exchange with Israel, if it meant the annihilation of that Jewish state. So, let us not play by the rules. That they will not expect. Let us generate a psy-op against SAVAMA and the NRI. And let's squarely attack their government's leadership ideology.

"However, I am sad to say, attacking their curious form of Islamic ideology will not be sufficient. We need to attack the means as well. And what I have in mind is not the generation of a national financial crisis, but a ransacking of the SAVAMA and NRI budgets. And then, we must reinvest those same monies in ways that will discredit the SAVAMA, NRI, and government leadership in the eyes of the Iranian population at large.

"But most importantly, we must remove all physical trace of the temporal technology from their research laboratories and computers. And there is only one way to accomplish this. We must somehow, someway, destroy the NRI and SAVAMA facilities.

Sitting back in his chair, Cartwright announced, "Well. It seems that we all have some homework to do. Let's meet here again in two days, at the same time, for some serious planning. Now don't disappoint me. Dismissed."

*　*　*

Two days later, we gathered again at the Philology Annex. As I looked about the subbasement's conference room, I could not help but note that our number had grown, significantly. Buddy McGuire had brought along his entire IT team from Horizon Pass. Lieutenant Callahan now had two sergeants by his side. Young, Joey, Jung and I filled out the rest. All wore determined looks that needed a plan that could be executed as soon as feasible.

Cartwright, again called the meeting to order. "Alright everyone, here's how I see it. We need a phased approach to this operation and what I suggest for a start is the following. Phase I is the cyber stuff. Phase II we cash out their bank accounts and make some outlandish donations. Phase III is the dissemination of whatever dirt we can find. And Phase IV is an aerial assault on their facilities."

Pause.

"As you can imagine, all of these phases are extremely interdependent. Therefore, we must now establish priorities and their timing, so that the execution of these phases will yield the most damage possible.

Pause.

"To make things easier, may I suggest that we divide up into teams of common interest? The cyber team is you Mr. McGuire and your folks. Psy-ops are Jung, Richards, and Gregorieva. Dr. Young will led the financial team, and I will head up the aerial strike team.

"So cyber team, what are your priorities?"

So it began – a roomful of grim, creative vengeance. Curiously, I found myself smiling and remembering back to when Rosovec spoke of his envy of American free-wheeling inventiveness. If only he could see us now.

* * *

While the execution of an act is important, its timing could mean either total devastation or a clean miss. Joey compared it a boxer, who was two beats out of rhythm. He's lost the match before it began. So in deference to the god of timing, Phase One, the cyber phase, began on an early Friday evening during the fourth call to prayer, the *azan*, just as the sun set over Tehran. Observing the cyber team on any other occasion might have been compared to watching paint dry, but not today. The three of them, huddled before their screens, now had a fourth member, Mr. X, a Farsi language specialist, who Professor Jung had thought might be handy.

It's truly difficult to describe the sheer electricity and excitement that was in the air. The NRI's email servers were the first to be penetrated, their contents copied, and then the whole trashed with a 256-bit encryption. Simultaneous to that act, access was made into the general network via a sloppy access point, where the central storage areas were found, copied, and encrypted as well. These two hacks took only several minutes, but the copying process took a tense thirty-four to complete the download. When finished, the entire network was encrypted, rendering it useless yet highly infective to any device that would subsequently connect to it.

With NRI so assaulted, copied, and fried, now was the time to do the same to the three email addresses which had hacked Horizon Pass. All led to a single IP address. This we assumed was SAVAMA. With a deft hand, the IT staff defeated its way through a series of virtual private networks. Now "inside", the team found a network made up of fourteen databases. These were copied, although three of them took a full fifty-four minutes. And as with the NRI network, this one was trashed as well with that highly infective encryption worm.

In a little over two hours, and much to the utter amazement of their audience, the cyber team had downloaded close to two terabytes of data. Grinning, fist-pumps were everywhere. McGuire, immensely proud of his people, quipped that the data had seemed to sizzle through the cables. But data, being data, is useless unless you know what you're looking at. Now, it was Professor Jung's late addition, Mr. X, the Farsi expert, who got down to work.

*   *   *

The next day Phase Two was scheduled to commence, and as with Phase One, it did so again at sunset, during the *azan*. This phase was Dr. Young's baby, assisted by the cyber team. An Oxford-trained economist, his brazen plan was to gain access to Iran's financial center, steal some money, and then deposit those funds in places embarrassing to the Iranian regime.

Using something called a "back door," the cyber team, using dormant SWIFT bank access points, courtesy of UN sanctions, broke into the Central Bank of Iran, the bank vault of the Iranian government. With again the help of the Farsi expert, Mr. X, several governmental accounts were identified as "suspicious", and so their funds were transferred into ten separate Swiss bank accounts, which Young had established for the purpose. In all, more than ninety-five million U.S. dollars moved in the blink of an eye.

I must say here and now that I have never before seen Young smile so much. He was truly having fun and should find the time and place to smile more often.

Now with the cash, it was time to reinvest, as Young put it, "all of his ill-gotten gains," as grants and donations to a raft of embarrassing causes and organizations. But not just now. Instead, Young carefully scheduled the transfer notices from the Swiss accounts containing the funds to the far more unsavory ones to coincide with timed, future events, so that they would catch the maximum media attention.

After about an hour and a half of this meticulously orchestrated financial mayhem, Young, positively giddy, stood up, stretched, and announced to us all.

"Damn that felt good! And the best part of it all, is that I have finally put to good use my Oxford studies in economics!"

*   *   *

A full two weeks after the aforementioned financial mischief was perpetrated, Phase Three was executed. During that hiatus, the Farsi files from NRI and SAVAMA had been sorted through and earmarked as worthy or not of world-wide publication.

It all began so innocently, even though Young's continued exuberant glee was beginning to wear on the nerves. Press releases were sent to *Al-Jazeera*, *The Times*, *The International Herald Tribune*, *The New York Times*, and *The Wall Street Journal*, that outlined Young's well-placed "surprise endowments." As one might expect the editorials that then appeared were as volatile as the releases themselves and ranged from "sheer blasphemy and a total betrayal of Quranic teachings" to "adroit portfolio management in the steamier and seamier sectors." The region's local and cable networks also aired the "dirty laundry," while their commentators, from a Sunni imam of the Saudi Kingdom to western economic ministers, alternately damned or wryly smirked at the news of the massive Iranian investments in corporate gambling, alcohol, pornography, and swine production.

Once the financial news had leaked its way to Main Street, Tehran, it was now our turn, the psy-ops team, to go to work. Our theme had to be shaped purely in black and white Islamic terms, specifically tailored to Iranian Shi'a sensibilities. So we began trickling out documents that graphically depicted the greed, hypocrisy, and obscenely venial nature of SAVAMA. Internal memos, surveillance reports, and secret directives were the coin that outlined the ongoing and rampant disregard of the Iranian citizenry. In actual fact, we had found so much within the SAVAMA files that we were challenged at how to categorize it all, much less release it.

The key to our success was timing and presenting both the heinous and the disgusting, which so fed the building storm of demographic frenzy. In the end, it would be the long legacy of domestic abuses that would call down upon the Iranian revolutionary regime, not only the wrath of its people, but also that of several United Nations' agencies. No one could deny the authenticity of the published documents, for to do so was to dig their graves even deeper. It was as if a media whirlwind had fallen upon the Iranian capital city. And with such external exposure came intense internal scrutiny.

*   *   *

Phase Four was without any doubt the most difficult to execute. At the very heart of the plan was that very special Gulf Stream V, which Horizon Pass "owned." Since planes do not fly themselves, or at least not yet, human assets, very highly trained ones, were found and recruited. And then there were all those "special arrangements" that had to be made for landing and takeoff clearances in distant lands, remote fuel purchases, and of course, the specialized munitions. All of this took planning, contacts, and money — bribe money, lots of it.

As Cartwright explained the flight plan to us before a digitally scrolling map on a massive flat screen, I was numbed. What he was asking the two flight crews to endure was nearly inhuman. But when I rather pointedly commented on this issue, I was told in no uncertain terms that these men were highly trained and that such endurance flights were common. That observation out of the way, the commander continued with his brief.

"The flight plan is as follows.

Outbound, Segment 1: Holloman AFB via Chicago and Gander, Newfoundland. Refueling at Gander. Gander to Lajes, Azores. Refueling at Lajes. Segment length: forty-four hundred miles.

"Outbound, Segment 2: Lajes to Larnaca, Cyprus. Refueling at Larnaca. Segment length: thirty-three hundred miles.

"Outbound, Segment 3: Larnaca to turn in point at Baku, Azerbaijan. Baku to wet launch point southeast of Ramsar, Iran. Segment length: thirteen hundred miles."

At this point, I just had to know what a "wet launch point" was.

"Over the Caspian Sea, Ms. Gregorieva," Cartwright answered tersely.

So chastened, I nodded and he continued.

"Total for all Outbound Segments: eighty-four hundred plus air miles. The return, or Inbound Flight Plan, will ideally mimic the Outbound, although two diversions have been planned."

"Are there any *more* questions?"

Blessedly, Professor Jung did have one. "Commander Cartwright, what is the payload?"

A bit surprised by the directness of the question, Cartwright thought for a moment, and then answered.

"Four U.S. Navy AGM-84K "SLAM-ER" cruise missiles. They are a medium range, air-launched, standoff, land attack missile. You fire and forget them as they are GPS guided initially, and then infrared and radar in the final stage."

"Very good commander. But how did you get your hands on four of these weapons?" Jung queried.

"Sir, you really do not want to know," was his answer.

Next Dr. Naysmithe asked, "Commander, what about our targeting? While I know that we have a set of hard coordinates on the NRI facility, what about the SAVAMA location?"

Cartwright smiled for the first time. "Thank you for that particular question. As it turns out, that RFID chip that Doc Allen planted on Jahan Manu Rabiei has been tracked by one of our global positioning satellites. So far we have established the man's movements over the past two weeks and ultimately his place of employment. We currently believe it to be SAVAMA's headquarters, and other sources, just let us say, have confirmed that assessment."

*　*　*

Throughout the entire execution of Phase Four, Cartwright, Jung, Callahan, Young, Joey and I were glued to four massive flat screens that McGuire and his team had set up in the second subbasement's conference room. Due to national and internal security, however, none of the cyber team could witness this phase, as we were linked real-time to the Gulf Stream V's telemetry via several USAF satellites.

Cots had been set up for those who wished to lay down during the long ocean over flights, but no one used them. We just milled around, watching, praying, and watching some more. This was reality TV on steroids. The coffee provided was military strength as well.

Once the plane refueled in the Azores, it began a delicate dance through the Mediterranean's airspace. Cartwright's succinct dialogue explained what the pilots were doing and why, and what they were evading and why. It all hit us like triple shots of espresso.

When the Gulf Stream went "feet dry," along the southeastern coastline of Turkey, the second and third flat screens went live as they depicted the flight path over a detailed topographical overlay.

"Notice folks," Cartwright chimed in, "that the flight plan calls for routes that avoid airbases, airports, and heavily populated areas. In other words, places with radar."

Then things got exciting as the waypoint near Baku was reached. In actual fact, I heard an audible intake of collective breath as the Gulf Stream banked southeast toward the Caspian Sea. Once "feet wet" again, over the Caspian Sea, the flight crew began its bombing run.

I cannot tell you how tense I was. My eyes hurt from the intense strain of watching the screens, looking at and seeing details, many of which my brain could not comprehend. And then there was that crushing sense of responsibility that we had sent four men on this journey.

That was when I realized, for the first time in my life, that I could never be a commander like Cartwright. While I could freely choose to place myself in harm's way, I could not do so for another. This revelation shocked me, for until that moment, I thought that I could do virtually anything. I was wrong. Then Cartwright's voice broke in.

"Okay folks, here we go. At a point twenty-three nautical miles from the Iranian coastline, the plane's launch doors will open and four cruise missiles will sequentially deploy from the rotary launcher. Once clear of the plane's slipstream, each missile's engine will ignite and their scissor-like wings will deploy. When they go live, the fourth flat screen will come on with four black and white in-screen images, which will be from the missiles' own cameras."

Then, we waited.

And waited.

Then, suddenly, the fourth flat screen came alive sequentially with four images. I was totally transfixed as I watched a constellation of lights that represented the Iranian shoreline. Coastal settlements blurred by to be followed by those of inland villages. It wasn't very long before the vegetation of the coast disappeared as the missiles made their way inland across the rocky crags of higher elevations. Then, just as quickly, the missiles crested and dipped down the rocky backside of that mountainous chain. I almost became nauseous, as the camera views jumped and juked about, just like a certain roller coaster helicopter ride, or better, a bad video.

The launch-to-target clock in the lower right portion of each of the camera views counted down. They were getting closer and closer to their targets.

At first, I thought someone was firing tracers up at the missiles, but then I realized that those illuminated streaks were just the lights of settlements, the northern-most suburbs of Tehran, which were being rapidly over flown.

"Okay people, the onboard computers on the missiles are now initiating the pop-up, or porpoise climb to one thousand feet."

Then at seven seconds, the views changed to a mixture of onboard radar and thermal images, which depicted the two targets from directly above. Almost comically, missile two of the upper right screen seemed fixated on a massive cooling vent on the roof of its target. And then it flew directly into it! Unconsciously, we took in a deep breath at the shocking maneuver. As the four in-screen images went sequentially blank, we all blinked in surprise. All the suspense was over.

It was only then that I noticed on screens two and three that the Gulf Stream V was already halfway across Turkish airspace on its return leg. By the way the cursor was moving across the screen, I could tell that the pilots were really pushing their engines hard.

Once the flight had gone again "feet wet," Cartwright stated for the record, "Ladies and gentlemen. You all have just witnessed history in the making. I don't know about you, but I could really use a cold beer right about now."

Then he got up from his chair, stretched, audibly cracking several vertebra, and then rolled the tension out of his neck. "Callahan," he said, "do me a favor and watch those screens carefully. If anything bad happens, you can find me in the Head puking my guts out."

"Yes sir. I've got your back."

Jung just sat there staring wearily at screens two and three, his chin in hand, wishing the retreating aircraft to go faster and faster, to get home quicker and quicker.

Young, with a dark set of rings around his eyes, looked exhausted, but triumphant.

As for myself, during the tension of the missile assault, I had latched onto Joey's right bicep and had not let go. Finally peeling my fingers off, clear red blotches appeared where they had been.

"Time to crash, Vesna." Joey quietly said as he took my hand and we stood up to leave.

CHAPTER XXVI
Early Cracks

It is still not clear to me just when Marvin J. Cruthers, U.S. Federal Senator, and Democrat from the Sunshine State of Florida, first got it into his head to raid this nation's black budgets. Nonetheless, this deep sea fisherman did indeed do precisely that, and with remarkable impunity. What is also important to remember is that Marvin Cruthers knew his audience, the length of their collective memories, and how to best please them. Consequently, Cruthers would do absolutely anything, and stop at nothing, to either line his pockets or provide his constituency with a new road project here or a public library there. As I look across the political canvass that is Washington, DC, I sadly must say that Cruthers and his ilk represent the vast majority of the ruling five hundred and thirty-six.

In the final analysis, I believe that it was the raid on Tehran that really had exposed Horizon Pass, for just too many balls had been put in the air, too quickly, for all of them to be caught, allowing the entire operation to be swept under the carpet.

In fact, I remember well Cartwright's own words, as he wondered aloud just when would the USAF finally "come a' knocking" with their "bill" in hand. After all, there was Horizon Pass' long history with the use of their satellites and fancy translation software, which had so facilitated the sensitive discussions between the two panels of the American and Russian Academy of Sciences. Perhaps it was the USAF's realization that we had begun encrypting those once profitable discussions, the text of which they could no longer "sell" to their intelligence agency colleagues. But regarding the Tehran raid, just where did Cartwright get those cruise missiles anyway?

And while I am talking about the USAF, I would like to point out that it really didn't matter that the SNOWMAN was in their hands, as was its Light Language recorder, at Wright-Patterson AFB. It really didn't matter that the genetic material from the Aten space craft, the location of which we provided to them, was still being analyzed in their research laboratories, or for that matter the dramatic digital photographic record of the craft. It really didn't matter that they were still in possession of the Kamil Crater's escape pod, again an alien artifact we had provided them. Besides, all of those artifacts were so darkly black, and deeply secret, that I seriously doubt that the Secretary of Defense herself has been briefed in on any one of them.

Now inject Cruthers into this bubbling witch's brew. He specifically ordered his staffers to look for small black budget items that he could more easily rape and plunder. Oddly, I'm told, his staff's first break regarding us came from a U.S.N. source, a petty officer third class, who helped manage the weapons inventory at the Jacksonville Naval Air Station, as in Jacksonville, Florida, Cruthers home turf.

Again, using all the skills and ploys that I had learned at the Directorate, I managed to track down this disgruntled seaman. It seemed that his initial contact with Cruthers' staff had occurred at a church barbecue, of all things, where the dear senator spoke to the gathered congregation, preaching the word of governmental waste and corruption. While Cruthers himself was very careful not to step on any military personnel, who were clearly in evidence in the congregation, he did nonetheless point to his two issues, and encouraged anyone present to come forward and help him clean up Washington's excesses.

Cruthers had already left the event and so was not present, when Petty Officer Third Class Jerome Burns indeed heard the calling, but his chief of staff, Johnny Wright, was. Apparently, what Burns told Wright was pretty interesting stuff. But the cagey chief of staff initially demurred, saying, in essence, that he needed hard evidence of what the petty officer third class was claiming. That is, if his senator was to step forward, something tangible was required. Sadly, here is where Burns really placed his professional career in jeopardy, for he provided that senatorial staff member with several damning photocopies that described the transfer of three U.S. Navy AGM-84K "SLAM-ER" cruise missiles to Holloman Air Force Base, in Alamogordo, New Mexico.

*   *   *

What happened next when the chief of staff told his senator about the missile transfer is anyone's guess. But what happened subsequently was clear enough. Given that the military love their paperwork in order to track their toys, a naked budget code appeared on the photocopied transfer notice. That code then led from this to that, and from that to this. Eventually, but only after many hours of research, the code was found as a line item on a black appropriations bill, only one of many, which the USAF managed.

Now so armed with a "magic" number, the real

digging began, because after all, what did that number represent? As I reconstructed the paper trail that Cruthers' staff followed it went like this: U.S. Department of Defense → Department of the Air Force → Air Force Intelligence, → Surveillance and Reconnaissance Agency (AFISRA). One of the units of the AFISRA is the 432nd Wing stationed at Creech Air Force Base, Nevada. There the budget trail ended, as Creech operated unmanned reconnaissance aircraft, some of which provide precision attack capabilities against fixed and time-critical targets. So, the transfer of three Navy cruise missiles to a well known testing facility was not such a stretch of the imagination.

Consequently, the senatorial chief of staff no doubt concluded that Petty Officer Third Class Jerome Burns was a seaman of that lowly rank for a good reason, and wrote off the entire investigation for what it appeared to be – a dead end.

But not so fast, for the budget number that Burns had provided, a valid and correct budget number, Cruthers staffers had not transcribed correctly. Someone, somehow, had left out two digits. This blunder was not discovered for several weeks, and so while one investigation was going on in one direction, another began heading off in another, all without the chief of staff's knowledge. Why? Because even among his junior staffers, it was a back-stabbing shark tank of East Coast Ivy Leaguers looking for any way to get ahead. Strangely, I understood this East Coast Ivy League culture and its motivation, for as a junior "watcher" of the Directorate, the very same sort of competition existed among our own people who wished early advancement.

Now, at least for me, things got most interesting. A junior staffer by the name of Claire Hagen had possession of the correct budget number and she knew it. And unlike her colleagues, her investigation led her to the Department of Energy, and in particular, the Office of Science, and not the USAF.

She knew that she was on to something, because when I had "interviewed" her, she stated for the record, "For Christ's sake! Why does the DOE want some cruise missiles?"

Hagen was right as the Office of Science is made up of ten laboratories, all devoted to some aspect of high energy physics. Then, ever the industrious one, Hagen began looking into each and every one of these facilities, and for whatever reason, became enamored with the 1.65 billion dollar budget of the Oak Ridge National Laboratory. And there, lo' and behold, under the materials science category, she found an exact match for the budget number. Its description had even caught her eye: Horizon Pass, New Mexico.

Now with a place name, Hagen began again, methodically, and nowhere in New Mexico could she find a Horizon Pass. Perplexed, Hagen, remaining methodical, went back to the number itself and asked herself the question: "Did it have a budget history?" So she investigated all of the former budgets, at least the ones that were available online, of the Oak Ridge National Laboratory. What she discovered was that her number was present in all the budget reports from 2000 to the present. This told her that whatever Horizon Pass, New Mexico was, it was an established facility of some kind, and established assets have to leave trails.

*   *   *

But even before Claire Hagen had begun her prescient investigation, it became rather obvious to all of us in the inner circle at the Philology Annex that the U.S. government and especially the State Department, while secretly overjoyed at Tehran's discomfiture, and also were extremely curious as to who had the balls to execute an operation of that scope. Even the UN was schizophrenically rocking itself to death between bombastically lamenting and condemning the plethora of documented human rights violations on the one hand, versus clear evidence of an unbridled act of war against the sovereignty of the Islamic Republic of Iran on the other.

All the while the talking heads of the media were in full frenzy, spreading specious speculations at every opportunity. (I really do sometimes wonder about the level of American public's gullibility.) By so doing, their greatest wish was that someone would step forward, soapbox opera-like, and bare all. And ever true to form, many a quack did. Equally amazing, only a few thought that Tehran's chastisement was perpetrated by one entity. In fact, the much favored *communis opinio* of the 24/7 cable news networks' was that someone, most likely Israel, had performed the masterful hack and smear campaign, while again most likely, Israel had supplied the missiles. That was the sum total of the media's contribution, as they were already jockeying to arrange interviews with the luminaries of the next global warming conference in Dubai. Rumor had it that Bono was the biggest ticket.

CHAPTER XXVII
Institutional Security

Joey and I first got wind of the Damokles' Protocol one month after Tehran and during a mandatory gathering of the Philology Annex's membership, which I flew in to attend. Such required attendance, I quickly discovered, were grounds for several of the university's faculty to air their displeasure. Dr. Young, ever the economist, then asked the three individuals whether they wished to severe their ties with the Annex. One bobbing head full of self-importance and unbridled ego actually did. To which Young smiled, and stated openly to the remainder of the audience that "Professor So-and-So, of Whatever Who Cares Department, has just declared that he wishes to breach his contact." Taking out his cell phone, Young then spoke very briefly into it, mentioning Professor So-and-So's name. Finishing, he then looked up, smiled at the individual, and again stated to the gathering.

"Ladies and gentlemen. Professor So-and-So, as you have just heard, wishes no longer to be a member of this organization. As of today, his generous stipend has been revoked. As of this very minute, the hard drive of his computer, located in his office, is being removed and replaced with another, less populated one."

At this point Professor So-and-So began to sputter and shout out his objections, all of which, Young surprisingly allowed to air. When the full professor finally halted due to a much need intake of breath, Young interrupted.

"Sir, you are an adult, despite this recent rude display to the contrary. Now, if you wish to pursue a law suit of any kind, allow me to suggest that you kindly re-read your contract and please do begin with Section Eleven. If that does not get your attention, then re-read the substance of the Non-Disclosure Agreement, which you also have signed, and I might add on your own recognizance, and under no duress. That document possesses even more teeth, and, I might add, the very real possibility of a sequestered, high-security trial and considerable imprisonment if you open your mouth in public, which you certainly seemed quite able and willing to do.

"Now, have I made myself crystal clear on all of these points?"

Pause.

"Hearing and seeing no response, now kindly leave this facility forthwith." Young stated with his arm extended and pointing at the door.

Another pause followed, accompanied by a rustling of clothing, low muttering, and the very sullen departure of Professor So-and-So.

Now pointedly looking at the other two miscreants, Young smiled and asked.

"Are there any other takers? No? Then let us proceed."

At this point, I actually liked Dr. Young.

*   *   *

In all, after that minor dust up, there were twenty-six of us, including Joey and me, and of course, Dr. Young.

"Ladies and gentlemen," he again began, "today we have to confront a serious issue: this organization's institutional security. "Mr. Roberts, would you please be so kind to dim the lights and power up the flat screen monitor."

Sitting now before us all was Dr. Charlie Naysmithe, who was obviously waiting for us, as his pony-tailed head was down, revealing a surprising amount of gray amidst the blond.

"Good afternoon Dr. Naysmithe," Young prompted.

Suddenly looking up from his prepared notes, Naysmithe smiled, rallied, and returned the greeting.

Damn he looks beat!

"Well, hello out there and thank you for coming together on such short notice. I know that making this meeting was difficult for some of you, but I can guarantee that your time will not be wasted."

Now folding his hands before him and leaning forward comfortably on his elbows, Naysmithe took his famous 'story tellers' pose.

"Prior to Dr. Borov's death, he left in my lap two outstanding tasks. The first dealt with the errant Philadelphia Experiment of 1943, which we duly investigated, but wisely, in my mind, chose not to fully pursue."

That comment caused a low rumbling murmur throughout the conference room as the hard decision not to pursue, while almost unanimously voted for, remained a universally unpopular one. For once the academics had to make a tough choice and they hadn't liked it.

"Borov's second task that he had left me was the creation of an institutional protocol, which could be executed at a moment's notice, whenever the security of Horizon Pass as a facility, or one of our devices, or both, was placed at risk.

"Now, many of you are already probably thinking, where was this safeguard when the Iranians hacked our servers? I totally agree. Where was it?"

Sigh.

"Well, I am here to tell you today that the protocol is now in place. Consequently, the purpose of this teleconference is to share with each and every one of you just what it entails, and what your responsibilities are to it. I can guarantee each and every one of you that the implementation of this draconian protocol will not be easy, but it has to be done nonetheless. If in doubt, then consider this: our current reality depends upon it. Now, can any of you think of anything that trumps that?"

Extended pause as ears were pulled, noses scratched, and jaws were rubbed.

"I didn't think so. So here goes. It's called the Damokles' Protocol. For those of you who slept through your ancient history class, this security protocol is nick-named after an ancient Greek legend of a king, who had placed a fawning courtier named Damokles on his throne. Once so seated in such a place of power and luxury, the king directed that a sword be suspended above his throne by a single horse hair. The lesson learned: with power and privilege also comes danger and insecurity."

*   *   *

Forty-five minutes later, twenty-six wide-eyed, muttering, and mind-numbed individuals left the Philology Annex's second basement's conference room. Many of them yearned for the good old days, defined as the innocent pre-Internet days. Several of them actually blamed Al Gore for their predicament. Several others, far more informed on the history of technology, DARPA. Only a handful of us really knew why the protocol had been so swiftly put into place, to staunch any blow back from the Tehran adventure.

CHAPTER XXVIII
Hemorrhage

As I have flown in and out of Holloman AFB many times, I have made my fair share of acquaintances. Although the following narrative was the result of an intense interrogation session that involved ridiculous amounts of beer, I nonetheless believe every word of it. Especially, since the subject of my interrogation was none other than the base commander himself. Furthermore, the many and varied ruminations of Claire Hagen were similarly procured, but her drink of choice had been John Barleycorn. Raybob Smith also made his memorable contributions, especially during a ride I gave him from Santa Fe. So, after putting two and two together from all of these sources, and of course knowing what I do and how I do it, I'm fairly confident that the following reconstruction is pretty close to the truth.

*　　*　　*

Just as Cartwright had warned us all, the USAF did indeed have a bill that it wanted paid, and paid in full. As to what that amount precisely was remained unclear. But given the recently televised events in Tehran, the base commander at Holloman AFB wasn't about to take any chances with his own personnel jacket.

As was so often said, "the shit really hits the fan" whenever a base commander "greets" your still taxiing Gulf Stream V with four MP Hummers at your hanger. From there, the four pilots, exhausted and spent from their Tehran adventure, were "escorted" to his hooch, or command headquarters. For good measure, the airframe was impounded.

Once in his august presence, the four pilots flatly refused to comment on either their unfiled flight plan or any of their activities during the last thirty-four hour period. Now as one can readily imagine, this royally pissed off the commander as he considered his base his kingdom, and nobody, absolutely nobody, dared to deny him what he wanted to know. But the commander was in a real bind.

The USAF did not own the Gulf Stream V in question. Therefore, he legally could not impound it. Although, through a dummy corporation, Horizon Pass did lease its hanger and support facilities from the USAF. Add to that, the four pilots had not gone AWOL, as all of them were on approved leave. So, the commander, still quite vexed, decided to "entertain" the pilots for the next twelve hours, after which he released them to their quarters. As for the Gulf Stream, he ordered four of his best crew chiefs to "inspect" the plane for any safety infractions so that he could ground it permanently. So armed with a long check list, they began their "safety" inspection. Instead, the four chiefs fell in love with the plane and all of its innovative features. Clearly, to them, it was a black ops aircraft and nothing more. And yes, the plane was given a clean bill of health, which released it from impound much to the base commander's displeasure.

*   *   *

About two months later, I was quietly told by Dr. Naysmithe that Holloman AFB had received an official visitor. This was confirmed by the base commander, several of his men, two onsite Horizon Pass employees, and my dear friend Raybob Smith. What happened next was unbelievable.

The visitor threatened to tear new bodily orifices if she did not receive full cooperation. Specifically, a certain Ms. Claire Hagen, special investigator to Senator Marvin J. Cruthers, had arrived bearing a document that stipulated:

> Kindly extend to my representative any and all courtesies forthwith, as Ms. Hagen is my specially appointed representative regarding these matters, which are under Federal investigation.

Standing before the base commander, this plucky five foot something, wearing a gray pin-striped pants suit with a tight and neat pony tail, pulled from her file folder several photocopied transfer documents for naval munitions. Handing them over, she said, "Commander, I respectfully request to examine your base's inventory files to see whether these munitions, in fact, were delivered to your base."

Completely surprised that someone had the brass to order three air-to-ground cruise missiles, and naval ones at that, was indeed disturbing.

So the red faced base commander replied, "By all means, Ms. Hagen. I'll call up Tech Sergeant Green right this minute. He would know the status of this transfer, as he is part of our munitions inventory team. Also consider him your base tour guide as well."

An hour later, and duly surprised by the efficiency of Tech Sergeant Green, Hagen had her USAF delivery document in hand. Indeed the base had taken delivery of three naval cruise missiles. The circle was now complete, but more than that was the hand written note at the bottom of the document, which referred to another receiver number. Curious, Tech Sergeant Green pulled out that document as well, and lo' and behold, this receiver listed the delivery of yet another cruise missile, of precisely the same type, which had originated from the Naval munitions depot in Norfolk, Virginia.

Hagen, stared with total astonishment. A total of four cruise missiles were ordered and delivered to this base! All within a two day period!

Then, carefully searching both documents for any budget numbers, she found them, and both were the same, identical, string of numbers.

Staring so hard that her eyes hurt, Hagen then innocently asked the helpful Green, "Sergeant, these numbers on the receivers are the same. What do they represent?"

"Oh, those are budgetary notations. Those numbers tell us who's paying for them."

"Okay…but is there any way to put a name to a budgetary notation?" She dared to ask.

"Oh sure. Let's go over to my terminal, and I'll pull up the Cardex right away."

As the moments crawled by while the computer terminal booted up and Sergeant Green performed his inquiry, Hagen was silently going out of her mind.

"Here it is Ms. Hagen. I found it. That account number belongs to Horizon Pass."

"Oh. And who is Horizon Pass?"

"I dunno, but they own a really sweet looking plane over in Hanger Five. In fact, they even lease that hanger from us."

"Can I see it? I mean, the plane that is?"

"No problem. The commander said that I was your tour guide. So let's go touring," he said with a good natured grin.

* * *

The two airframe mechanics, actually Air Force retired employees of Horizon Pass, could not believe their eyes when this goober of a tech sergeant, with a civilian in tow, dared to brazenly enter their world.

"Holy shit! What's Green doing here with that!" said one very startled Tony Flynn to his companion, Jeff Fielding.

"I don't know, but alert our friends, while I get rid of these bozos." said the tall Fielding.

Stopping Green and Hagen dead in their tracks and not twenty feet into the open hanger, Fielding put out his hand.

"Stop you two! Right there, and not one step further. This is a private hanger and is not Air Force property. You're trespassing!"

Hagen, while surprised, also noticed that the fit man with the blond crew cut coming toward them was wearing a side arm. So she stopped and announced with her best Washingtonian bluff.

"No, I'm not trespassing. I am a senatorial investigator from Washington, DC. And I have been granted full run of this Air Force Base."

Now standing right before the five foot something, Fielding could not help but grin ear-to-ear at her self-important moxie. "Well, isn't that just *precious.*

"Tech Sergeant Green! You should know better than to lead this young lady into a private section of this base. Get her out of here like yesterday!" he emphasized with an extended left arm and index finger, while his right hand had unconsciously drifted to his right holster.

Totally flustered, Green indeed led Hagen away, but not before the senatorial investigator had managed to surreptitiously take a video of the scene with her smart phone.

*   *   *

Hagen thanked the base commander for his time and cooperation, and in the process told him, in front of Green, what a wonderful help that he had been. And yes, she got all and more than she had ever expected to find. At no time did she mention the incident at the private hanger. That battle, she vowed, would be fought at another time.

So while she waited for her return flight the next day from Alamogordo to Washington, DC via Atlanta, she reviewed her video in the privacy of her hotel room and was pleased that it had captured two men and an oddly shaped commercial airplane.

Damn, that thing almost looks pregnant.

Gathering her thoughts, she concluded that Horizon Pass, New Mexico, was indeed a reality, but what kind of reality? After all, it was a very modest black budget item on the DOE's books that went back to at least 2000. It spent some money on four naval cruise missiles. It owned a private jet. It leased a hanger at Holloman, but not at Alamogordo's public airport. How odd. It has at least two employees, who maintained the jet and looked military, probably ex-military. Well, maybe, not so odd. But such employees needed a salary, a place to live, and food to eat. So the real question is: where is Horizon Pass? Or, is Horizon Pass the same as Holloman AFB? After all, they both begin with the letter "H".

Not liking that train of thought, Hagen began again.

Okay, Horizon Pass, New Mexico, is on the budget of the Oak Ridge National Laboratory. That facility works exclusively with high energy and nuclear research. Therefore, it is possible that Horizon Pass, New Mexico, is also a high energy and nuclear research facility. Clearly, there is nothing on Holloman AFB that is that, but White Sands does exist just to the west, and that surely does have a long history with high energy – the nuclear kind. I just wonder, if the mysterious Horizon Pass, New Mexico, is out there somewhere in the desert wilderness? But if that were so, then why would they buy four naval cruise missiles? Why would they have a jet? And a jet on a military base? Purely for security? I suppose that's possible.

Hagen, who needed white noise to think since college, had the television on. The cable news network, since it was a slow day, had decided to run the graphic videos of the now two-month-old Tehran missile raid. The announcer, describing the aerial carnage, mentioned two things that lodged in Hagen's subconscious: the NRI research center and four missiles.

Blinking rapidly as these two facts surfaced to the conscious side of her brain, she gasped and furiously wrote down her thoughts.

Is it possible that Horizon Pass, New Mexico, a high energy and nuclear facility, could have attacked an Iranian high energy research facility and one other building as well? Absolutely! It owns a jet and it bought four cruise missiles. So, was the missile strike on Tehran really about a U.S. attack on Iranian high energy and nuclear research, instead of some kind of an Israeli attack?

Is it even possible to privately mount such a strike?

At this point in Hagen's brain-storming, she innately realized that Horizon Pass, New Mexico, was not Holloman, but had to be a separate and very secret facility. And such facilities had employees that had to be paid.

So, Claire, let's find us a supplier, a warehouse, that could provide, on a regular basis, a secret facility out in the desert.

After only ten minutes of searching on her laptop, she found that Alamogordo had only one such warehousing and trucking concern with sufficient capacity to supply a facility of about, she guessed, fifty individuals. And being that it was a Thursday, and that she was flying out on Friday afternoon, Claire Hagen, special investigator for Senator Marvin J. Cruthers, decided to stake out this warehouse. After all, what did she have to lose?

*　　*　　*

Given that Hagen was an early riser for New Mexico, since she lived in Virginia's Eastern Time Zone, she rose the next morning in the dark. Not deterred, she got dressed, jumped into her rental car, and grabbed some take out from McDonalds. Now with her goodies on the passenger seat and two large coffees stowed in the console, she parked her car a half block away from the warehouse and began to eat. After a bit, she was surprised to see that the warehouse was going full tilt at this hour. A sixteen wheeler had jockeyed up to a cargo bay, and by the look of it, a fork lift was busy loading it up. Then a Chevy pickup arrived, parked, and its tall, lanky, and fit-looking driver jauntily mounted the sixteen wheeler's cab, and took out of it a clip board full of papers. He then disappeared into the warehouse. Noting that this warehouse was not gearing up for any other loads, Claire decided to follow this truck for a bit, just "for grins."

Ten minutes later, the truck now loaded and with its tall, lanky, and fit driver in place, the truck pulled out onto the road. Alamogordo, not being a big town, the warehouse fronted on Highway 52, which led in a southerly direction out of town and into the New Mexican desert. Being that it was still dark and that the town was still very much asleep, Hagen followed the truck's lights at a distance with hers off. Just as she was beginning to seriously question her sanity, the truck's brake lights lit up as the big rig slowed and turned off into the desert toward White Sands. Slowing her car and coming to a stop, she could barely make out the start of the desert trial. Looking around, she made a note of the nearby mile marker. It said "32".

"So that's where Horizon Pass, New Mexico, is!" she whispered with a tight fist in complete triumph.

* * *

One week later, on a Thursday afternoon, four C-130H Hercules troop transports, who identified themselves as a mechanized Marine platoon from Fort Bragg, North Carolina, requested permission to land at

Holloman AFB. Their presence represented a last minute, unscheduled surprise.

Upon landing, Lieutenant Joshua Sondheim and a civilian presented to the base commander their orders. While the commander didn't know this Marine lieutenant from Adam, he did recognize the civilian, that plucky, little, five foot something of a senatorial special investigator, named Hagen.

"Not to worry base commander, we're here to do some desert research. We should be gone by tomorrow afternoon. Do you mind if we bivouac on your base for the evening? We're all kinda' burned out from the direct flight from Bragg, and would like to get an early start in the morning."

* * *

Raybob Smith, per the usual, managed to arrive at the warehouse fifteen minutes before his usual TGIF drive into the desert. This weekend he had big plans to do some for-real door rubbing, road racing up at Sandia, but this morning his venerable and much-beloved Chevy pickup had almost refused to start in the cool morning air. After several pumps of the gas pedal, it had caught, but the bad start did not end there, for as soon as he had arrived in the warehouse parking lot, his world took a turn for the worse.

By his own count, eight mighty serious looking Hummers, packing heavy ordinance, were all parked in the back. Their presence blocked from anyone driving along Highway 52. Trying hard to be his usual jaunty and confident self, Raybob went to the sixteen wheeler's cab to grab the day's manifest, but was surprised to see that its passenger seat was filled with a no nonsense U.S. Marine, who was packing some really heavy shit. Frozen for a moment in mid-entry, the Marine just said.

"Go ahead. Take the clip board. They're waiting for you inside."

*   *   *

As Raybob pulled out the big rig from the parking lot, his mind was a whirl.

Holy Shit! This must be the big bust that Professor Naysmithe had been warning all of us about. I just have to get out the word before all those jarheads in the trailer cut loose on all of those fine folks. Remember: be patient Raybob. Just like the Professor said. You can do this. Just be patient.

And so as the trucker eased his rig onto Highway 52 South, he deftly triggered the ALERT button that had been hidden on his steering wheel. His passenger was none the wiser.

Once that was accomplished, Raybob settled down to what he knew was his final delivery to Horizon Pass, per the book, and with nothing out of the ordinary. After all, those had been the Professor's direct orders.

"Do not do anything heroic or stupid Raybob." The director of Horizon Pass had said. "Trust me when I say that I will take care of you, no matter what. Just remember: we are family and we'll cover your back, no matter what."

And so during the entire drive through the desert, Raybob, scanning to his right and left, tried to take it all in one last time and enjoy the moment. In the hazy dust cloud behind him, he could occasionally pick out the shadowing mechanized column of Hummers. And as he backed up his trailer to the camouflaged cargo dock, Raybob put the truck in park and shut it down. Then, he just sat there with his hands on the steering wheel.

Hearing the trailer opening and the Marines within scrambling out, he looked over to his baby sitter and said, "Okay, now what Marine?"

CHAPTER XXIX
Damokles

I was at Horizon Pass when Robert James "Buddy" McGuire, Horizon Pass' head of IT, Marla von Epping, a bright-eyed, fresh out of college analyst, and flat out security systems genius, and Ron Marston, the hardware guy, informed Dr. Charlie Naysmithe that Damokles was operational. That was back shortly after the Iranian hack and our response to it. They, as a team, had been tasked not only to reconstitute their entire system security, but also to incorporate it into the Damokles' Protocol. And what they came up with, implemented, and then deployed in less than one month's time made Naysmithe smile with genuine pride. Now, we all just hoped that Damokles remained that insurance policy that we would never have to execute. Unfortunately, today was that day.

*   *   *

I was told that back in the early sixties, when Horizon Pass was first conceived, Dr. Borov had insisted upon the addition of an escape route for the entire staff. The physicist reasoned that if his people were to live, work, and sleep underground, then they damn well should have a way to get out in the event of an emergency. In short, the facility needed a magical rabbit hole, much like the one in the *Alice in Wonderland*.

So, just such a provision was indeed built. Initially, it looked like a deep canal that had been bulldozed out of the wild desert, which went for about three quarters of a mile in a northeasterly direction. Next, an endless parade of trucks came with their concrete, preformed sections, each over twenty feet long with an eight by eight interior. These were carefully placed by crane, trued, and leveled in the bottom of the trench. At the exit of this tunnel were installed two sets of steel stairs that led to escape doors. Beneath these stairs were fully stocked weapons lockers, sealed bins of stenciled desert fatigues for each staffer, bush hats, and a cache of water bottles.

In all, it took almost two hundred of these interlocking sections, provided by the concrete outfit in the town of Truth or Consequences, to complete the escape tunnel. Once the necessary wiring had been put in place, the whole tunnel was then bulldozed in with the surrounding fill, smoothed, its entire course graded, and all trace of the dirt track that the hauling trucks had used, removed. It is said that Dr. Borov himself seeded that entire stretch with desert wild flower seeds. And looking at the area today, and having jogged through and over it many times with Joey, I believe it, for it is a lush riot of color in the spring and early summer.

John Jacobs and Dick Harwood were the reasons why the tunnel had been provided with electricity. Both men were retired carnival hands, who knew their roller coasters inside and out. Working closely with two of the facilities electricians, John and Dick first rigged up a continuous string of caged lighting fixtures, which were hung uniformly in the upper left corner of each concrete section's center. Once the lighting of the tunnel was completed, they got to work on laying God only knows how many concrete rail road ties. Legend has it that they wore out five forklift motors just maneuvering all of the ties into position. Then came the positioning of the three rails themselves, the endless adjustments to the ties, the checking and rechecking of their true, and only then, did they get their final bolt down and attachment to the electrical grid. What rode atop these rails was a low-slung fifteen car roller coaster that carried forty-five seats, including the operator. Traveling at a top speed of thirty-five miles an hour, Dr. Borov knew that he could evacuate his entire staff and the security detail quickly, and in just two trips. And I totally believe it, as Joey and I once were treated to a "thrill ride" conducted by old Dick Harwood himself. Dick was such a pleasant man, who was so very proud of his creation, and was even quicker in his praise of his late friend John.

As for the entrance air lock that provided access to this emergency tunnel, once all the staff had been evacuated from the Horizon Pass facility and the air lock sealed, an option was available to release, throughout that underground complex, an aerosol flood of an odorless, tasteless, nerve agent that was non-lethal. Producing extreme headaches, nausea, and mild muscle cramping, the idea was to discourage and incapacitate any assaulting force as humanely as possible – all to buy as much time as possible for the staff's escape.

*　　*　　*

A lot of thought had been put into local threat detection at Horizon Pass and both Joey and I were made aware of it early on during our runs in the desert. While it is very true that the immediate perimeter was walked on a daily basis by the facility's roving security force and was monitored by carefully calibrated infrared sensors, Tuna Cartwright had embedded into the facility's overhead bedrock peaks radar sensors of extreme sensitivity. Anything larger than a turkey vulture was noted, categorized, and recorded. This detection system granted the facility about eight minutes time in which to react. But for Tuna, this line of defense was not enough, for he believed in two things: redundancy and a layered defense. Consequently, focused radars were emplaced at the exit and interior of Strawberry Pass to the southeast, which was the usual corridor for any helicopter or supply traffic coming to the facility from the direction of Alamogordo and Holloman AFB. This second layer effectively bought Horizon Pass another five minutes.

* * *

The final level of threat detection came from the bi-weekly supply trucks themselves. Tuna, always a big war game fanatic, as Joey would be more than willing to attest, had figured that if he were to attack Horizon Pass, then why not commandeer one of the bi-weekly supply trucks, take over its cab, fill its trailer with troops, back up the semi-trailer to the facility's dock doors, and execute a classic Trojan horse attack. So, the question on the table was, how do you foil this clever approach?

The strategy that Tuna eventually adopted hinged upon the fact that only the truck driver knew how to get to Horizon Pass through the desert, a drive of about an hour and forty minutes. Thus, Tuna reasoned that the driver would be retained by the hostile force, but would be driving under duress. Somehow the driver, probably at gun point, had to be able to subtly trigger an alert and transmit it over the truck's radio, all without being caught. The solution that was finally adopted was the installation of a small black button on the backside rim of the steering wheel. Covered with a flip up cap to prevent its accidental activation, all that the driver had to do was flip it up with the edge of a free finger, press hard, and flip it back down. Job done.

* * *

What the Horizon Pass IT team of Bobby, Marla, and Ron contributed to the Damokles' Protocol was an automated system security shutdown that itself had to be manually triggered. If in fact the threat to Horizon Pass was deemed real, the following would happen. An encrypted worm would be sent through a specially "armored" and dedicated core system pathway to all devices at Horizon Pass, the Philology Annex, and the terminals of its core membership in Chicago. This encrypted worm, using a 256 encryption, layered over the two thousand-odd Egyptian hieroglyphs of the Gardiner fonts, would burn through a typical five hundred gigabyte hard drive in approximately two minutes flat, rendering it unusable. The only warning that a user would get that the shutdown was in progress, would be a pop up window that said:

Damokles' Execution – Encryption Underway
Have a Nice Day!

In the meantime, the screen's background would begin to fill with totally random hieroglyphic characters.

Now with the external and internal databases made

trash, Ron, or one of his colleagues, would quickly remove the actual hard drives of Horizon Pass' data storage farm. This was possible as all of them were installed within handy racks with a pull handle, each secured in place with large, plastic thumb screws. The hard drives, once so removed, would be dumped within an externally vented chamber and then sealed. A simple button then triggered within the chamber a Thermite charge. How do I know all of this? For every member of Horizon Pass' staff was cross-trained in the event that they would have to perform someone else's tasks. In fact, because of my university background in computer software, I was the fail safe backup for the entire IT staff. In essence, I could initiate the entire IT side of the Damokles' Protocol by myself.

Another manual task to perform was that once the Tombstone research laboratory had been evacuated, the permanently installed temporal device, the Soap Bubble's laboratory bench version, had to be destroyed. Since the massive double doors to this modified natural cavern took a full two minutes to completely seal, the Thermite charges that were attached to the temporal device had to be remotely detonated once the blast doors were shut. The charges themselves, two for each pylon and four for the drop ring, would reduce the bench version into a bubbling puddle of spent carbon and metals.

Then there was the final disposition of the portable temporal device: its four pylons, drop ring, portable generator, and calibrating laptop computer. All of these already had Thermite charges incorporated within their designs to facilitate their near instantaneous disposal and destruction in the field. The real issue was whether this last vestige of Dr. Borov's legacy should in fact be destroyed, or, instead chance its safe transport to another secure facility. That decision would remain one to be made, if, and whenever, the time would come.

During a test of this shutdown procedure, from its manual initiation to the complete personnel evacuation and sealing of the escape tunnel's air lock, it took five and a half minutes to complete. This day that record would be broken.

CHAPTER XXX
Exodus

As neither Joey nor I were at Horizon Pass on that day of Damokles' execution, I learned all about it from Lieutenant Callahan, Dr. Naysmithe, and of course, Raybob. In fact, it was up to Lieutenant Callahan to decide whether to leave the portable temporal device behind, or to dare and take it along during what we now call "the Exodus." Callahan, being Callahan, dared.

According to Dr. Naysmithe's own watch, the last evacuee into the escape tunnel did so in four minutes, fifty-six seconds. Without pausing to reconsider, he then flooded the entire facility with the non-lethal nerve gas. Completing that task, the roller coaster was already on its return leg to pick up the rest of the staff. Like a captain on his sinking ship, Dr. Naysmithe was the last to mount the coaster.

Since the vast majority of the Horizon Pass' staff had been military at one time or another, they understood the need for speed and efficiency. All found and donned their desert cammies, hats, secured their firearms, and each took their water bottles. As they emerged from the two escape hatches, the sky was still a pre-dawn dark.

With Callahan and his men acting like sheep dogs, fifty-one souls walked away from their past occupations and into their futures. This silent horde was already a full kilometer away from the escape tunnel before Raybob had reached his turn off at Mile Marker 32. After hiking another three kilometers, three camouflaged school buses were reached, each carefully stored in their own ancient and camouflaged Quonset hut, reminders all back to another time of high energy nuclear research in this lonely desert.

The firing up of these bright yellow conveyances took some time as they were each wrapped in yards and yards of clear plastic shipping wrap. As it was, one bus absolutely refused to fire up, but the other two did right away. Again, Cartwright's redundancy rule had proved to be a blessing.

By the time Raybob backed up to the camouflaged shipping dock at Horizon Pass, the yellow school buses were only thirty minutes away from Alamogordo's airfield, where a private commercial jet awaited their arrival. And much like rock stars, who had ditched their weapons as one in the desert for some lucky person to find, they all boarded with a sigh. As for the portable temporal device, it had been placed within the lone cargo carrier in the plane's belly and secured.

*　　*　　*

As for Raybob's late arriving sixteen wheeler, his usual lead foot had somehow left him as he had milked the run for a full two and a half hours. The wily road racer, who so dearly loved his jet black number forty-three Camaro, smiled inwardly.

Damn Professor! Now you owe me for overtime!

Now backed up to the vertical door of the cargo dock, the Marines had easily defeated its locking mechanism, opened it, and rushed inside, the whole lot of them, where they slowly began to develop headaches, display nausea, and some muscle cramping. Fully one quarter of the platoon had been affected before they realized that they had been gassed.

* * *

Five hours later, and after the entire complex had been explored, Claire Hagen finally tore off her gas mask and stood under the unrelenting glare and heat of the midday sun. Thirsty, hungry, with a deep creased ring around her face from the mask, and soaked to the bone in her BDU, she stood before the amazingly beautiful twin rock outcrops of red sandstone and asked herself why she was there.

A single line of a black budget uncovered this, this secret lair out in the middle of nowhere. From the look of it, it once easily housed over fifty people and had been evacuated at the drop of a hat. How we don't know. Where they went we don't have a clue. And then there is that one chamber with a bank vault door that we can't even get into. Perhaps they're all in there, but by the looks of it, I really doubt it. These guys were good.

And so while Hagen was walking around the twin outcrops, the toe of her boot caught on something solid. Looking down, she then saw it. She was standing on a partially sand covered concrete helipad. Scrapping around with her boot, she began to uncover the much scarred lenses of landing lights. Turning abruptly around to again look at those majestic twin peaks she then said.

"Okay Horizon Pass, New Mexico. How many more secrets do you have?"

CHAPTER XXXI

Reunion

Obviously, the story that is Horizon Pass does not end here. Fortunately, Lieutenant Callahan filled me in one all the particulars, both sad and otherwise. As it turned out, the private flight took off from Alamogordo and landed in Denver, where many heartfelt farewells were said with hushed and choked voices, all accompanied with rivers of tears. To any passerby, all these uniformed people looked just like a military reunion that was in the process of breaking up. And in many ways, it was just that. For many, recruited by Dr. Borov himself, the facility had become family, and now, it was scattering to the four winds. How terribly sad.

As for Callahan and his twenty-four men, they continued on to Chicago with their precious cargo, as did Dr. Naysmithe. Once at O'Hare, they were picked up by a bright yellow school bus, which the venerable Cartwright himself was driving. And, per the usual, he was bitching a blue streak for everyone to "shake a leg as his wife's dinner was waiting." Once at the Philology Annex, they all disembarked from the bus in the alley and headed for the annex's secret gangway entrance. From there, they made their way to the second subbasement for their debriefing.

In the conference room, an ancient looking Professor Jung, Dr. Young, and Joey were waiting for them with a full spread of sandwiches, chips, water and cold beer. The spread had been Jung's idea. Joey said that Milson would have insisted on the Silver Bullets.

No one took any of the water bottles. Uncharacteristically, the Dean of Humanities hugged each and every one of them as they entered, as if each were a long lost relative, even though he didn't know most of them by name, much less face.

After everyone had eaten and had several beers, Dr. Naysmithe called the group to order and said.

"Gentlemen, we have one more mission before us. We have left one of our own behind. Our truck driver Raybob Smith is no doubt in some form of military or federal custody. We gotta' spring him.

"Lieutenant Callahan. Do you have any ideas?"

* * *

I was in Santa Fe at the time of "the exodus" and knew about its execution only because Dr. Naysmithe had left a coded message on my smart phone. So I waited for further instructions. Then Dr. Naysmithe called me from Chicago, told me about Raybob Smith's plight, and asked me to "stand by for a phone call." That's all the man said. So I waited some more. And as you well know, I am not a patient one.

Put simply, the Marine platoon commander, Lieutenant Joshua Sondheim, did not know what to do with Raybob. Yes, he strongly suspected that the driver was an employee of this secret facility, but he considered him a compartmentalized asset, one who clearly didn't know squat about anything, in his opinion. He was just like any UPS, or FEDEX, or DHL delivery man for that matter, who dropped off packages at the CIA. Did that make him a spook? Furthermore, Smith had cooperated to the letter, and for Sondheim that meant something too. Actually, quite a lot.

But Claire Hagen didn't see it that way. Not one bit. In fact, Raybob Smith was her only living evidence that proved the existence of Horizon Pass, New Mexico. No, as far as she was concerned Smith was hers, and he was going back to Washington with her come hell or high water. After all, Smith represented Senator Marvin J. Cruthers chief evidentiary witness. And what was left unspoken, Smith was her ticket to advancement as well.

Meanwhile, this once plucky five foot something was really beginning to wear on the base commander, as were all her Marine friends. And the more he thought about it, the hotter he got. And when he found out that Smith hailed from College Station, Texas, was a decorated U.S. Army Abrams tank driver, a guy who had done his stint in Desert Storm – that broke the camel's back.

So the base commander went down to the brig and made a confidential visit. He learned that Smith did indeed have local kin in Santa Fe.

"Yes sir, she would be more than willing to come and get me.

"Yes sir, I will keep this entire discussion on the Q.T.

"And yes sir, thank you sir, for so kindly thinking of my welfare."

Needless to say, once I got Raybob's call, my VW flew down from Santa Fe to Alamogordo in record time, and by the time I had arrived, it was already near midnight. And as it turned out, that was perfect for our escape.

After we were a full two hours into the drive back to Santa Fe, I rang up Dr. Naysmithe's cell and woke the poor man up in Chicago. Even though he was asleep, when he had heard what had transpired, he almost jumped though my phone!

"Let me talk to Raybob!" he said excitedly.

"Raybob, is it true that THE most gorgeous woman on the planet just saved your sorry ass?"

I chuckled as the cell was on speaker.

"Indeed Professor! She truly is, and, did just that, but what really sealed the deal was the base commander. What a fine dude! He was the guy that really made it all happen."

"Well Raybob, I am just pleased as punch that you're once again a free man. Now, let's talk about your future for a moment..."

Dr. Naysmithe totally rearranged Raybob's life, walked him through the drill, and reminded him where he could find his new identity papers, the works. To this day, that conversation reminded me a lot of Peter Borov, John Milson, and even my own father's loving words of advice and encouragement.

* * *

The next day Claire Hagen was one very angry young lady, when she discovered that "her prisoner," her words, had been released during the early morning hours on his own recognizance. The base commander, a man in his mid-fifties, just sat in his chair and allowed her to vent, and boy did she vent, and threaten, and swear, and vent, and threaten the collective wrath of Washington, DC., and then she began to get personal, real personal, which for Base Commander William M. Richards, was just fine as he had the foresight to record the entire "love fest" on tape.

With her face so red that Richards began to worry some for her health, he finally spoke his first words.

"Ms. Hagen, are you finished?"

"FINISHED? Well Mister, I have just begun..." she began anew.

And then Richards began laughing.

After a second, Hagen began viciously biting off her words. "So commander, just, what, the fuck, is, so, funny?"

It was then, I am told, that Commander Richards showed the senatorial special investigator the running tape recorder.

At the sight of it, she turned ash white, put her hand over her mouth, and stormed out of the commander's office. She, her Marines, and their four C-130s left one hour later.

As for Base Commander William Joseph Richards USAF, in case you haven't already guessed, he is the younger brother of Captain John Richards, USAF retired. John was Joey's father, which made Bill his uncle and god father. Joey even carries his middle name. And by a happy circumstance, Bill too, in league with Cartwright, was part of the Horizon Pass' early warning system.

His docking of the Tehran flight crew and its airframe were per the book for any major military engagement. That is, of course, if you could even prove that. The crew, clearly exhausted and stressed out on their military issued amphetamines, needed observation, hydration, and a good old fashioned rest. The Gulf Stream V too, needed to be gone over with a fine toothed comb in order to identify any potential battle damage. Fortunately, there had been none. Yet another evidentiary fact that argued against such a purported military incursion.

Additionally, Bill had spent many a weekend with his good friend Peter Borov fly fishing. And his successor Naysmithe, although a good chap, really couldn't drink his beer, so when Naysmithe had called about Raybob Smith, he was as good as home, nice and snug as a bug in his bed. But as for Smith's cousin, who had come to fetch him, well, in the base commander's own words, "Damn that was sure one classy chassis!" And for that kind compliment, I bought him another beer.

Chapter XXXII
Stalk & Destroy

For someone with my skills, Washington, DC was a target rich environment with preening egos abundant and everywhere. But at the moment, I already had two targets, and one would naturally lead to the other. That's just the way that I like to do things, thoroughly, from the bottom up.

That meant that my first target was Senator Cruthers' chief gopher Claire Hagen. After all, she had singlehandedly torn down the entire Horizon Pass edifice, whereas the Secret Service of the Islamic Republic of Iran and Russian *Spetsnaz* had failed to do so.

Since I like to know who I am stalking, I asked myself, *just who is this bitch?* So I contacted a good colleague knowledgeable in the intricate ways of the Washington scene, and here is what he sent to me.

> Born in an affluent northern suburb of Chicago, Claire Marie Hagen was raised a Methodist as the daughter of a very successful dentist and occasional local politician. Having done well in high school, she was accepted to Wellesley College in Massachusetts and double majored in political science and psychology. Graduating in only three and a half years, Hagen, apparently a driven personality, immediately enrolled into the Yale Law School. There she excelled again, earned her *juris doctor*, and came in fourth in her class – no mean feat. Clearly looking for new lands to conquer, Hagen joined the Capital Hill staff of Senator Marvin J. Cruthers of Florida. The reason

behind this decision is unclear, except that Hagen was probably looking for a temporary foothold with which to launch her own political career. Another rumor speculates that Senator Cruthers and her father had been old college friends. Regardless of what motivated her decision, especially given her impressive college and law school credentials, Hagen's initial starting salary was a clear cut above the usual. She now lives in a gated and gentrified condominium community in Virginia. She drives a Prius. In short, she seems to live, eat, and sleep her senatorial staff position, and apparently, the senator trusted her judgment enough that he allowed her to run the entire Horizon Pass investigation, which she had uncovered. Since her highly publicized successes in New Mexico, Hagen has established herself with the media as an attractive source for an opinion. Most recently, no doubt to hang on to her, Hagen has been promoted to the position of assistant counsel to the senator. By all accounts, Hagen's star is clearly in the ascendant.

What I needed was an "interview" with this recently christened media darling, as her exploits of daring duo in the New Mexican desert had been garishly splashed across America's media networks. So I became a Russian journalist, out to discover the next relevant force of Nature in American politics. I figured, with that pitch, how could she refuse me?

Well, she didn't, as her assistant had so gushingly emphasized, when she called to confirm our luncheon date, that was of course on my tab, and yes, at Hagen's preferred posh locale on Constitution Avenue. And yes, at 11:30 sharp.

Frankly, the restaurant's décor was a bit too sterile, open, and bright for my tastes, but when in Rome, as they say, play along. So I dressed the part in a severe black shift, small matching hand bag, tall pumps – *must have those*, and with my long dark hair cascading down my neck and shoulders. For my Sasha, I wore his pearl earrings. If I wasn't so tanned by the glorious New Mexican sun, I could have easily auditioned as a vampire with my redder than red lip gloss. Early on I decided that I would take compete control of this interview, and so I dressed for the part.

I arrived ten minutes early and stood next to the bar with a chilled glass of Chablis in order to take the temperature of the place, its smells, and note its clientele. Frankly, I fit right in and that pleased me no end. And so like any good hunter, I waited for my prey to arrive, and I was not at all surprised, when she finally did, precisely fifteen minutes late.

Oh how I love games like this!

By the looks of her, she had just emerged from the lady's room with her hair and makeup perfect. Dressed in a finely tailored gray pin striped pants suit, she fit the part of a successful lawyer/senatorial staffer, but next to me, she still looked like a man.

Now let the devastation begin, I thought, as I left my untouched glass of wine at the bar.

She just stood there, at the entrance, looking around like a doe in the middle of a clearing, and even had the gall to glance at her watch. I timed my approach, while her head was turned.

Perfect!

"Dr. Hagen, I presume?"

I noted several things: a truly surprised widening of

the eyes, a one step retreat, and a slight drop of her jaw line.

Perfect!

"Hello Dr. Hagen," spoken with a mildly thick St. Petersburg accent. "I am Gregorieva. Vesna Borisevna Gregorieva, of *The St. Petersburg Times*," as I simultaneously extended my hand.

Looking down at it, clearly still in shock, she finally took it.

"And here is my business card."

At that point, I turned, took command, and asked for us to be seated, which the *maître d'* did most willingly as my charms had so captured his attention.

I then gestured to Hagen to follow him to our table, which gave me a long opportunity to judge this woman, her carriage, and just to make her nervous.

Now seated, I placed my slightly opened clutch purse to my left, put my hands in my lap, leaned forward, gave Hagen my most winning smile, and said quietly over the table.

"So Dr. Hagen, what do you wish me to tell my readership about you?"

Her face went blank at the question. She blushed and looked down at her lap. Then she said.

"The truth."

"And that is?"

"That I am a hard working lawyer. That I believe that our government is full of waste and corruption. And, that I wish to be a part of the solution."

I waited for a dramatic moment before I probed a bit further into this idealistic one's sense of place and purpose.

"So, you say that your 'government is full of waste

and corruption.' Do you mean to infer that Senator Cruthers should be included in that assessment?"

Then came this surprisingly quick and sharp reply. "I did not infer that at all, Ms...Ms. Gregorieva. In point of fact, Senator Cruthers is the solution. And I support him to the hilt in his desire to clean up Washington's wasteful spending, on any number of overblown and overfed black budgets."

At this point, the waiter arrived and took our drink orders. I again chose a Chablis. Hagen a Scotch and water.

Oh I had gotten under her skin!

Once again alone, I asked, "Dr. Hagen, regarding your most recent victory in this regard, this entire Horizon Pass business. How did you discover it? I would really like to hear from you, one professional to another, what it was like to break a story as big as that."

"Well," she began, "consider this Ms. Gregorieva. For Christ's sakes, what did the DOE want with some cruise missiles? That was what drove me, pure and simple. Here I had the munitions transfers in my hand, and it just didn't make any sense. So I began digging. And, after one hell of a lot of work, the name Horizon Pass, New Mexico, appeared in Oak Ridge's budget. And that, Ms. Gregorieva, is how it all began."

"Now that is a simply incredible story, Dr. Hagen. I only wish that I could have such an opportunity in my country, which is, as you very well know, a land of opportunity only for the very well connected," I said. "But how did you make the connection, no, that is not the word, how did you find the location of this 'Horizon Pass'?"

In a rare moment of honesty, that frankly stayed

my hand and potentially saved her career as well, Hagen said, "Luck, Ms. Gregorieva. Luck. Damn, stupid, luck."

At this point in the conversation, it was she who was now leaning forward over the table with her elbows on it.

"Imagine this. Here I am deep in southeast Jesus having just proven that the munitions transfer had taken place, but I still didn't know where this Horizon Pass, New Mexico, was. At one point, I even entertained the cockamamie idea that Holloman AFB and Horizon Pass were one in the same. I was at wits end. But then I considered that this Horizon Pass, New Mexico, must have had employees, and employees eat, so, who was supplying their food. After some research, I discovered that there was only one refrigerated trucking and warehouse facility in Gordo that could do it."

At this point, I politely interrupted.

"'Gordo?'"

She waved her hand in dismissal.

"Yeah, that's what the locals call Alamogordo."

"Oh, I see. It's an abbreviation. Please go on."

And she did, in exquisite detail, on through the entire lunch. In fact, she had left out only three rather seminal details – the nerve gas, the incarceration of Raybob Smith, and her volcanic run in with the Holloman base commander.

Oh, I thought, *this will indeed be delicious.*

Then as we were nearing the completion of the lunch, I asked, "Dr. Hagen, now that you had found your Horizon Pass, New Mexico, can you reveal to me what sort of facility it was?

At this point, by my count, Hagen had finished

three Scotch and waters, so her tongue had loosened considerably.

"Ms. Gregorieva, I'm so very sorry, may I call you by your first name?"

"Certainly doctor, it is Vesna."

"Okay Vesna, and by the way I'm not a doctor, just a lawyer. As for Horizon Pass, that place is one really spooky mystery. It's underground, with all of these tunnels, and rooms, and even a hospital, but what it was for we haven't a clue. But there is this one room or something that we couldn't get into. It was sealed with this huge door that looked like it came from a bank vault. Maybe, whatever is in that room might give us an answer to your question."

"Doctor, please excuse me, Ms. Hagen, I only have one more question. What happened to all of Horizon Pass' staff, its employees?"

Thoughtful silence, and then, "Vesna, I really don't know. The entire place was like one of those ghost ship stories you read about, with mugs of still hot coffee left in the cafeteria. When we entered the place it was a ghost town."

"You don't say." I stated with considerable interest.

"Yeah, pretty strange, huh. Well, it has been a real pleasure to meet you, Vesna. And thank you so much for lunch. It was truly delicious. And here's my card if you want to get in touch with me again."

But just as she was about to rise from her chair, I quietly asked, "Ms. Hagen, have you ever heard of a gentleman named Mr. Raybob Smith?"

The question must have truly registered, as the gravitational forces on the other side of the table had caused Hagen to plop right back down in her seat. With an ashen face and a barely contained snarl she said, "What did you say?"

"Mr. Raybob Smith. Have you ever heard of that name?"

Now with slitted eyes full of instant suspicion and hate she warned.

"Be very careful Ms. Gregorieva. You are now standing on some pretty thin ice."

With a relaxed and placid composure, I answered.

"No, Ms. Hagen, rather it is you who are on thin ice. The incarceration of a United States citizen, without just cause, and on a military base, is rather, let us say, irregular. Further, did you know that Mr. Smith was a highly decorated veteran of the First Iraq War?"

Pause.

"No, I didn't think so.

"Instead, you used Mr. Smith, actually made him drive, under duress, his sixteen wheeler to Horizon Pass, and then you and your merry band of Marines followed him in. In actual fact, Mr. Smith showed you where Horizon Pass was. He took you there, but at gunpoint.

"In summation Ms. Hagen, you didn't find Horizon Pass single-handedly at all as you told the media. And, when all was said and done, all you had was Mr. Smith. And as you yourself said, the rest of the facility was like a 'ghost ship'. And so you imprisoned the very man, who made you famous. How does that make you feel, Ms. Hagen?"

At that, I stood up, and left one devastated young lady with the bill. As I closed my purse, I turned off the tape recorder. Now I had two tapes of this egotistical monster: Base Commander William Richards', and now my own. That's what I call an insurance policy.

*   *   *

Target One so devastated, I then moved on to Target Two, Senator Marvin J. Cruthers, Target One's boss. Allow me to describe him, and while I do, ask yourself if anything about this man sounds familiar. Athletic build in a two-piece silk suit, longish, roguishly blond hair graying at the temples, a tan, French cuffs with his alma mater's cufflinks, a power tie – color du jour, a clear complexion with just a hint of crow's feet at the corners of eyes – his so-called "laugh lines," a straight aristocratic nose, strong chin, and deep dimples whenever he smiled. That stereotypical image *is* Senator Marvin J. Cruthers in a nutshell. He's a testament to what liposuction, hair grafts, tanning booths, and three facial surgeons can produce – pure Hollywood, which today, unfortunately, also happens to be pure Washington, DC.

I could go on and on providing reasons to hate this man, but I do not wish to be redundant or even worse, to be boring. If you regularly read the newspaper or kept current with cable news, then you already know what I am talking about.

Without any doubt, getting to this target would represent quit a challenge, but then again, I just love challenges. So I waited for the arrival of the college football season. Cruthers, a simply rabid university alumnus and hedonistic frat man from way back, was to attend the Homecoming Pep Rally and the big game the following day. Marjorie, his wife, knew better than to accompany her husband of some seventeen years for that particular weekend. It was understood that Marv needed his annual "fix" and this was to be it.

So during the furious frenzy at the rally, where beer kegs proliferated like mushrooms after a warm spring rain, and with an atmosphere densely dosed with young pheromones, I decided to show up to see if I could catch the good senator's eye.

Well, I have to say that I filled out that cheerleader outfit quite well, and given my extraordinary dancer's flexibility, that hadn't hurt either. So after the brief limo ride to his hotel, where I was careful not to touch anything that could hold a print, I finally got down to business.

As it turned out, the senator, when drunk, and at that moment he was quite drunk, turned out to be quite a brutal beast. But not to me, as I quickly and quietly subdued him. Frankly, I think he loved it. But when I tied him up with my panty hose, he really lost it, so I stuffed his mouth shut with his socks.

Now spread-eagled on the cheap bed, and armed with a cocktail straw that I took from the limo, I blew a line of cocaine into each of his nostrils. With the senator very much in la-la land, now wearing surgical gloves that I had hidden in my uniform, I cleaned up myself, the senator, and the room, having learned with the three physicians in Moscow not to leave any trace of DNA behind. Satisfied, I seeded the bed stand, and his personal luggage, with controlled substances. With the stage so set, I left the deliriously happy senator.

Once I was about two blocks away, I called my friend in DC, you know, the same fellow who had so kindly provided me with the background information on Hagen. By a strange twist of fate, he just so happened to be in the vicinity with his television crew, who were covering some local event. So I made a suggestion and provided my dear friend with the hotel's address and a room number. "Yes," I said, "I left the door wide open."

*　　*　　*

The evening newscaster smirked and could not believe what was being pitched to her. It was just all so juicy that she couldn't believe her luck. To break a story on a federal senator caught more than just red-handed, and so deliciously kinky too! She just didn't know where to begin, there were just so many possibilities, so many angles. So her colleague made some suggestions and she just ran with it.

"Good evening ladies and gentlemen. It is not often that a story quite like this one comes across my desk…"

*　　*　　*

One last point. While her benefactor and boss was being grilled by the media and disowned by his wife in the aftermath of "Cocaine Hotel-Gate", Claire Hagen, for whatever reason, thought that this was *her* time to shine, when the media eventually got around to interviewing her about her boss' dalliances. In typical shark tank fashion, Hagen threw the man under the bus, even to the point of intimating that he had physically taken advantage of her as well.

At this point, I again called up my friend in DC, and asked him if he would be interested in the two tapes that I had on Hagen. Once he heard about their general content, and their damning implications, he said that he was, and so I sent copies of them next day delivery. About two weeks later, I received an email from my friend alerting me to watch that evening's news. Not only was Senator Cruthers put through the ringer once more, but one of his staffer's was there as well, a lawyer of all things, who had illegally imprisoned a U.S. citizen and decorated veteran. Just before I changed channels, the on-air reporter was demanding the senator's impeachment and his staffer's disbarment.

How delicious.

CHAPTER XXXIII
Going Home

There is something that I forgot to mention that has just occurred to me. When Horizon Pass became a functional facility, after almost two years of construction, Dr. Borov skimmed a full fifteen percent off the top of that third year's operating budget. Those monies he invested in various financial instruments, initially as seed funds, but thereafter that core was supplemented each subsequent year with an additional fifteen percent of skim. Why? Dr. Borov was building a private pension fund.

So did Dr. Borov continue this quietly for each and every year? According to Cartwright, one of Dr. Borov's closest friends, after the fifth year the fund had grown considerably, as well-managed funds beyond the government's reach often do, enough so that he could finally announce to the permanent staff in New Mexico and Chicago, excepting the twenty-six members of the academic council, what his grand plan was for their future. Since most of these folks were former military with their own pensions, Dr. Borov's idea was to grant anyone leaving his employ, after a minimum five-year vesting period, a lump sum amount. Obviously, the longer you stayed on, the greater the separation became. And, as the New Mexico and Chicago facilities were black projects, so too were the pension monies off the books, and black as well.

So, when the Damokles' Protocol was executed, so also were the pension funds dispersed. And this was logical, for fifty-one individuals suddenly had to reestablish themselves somehow, someway, into their new lives. That nearly all of them were now newly minted millionaires certainly helped. As both Joey and I were considered permanent staff, we consequently received a little something as well.

*   *   *

Well, following that university homecoming, I decamped from Santa Fe and moved to the city of Kralendijk on the awesomely lovely island of Bonaire. There, the Banco di Caribe, NV, was more than happy to accept my funds transfer, which was managed via the SWIFT system. Remember that? The transaction was totally seamless, as the transfer was executed directly from Dr. Borov's pension fund into a pre-existing account that I had established and under a different name. For this I must thank the foresight of Joey, who just so happens to bank across the street, where his book royalties have been slowly piling up.

The move to Bonaire from New Mexico was quite a shock to my system. Yes, there is the sun, but now I had to acclimate to sea level humidity, rain, and tropical storms, and oh yes, the insects. I quickly learned not to enter a room at night without the light on. But truth be told, I didn't suffer that long, and as you well know, I adapt well to change.

So, under my new identity, I entered into a rental agreement with a well-to-do condominium community with an international flavor. In the meantime, I stayed in a reasonably priced hotel that was favored by the diving community. All was going swimmingly, including my newest passion, snorkeling, until Joey emailed me with a very special request.

Dearest Maatkare:

I have decided that because of the current situation here, and given certain developing circumstances that have occurred of late, I would like to take that job offer in Memphis. However, to do that, I will need your assistance. Let me know your status, soonest.

I knew what Joey had in mind, but seriously doubted that anyone back at the Philology Annex would approve such a thing. Nonetheless, I began to nose around, as that seemed to be my greatest skill and talent at the time.

After several inquiries, I did indeed discover just what Joey had meant about "the current situation" and "certain developing circumstances," all of which were ongoing at his university. Remarkably, several members of the academic council had actually gone public and were bringing a class action law suit against the Philology Annex over the execution of the Damokles' encryption of their hard drives. Their claim was the irretrievable loss of years of research.

Remarkably, the first thing that came to mind was: a) they had signed a contract and had financially benefitted from it, and b) they had signed a military-grade confidentiality agreement. With their law suit, they were flying in the face of both of these documents as if they didn't exist. The next thing that came to mind was: just who do they intend to sue? Horizon Pass had been abandoned. The Borov pension fund had been dispersed. Then it hit me, the portable temporal device was still at the Philology Annex, and Dr. Young and Joey were still on campus. Strangely, I intuitively knew that Young could stand on his own. If that was not the case, then he probably was already in the process of executing his own disaster plan – probably on some British-held island group. But Joey? I wasn't so sure.

So I e-mailed Callahan. After all, it had been his decision to take the portable version of the temporal device from Horizon Pass, instead of destroying it there and then. And to my happy surprise, ten minutes later he responded, outlining pretty much the same concerns that had Joey, and that he had already removed the device from the Philology Annex three days prior, as he had gotten a really bad feeling that, in his words, "the shit was about to hit the fan."

So I replied back.

Sir:

It seems to me that movie making and sound equipment quite often is taken to Egypt. Advise that you and several of your "best boys" do just that, and quickly.

Let Mayneken know so that you can coordinate the movie shoot.

Let Maatkare know as well as she will want to help out.

Exactly fourteen minutes later Callahan responded positively to the movie proposal and that Mayneken, who was at his side, had totally concurred. Then they both encouraged me to book early and often.

* * *

Two days later I landed in Cairo. I could have gotten there sooner, but flights to Egypt from South America are not exactly plentiful. So with my Dutch passport, I flew from Puerto Rico to NYC to London to Cairo. Upon arriving, I was really beat, but I immediately brightened as Callahan, three of his "best boys", and Joey were all there to greet me outside of customs. As it turned out, their "special gear" rested in a rented baggage cart between them, covered with the decals of a prominent cable network and with heavy labeling identifying just what was what. Believe it or not, the containers had not even been opened, just x-rayed at O'Hare. Once so blessed, they had been passed along through the international airline baggage system all the way to Cairo. Callahan explained that all of the Thermite charges had been removed in order to pull off this "stunt", as he called it.

So we all jumped into a large SUV taxi and went to the Mena House at the base of the Giza Plateau. Only Joey, per the script, had made a room reservation. But with it, we all dumped our gear there and then went to dinner, our "last supper."

The conversation was initially stranger than strange, but after several of those big Egyptian beers – yes, even I, ever the princess, drank some beer – the conversation turned to topics of the future, what are you going to do with your share of the pension, and the like. Only one of us was excited about the past.

Frankly, Joey's last deployment went as smooth as glass from our point of view. He dropped cleanly in the open desert that night high atop the Sakkaran Plateau, into that marvelous star-studded night sky of the Egyptian late Eighteen Dynasty. This we know. My only concern was for his damn PDS, as I wasn't there to guard over him until he revived.

I have believed to this very day that after a couple of minutes, he did indeed revive, and came to his senses. Without any question, his future in the past was guaranteed to be a very bright one. After all, he was the adopted son of the high priest of Amen Re, personal confidante and ambassador of a queen, his uncle the high priest of Ptah in Memphis, and the adopted brother of a Memphite prince, who would soon become pharaoh. Can anyone have more connections than that?

While I truly miss him dearly, and my heart absolutely ached once he dropped, I always knew that Joey would make a fine high priest of Ptah. And, I will never forget that look on his face, when his uncle Ptahmesou had first offered him the opportunity. When you consider his many fine attributes, that of a natural teacher, a warrior, and such a kind and humble human being, all of these things truly made his final decision a most logical one.

As for the portable temporal device, we tore it down after Joey's drop, and frankly could not bring ourselves to destroy it. The following day, we did however pay a visit to the Director of the Egyptian Museum, a certain Dr. Sharil Moussa, and asked her if she happened to have a place of safekeeping. She said that she did, and that Joey knew of it as well, so that whenever he wanted to retrieve it, it would be there waiting for him. To this very day, I will never forget that conversation without tears streaming from my eyes. As for me, I will be forever waiting for him as well.

A NOTE ON RUSSIAN NAMES

Westerners typically are not aware of the proper use and structural hierarchy employed by the Russian naming system. Americans, in particular, are very informal in their personal address and use of nick-names. Not so much with our Russian neighbors as their personal names are made up of three parts: the first name, your father's name, and lastly, the family name. So, Karlov Gregorievich Drazinzka is a example of this phenomenon where "Gregorievich" stands for Karlov's father's name "Gregorie" plus the patronymic masculine "vich" ending, which itself can come in various forms depending upon the father's name. But note, as Russian is a very gender specific language, Vesna Borisevna Gregorieva, her father's name is "Boris" plus "evna", one of the accepted feminine patronymic endings.

Another twist to be aware of is that the last name itself also will reflect the gender of its owner. Thus, Karlov Gregorievich Gregoriev, while his sister's last name would be formed as Vesna Borisevna Gregorieva, or, as with the name Konstantina Iosifeva Markova, instead of the masculine form "Markov."

Finally, Russians do not abbreviate their first names, even if they are extremely close friends. It just doesn't happen. So, for example, the feminine name Konstantina would never be abbreviated to 'Tina'.

Rules regarding proper address between the young and old, between subordinates and their superiors, also exist. For example, good friends would refer to each other with first and patronymic names, thus: Karlov

Gregorievich, but a youngster or subordinate would never dream to do so with an elder or superior. Consequently, the harsh use of just "Gregorieva" as a form of address, would indicate that the speaker was her superior, and the situation most likely military. Otherwise, it would constitute an outright insult.

Ancient Egyptian Chronology

During the third century BC, King Ptolemy I of Egypt commanded Manetho, high priest of the sun god of Heliopolis, to write a history of Egypt. Unfortunately, that work now only exists in the form of tantalizing fragments, which merely list kings, how long they ruled, and their dynastic divisions. Fortunately for Egyptologists, they have at their disposal several papyri and temple inscriptions, which help to fill in the blanks.

But truth be told, king lists are just that – lists, which do not provide us with an absolute chronology. Occasionally, however, hints do appear in the historical record, specifically the recording of exceptional astronomical phenomena, from which can be calculated an absolute date for a given event. Consequently, the absolute dating of precisely when such and such a king ruled has become a sort of scholarly contest between whom can count the most accurately between these astronomical benchmark events.

As if that were not enough to trouble the mind of a conscientious historian, one must contend with the difference between the established Egyptian civil calendar and our own. Unlike our modern calendar that begins on January 1st, the first month of the Egyptian civil calendar began at the Inundation of the Nile River that occurred between June 15th and June 30th. Then there is the tendency among some Egyptian dynasties – and in our case the Eighteenth Dynasty – to employ the use of a regnal calendar as well; meaning that time was recorded in years from the date of a pharaoh's accession to the throne. For example, some have speculated that the Pharaoh Amenhotep IV ascended the throne sometime during the fifth month of the Egyptian civil calendar. Since the start of the civil calendar occurred between June 15th and June 30th, then Amenhotep IV, according to these scholars, was crowned pharaoh sometime between October 15th and the end of that month. Hence, the game.

Whether dealing either with the Egyptian civil calendar or a specific dynasty's regnal calendar, one always must recognize that modern equivalent years often will overlap. For example, the first regnal year of Amenhotep IV lasted from approximately October 15th/30th, 1377 BC, through approximately October 14th/30th, 1376 BC of our modern calendar.

Sadly the debate does not end here, for scholars have over the years argued long and hard on the actual years that should be assigned to a given civil or regnal year. Again, here a game of sorts is played as well as to whether one prefers a so-called high or low chronology. Consequently, as in the example above, the first regnal year of Amenhotep IV could be assigned as 1377/76 by one scholar using the low chronology, while the very same regnal year for this king could be assigned at 1358/57 using the high chronology. This is why this author has tried to avoid attempting to correlate ancient with modern dates. Instead, he has preferred to enlist regnal dating, i.e., Year 16, to date the events that occurred during the sixteenth year of such and such a king.

The recent discussions of the high and low Egyptian chronology are that of K. A. Kitchen ("The

Basics of Egyptian Chronology in Relation to the Bronze Age," in P. Åström, ed., *High, Middle or Low*, Gothenburg 1987 I: 40-43, 47, III: 153), Jürgen von Beckerath (*Chronologie des pharaonischen Ägypten*, 2nd ed., Munich 2001), and E. Hornung (et al. ed., *Ancient Egyptian Chronology* Leiden, 2006).

ON EGYPTIAN PRIESTS & THEIR PRIESTHOODS

The duties of Egyptian priests and their many priesthoods, varied during the three thousand years of pharaonic history. By the New Kingdom (1567 – 1085 BC), the vast majority of religious functions was performed by the priests devoted to each god on the behalf of the king. As one might expect, due to the formation of so many religious organizations, priestly bureaucracies formed to manage the resources of the god's estate. Just as naturally priestly hierarchies developed in order to apportion and manage the many tasks associated with the care and maintenance of a specific deity. At the top of this priest ranking stood those who served the god, the high priest, literally "the first servant of the god," who in turn was followed by the "second," "third," and "fourth servant of the god" as well.

In opposition to these administrative rankings, the vast majority of Egyptian priests who undertook the day-to-day temple duties were the common priests, the *wab*-priests, literally "the cleaners." This is not to say that specialty priesthoods did not exist, for they did, especially those devoted to mummification and the necropolis. But one class of priests, the *sem*-priests, appears to connote a ranking of importance unto their own. While certainly not as powerful as high priests nor as lowly as *wab*-priests, the *sem*-priests were those associated with cultic activities and even the royal palace itself.

A Note on the Vocalization of Ancient Egyptian

Regarding the vocalization of ancient Egyptian, the fact of the matter is simply this: the language is a very, very dead one – meaning that what it sounded like has been long lost. Its closest linguistic cousin, Coptic, is itself a dead language, but at least one that included vowels within its script. On this shirt-tailed basis, Egyptologists have carefully compared the vocabularies of the two languages and have constructed a scientific vocalization scheme to approximate what the Egyptian tongue might have sounded like. But even if the assigned vowel placements are accurate, their quality remains just as uncertain as is their emphasis, or where the accent falls on a particular word – not to mention that there is evidence to suggest several regional dialectics during the course of any given dynasty. To add even more fuel to the fire, different vocalization schemes have been put forward by the dominant Egyptological schools of thought be they American, British, French, Italian or German. As a consequence, the vocalization of ancient Egyptian becomes more a matter of one's cultural preference than anything else. In short, just what the language really sounded like during a given time period and within a given region is up for grabs.

With the above caveats and considerations in mind, the author offers the following possible pronunciations for the ancient Egyptian names and words that appear in this manuscript.

Akhenaten (a.k.a. Amenhotep IV) – King of Egypt: *ach-en-a-ten*

Akhetaten – capital city built by Akhenaten – *aa-khet-a-ten*

Amenemhet – high priest of Amen Re: *a-men-em-het*

Amen Re – chief divinity of Thebes: *a-men-ra*

Ankhmes - court royal physician: *anch-mes*

Hapi – Egyptian god of the Nile: *haa-pee*

Horemheb – Prince and future pharaoh – *hor-em-heb*

Maat – divine order: *maa-haat*

Mahu - Chief-of-Police of Akhet-aten – *maa-hoo*

Mayneken – *sem*-priest of Ptah: *may-necken*

Mekbet – young, Pre-Dynastic village girl of Memphis: *mech-bet*

Meryptah – high priest of Amen Re: *mary-p-taah*

Nebmare Amenhotep – King of Egypt: *neb-maa-ra a-men-ho-tep*

Neferneferru Nefertiti – Queen of Egypt and Chief Wife of Akhenaten: *nefer-nefer-roo nefer-tee-tee*

Pahamneter – high priest of Ptah: *paa-haam-neter*

Perunefer – the harbor of Memphis: *pear-oo-nefer*

Piankhhotep – seer and *sem*-priest of Ptah: *pee-anch-ho-tep*

Ptah – chief divinity of Memphis: *p-taah*

Ptahmesou – high priest of Ptah: *p-taah-mes-oo*

Sekhmet – goddess of war: *sech-met*

Sennufer – major of Thebes: *senn-noo-fer*

Smenkhkare – King of Egypt: *ss-menk-ca-ra*

Sia – divine understanding: *see-ya*

Sobek – Egyptian crocodile god: *so-beck*

Thoth – god of writing and civilization: *thoawth*

A Note on the Editing of Papyri & Inscriptions

The study of inscriptions, known as epigraphy, possesses well-known philological shorthand for the recording and interpretation of such ancient monuments – be they handsomely carved stone inscriptions, painted surfaces, or hastily scratched out graffiti. This methodology was first established by Theodor Mommsen, the founder of the *Corpus Inscriptionum Latinarum*, or *CIL*, in 1853. The *CIL*, which celebrated its 150th anniversary in 2003, is a vast compendium of nearly eighty volumes of inscriptions that relate to the Roman Empire. The continued study and publication of newly discovered inscriptions from this period of history is the patient and laborious task of the Berlin-Brandenburgische Academie der Wissenschaften, *Corpus Inscriptionum Latinarum*'s staff and its most able director, Prof. Dr. Manfred Gerhard Schmidt.

Needless to say, with such a ready tool available historians and philologists of other ancient time periods naturally gravitated to the *CIL* methodology of philological criticism and commentary and either wholly adopted it or did so with few exceptions.

Consequently, all of the ancient Egyptian texts contained within this book follow the *CIL*'s editorial conventions and use the following symbols to indicate:

a|bc	Breaks in the text, usually a line break
a||bc	Text located outside of an inscribed field or displaced text
(vac.)	The presence of a gap in the text

[[abc]]	An ancient erasure of text
<<abc>>	Ancient text inscribed on an erased background
abc (!)	An ancient grammatical error, misspelling, or philological irregularity of some kind
abc (?)	Uncertain reading of the text
(abc)	Either the modern explanation of an abbreviation or philological convention
a[bc]	A modern editorial addition, explanation, or change to the text
{abc}	A modern editorial deletion of text
<u>abc</u>	Letters once read by previous editors, which are currently lost or unreadable

About the Author

"Can't was killed in the Battle of Try!"

As a fifth-grader the author took Sister Mary Stephana's clever and memorable words to heart and ever since has found the confidence to take on challenges that others shy away from. When confronted with retirement, Cherf said, "Heck, I've always wanted to write a book without footnotes, to tell a fascinating tale, that is so real, that my avid readers would be left puzzled over what was real, and what was Memorex."

To craft such a tale takes wit, a love of science and science fiction, and above all a deep reverence for ancient history and archaeology. All of these qualities are stitched together beautifully in his books, because Cherf has been there, dug that. This is a guy who has seen the sun rise from atop the Great Pyramid.

Cherf tells a story about when he was eleven years old and had become bored with dinosaurs. While exploring the Field Museum along Chicago's water front one Saturday morning he discovered Hall N – the ancient Egyptian collection. From that time forward Cherf was terminally smitten as that truly was his life-changing "Ah ha!" moment.

Needless to say Cherf's books have been generously reviewed by his readers, who have in turn eagerly shared their joy. The *Historical Fiction Society* in 2013 rated *Bow Tie*, the first of this series, an Editor's Choice. For an author, such sentiments are an embarrassment of riches; precious words like honey deliciously, drizzled.

At his core Cherf is a teacher and his books do just that. They are a passionate sharing of a much-beloved subject. His readers tend to be adults who are looking for an adventure, who enjoy lively description, an involved plot, and the intellectual satisfaction of learning something new.

Cherf has excavated in Israel and Greece and toured and photographed many of Egypt's ancient sites first hand. He is a big fan of vintage Tom Clancy and Michael Crichton. But Cherf is quick to point out, whenever he can, the four men that professionally shaped him. Rufus J. Fears first lit the fire; Edward W. Kase stoked it; George J. Szemler refined it; and Charles K. Wolfe, Jr., set him free.

Degreed in Anthropology, Egyptian Archaeology, and with a Ph.D. in Ancient History, Cherf remains current as an officer of Denver's Egyptian Study Society. He is also a member of SERTOMA – Service to Mankind, a national service organization.

Living with his beloved wife Sue, they keep Foxbat 1 out in the garage. They enjoy playing golf, road racing (that's where Foxbat 1 comes in), jawing around a fire pit on a cool evening while sampling craft beers, and rooting for the Cubs – clearly Cherf is a hopeless romantic.

Visit www.wjcherf.com to access free sample chapters, peruse the latest news in Egyptology, and continue following the temporal adventures of Egyptologist Joseph Richards and his colleague Vesna Gregorieva.